This book is donated by

*The Friends of The
Fort Jones Library
&
The Pilcrow Foundation
Cottage Grove, Oregon*

Bridget Wilder
Live Free,
Spy Hard

Bridget Wilder
Live Free, Spy Hard

Jonathan Bernstein

 KATHERINE TEGEN BOOKS
An Imprint of HarperCollins Publishers

Katherine Tegen Books is an imprint of HarperCollins Publishers.

Bridget Wilder: Live Free, Spy Hard
Copyright © 2017 by Jonathan Bernstein
All rights reserved. Printed in the United States of America.
No part of this book may be used or reproduced in any manner
whatsoever without written permission except in the case of brief
quotations embodied in critical articles and reviews. For information
address HarperCollins Children's Books, a division of HarperCollins
Publishers, 195 Broadway, New York, NY 10007.
www.harpercollinschildrens.com

Library of Congress Control Number: 2016935935
ISBN 978-0-06-238272-6

17 18 19 20 21   CG/LSCH   10 9 8 7 6 5 4 3 2 1
❖
First Edition

To Laura Bernstein

CHAPTER ONE

The Hills Are Alive with the Sound of Musical Mops

"The universe whispered one little word in my ear: moptunes."

What am I doing here? Why am I sitting at a table in Reindeer Crescent's Three Trees Hotel listening to a woman talk about inventing a mop that plays music?

I thought I was here to see my mother, Nancy Wilder, receive the supposedly prestigious Reindeer Crescent Businesswoman of the Year award for managing her courier company, Wheel Getit2u. I thought my younger sister, Natalie, and I were here to provide support since my dad had a work thing that couldn't be shifted, and my brother, Ryan, responded to the invitation with a heartfelt

"I'd love to be there, but I just died of boredom."

But as the award ceremony drags into its second hour, I realize that every businesswoman who showed up is automatically guaranteed her own award.

"And that's how I achieved mopularity!" the woman gushes.

I look to my left. Natalie is watching Mrs. Mop and mouthing "So inspirational." I look to my right. My mother, who should be *fuming*, is smiling, nodding, and making notes in the margins of her acceptance speech—which I pray she gets to deliver sometime before my forty-fourth birthday. The woman gestures to an assistant, who hands her two mops, both with red, white, and blue handles. "To commemorate the upcoming election, I am happy to present supporters of President Brennan with their own mop." Pink Suit holds up a mop that plays a tinny version of "It's a Grand Old Flag."

"And if you're thinking of voting for independent candidate Morgan Font, I have a mop just for you." "I'm a Yankee Doodle Dandy" tinkles out of the second mop. The businesswomen clap along.

Although I'm only here as a barely awake audience member, I technically qualify for an award. I *am* in the spy business, and I *am* a resident of Reindeer Crescent.

I look around at the women sitting at the other

seventeen tables in the hotel conference room, clapping like seals along to the sound of mops, and I find myself wishing they could hear *my* acceptance speech.

"Businesswomen of Reindeer Crescent, Sacramento, thank you for this beautiful award," I would begin, holding my gold-plated figurine representing Hermes, the Greek god of merchants and commerce, high in the air. "It's an honor and a privilege, but I didn't get here on my own. I know you look at me and think, wow, she makes the world safe for the rest of us mere mortals. But it took a lot of people to make Bridget Wilder the spy she is today.

"I'd like to thank the evil agency Section 23, who attempted to use me to capture my biological father, Carter Strike. In doing so, they made me into the awesome spy who brought about their downfall. I'd like to thank another evil organization, the secret criminal operation known as the Forties, who kidnapped Carter Strike and introduced me to my birth mother, the international assassin Irina Ouspenskaya. And then I brought about *their* downfall. I'm good with the downfalls.

"I'd like to thank the CIA, who put Strike and Irina in charge of a rebooted version of the Forties that occasionally sends me on missions involving young people. I just vetted a bunch of contestants for that TV cooking competition for kids, and, of course, I did an impeccable job.

I didn't find a single evil villain among the *Little Chefs*. I'd particularly like to thank someone who's very special to me. Someone I keep close at all times . . ."

At that point, I'd hold up the second finger of my left hand and let the audience gaze at what they'd see as an ordinary ring with a big crimson stone. "I would like to thank Red, the plucky, loyal, unbreakable nanomarble, who has become my closest friend in times of crisis." The Research and Development team at the Forties came up with a clever way for me to hide Red in plain sight. They attached him to a magnetized bezel, which, they informed me, was the part of the ring that holds the gem. "To unleash him," they told me, "just squeeze."

"We made it, buddy," I'd tell Red, fighting back tears. "Oh, and thanks to my mom, my dad, my sister, my bother—just kidding, Ryan—my friend Joanna, and Dale Took . . . actually, forget it, I'll stop there.

"Keep dreaming big dreams, Reindeer Crescent businesswomen, you can be anything you want to be . . . *ouch!*"

A sharp elbow from my left digs into my ribs. "Shut *up*," hisses Natalie. "You're mumbling to yourself like a crazy person."

To my right, my mother leans in and mutters in my ear. "I'm sorry you find this so boring, Bridget. Please try to pay attention. These are people who have done great things with their lives. You could learn something."

"About mops," I start to say. Then I focus on the conference room stage. I was so deeply immersed in my acceptance speech fantasy, I failed to register the new occupant.

"I'm Vidina Geiger," says the small, brown-haired woman on the stage. "Standing on this stage is the last place I thought I'd ever be."

I incline my head toward my mother. "Long boring speech alert," I mutter hilariously.

"Can you be quiet and listen to her?" Mom sighs.

"I never imagined myself starting my own business, let alone making a success of it," the woman continues. "I was happy and satisfied being the wife of Martin Geiger, and the mother of Sheryl and Nelson."

Pictures of Vidina Geiger's happy family appear on the video monitor behind her. Handsome husband. Pretty daughter. The son has kind of an egg-shaped head. The businesswomen all make *awww* noises. No *awwws* from Bridget Wilder. I'm not exactly sure what, but *something* about the picture of the Geiger clan has my spy senses tingling.

"They were my success story," Mrs. Geiger continues. "But sometimes you need to find your own identity outside of your family. My husband built Tastes Like Steak from a single restaurant to a nationwide chain. Could I build something? I asked myself. If I really put my mind to it, what could I do?"

"*Fart!*" I say out loud.

The woman's speech comes to an abrupt halt.

Oops.

Natalie throws her hands over her face. "I'm not with you," she hisses. "I don't know you."

Mom slumps down low in her seat as everyone swivels around to stare in my direction.

I jump up and gesture to my mortified mother and sister that I'm heading to the restroom.

"Sorry," I call out to the award-winner onstage. "Keep going. You're doing great."

"Bridget, *go!*" Natalie and Mom chorus in pained harmony.

So I go. But *not* to the restroom.

CHAPTER TWO

The Girl Who Cried Fart

That *Fart!* didn't come out of the blue. There was a reason for that *Fart!* Remember the part in my imaginary acceptance speech where I mentioned my last job for the CIA-sanctioned version of the Forties? The one where I vetted the contestants participating in the Reindeer Crescent heat of the *Little Chefs* cooking contest?

I *thought* I did a thorough job. I *thought* I'd checked the backgrounds of all the budding kitchen prodigies. I didn't find any evidence of cheats, ringers, dwarves, or geniuses with histories of winning similar contests. But then Vidina Geiger made a room full of businesswomen say *awww*.

I know the boy in her happy family photograph. The kid with the egg-shaped head. When I looked into his background and pronounced him suitable for inclusion on *Little Chefs*, his name was not Nelson Geiger, and he did not mention being the male heir to the Tastes Like Steak franchise.

One thing I do know: Tastes Like Steak has a deadly rival in the world of fast-food restaurants. That rival is a chain called Parmesan Marmoset that specializes in huge heapings of non-healthy but really yummy food. There is a Parmesan Marmoset in Reindeer Crescent mall. An episode of *Little Chefs* is shooting there *right this minute*.

Why would the son of the Tastes Like Steak chain be working in the kitchen of his father's biggest rival? I do not know, but I intend to find out.

I hurry out of the Three Trees Hotel after my *Fart!* while texting Strike and Irina to alert the *Little Chefs* producers that foul play may be afoot. As I charge out of the building, I see a bellhop pushing a luggage cart with a skateboard stuffed between the cases and bags. I pretend to text furiously and walk straight into the bellhop. At the exact same time, I squeeze my ring.

Before the bellhop has time to reply, I hold up the Red-less ring and wail, "My grandmother's diamond! It's been in the family for generations, and now I've lost it."

The bellhop cringes at my rising—and completely fake—panic.

"I'm going to get in so much trouble," I snivel.

"Don't panic," he says. "I'll help you look for it."

"I think I had it when I got off the elevator," I lie.

When the bellhop scurries off to look for the nonexistent diamond, I grab the skateboard from his cart and leave him a few dollars as compensation. Score! Then I squeeze my ring and Red flies back to his rightful home. I jump on the stolen board, *almost* pull off one of those cool kickflips that seem so effortless in skateboard videos, and fly the six blocks to the Reindeer Crescent mall.

I navigate the board through the food court. As I weave in and out of mall diners, the bright-red logo of the family restaurant chain Parmesan Marmoset comes into view. And so do the paramedics, rolling a gurney out the front door. I'm too late! A cameraman and producer follow the gurney out into the mall.

I see the producer shove a microphone into the face of the groaning man being carried away.

"How do you feel?"

"Sick," whimpers the man. "They poisoned me."

Alarm bells start clanging inside my head.

I propel the board past the paramedics and the TV people. The waiters are too busy calming the freaked-out diners to stop me from skating into the restaurant. I see a familiar face. Eleven-year-old *Little Chef* contestant Gigi Paredes (signature dish: Portuguese paella) is a red-faced, weeping mess.

"I've made it a million times," the girl sobs. "I never made anyone sick before."

Something smells rotten here. It might be the Hawaiian beef teriyaki nine-year-old Nate Wackman is about to serve to a table of four. I skate over to the table, where young Wackman stands proudly by, waiting to be complimented on his culinary expertise.

"Don't eat that," I tell the diners.

I turn to Wackman, who glares at me with open loathing.

"Who are you?" he snaps.

"Health inspector," I shoot back.

"You're too young to be a health inspector," says the know-it-all kid.

"You're too young to be a chef," I reply.

He rolls his eyes. "I'm a *little* chef."

"I'm a little health inspector," I tell him.

"You're a liar," he shouts.

There's no denying that. "Listen, Wackman," I say.

"Some guy just got rolled out of here moaning about being poisoned. What if your stinky beef causes the next victim?"

"*You're* stinky beef" is Wackman's childish response.

"Before you serve it up, I want you to think. When you were in the kitchen, did anything unusual happen? Did anyone act strangely or say anything that surprised you?"

"Dermot was really helpful," he says, after some thought.

"Does Dermot have an egg-shaped head?" I ask.

Wackman narrows his eyes at me. "How do you know him?"

I grab the plates of teriyaki and skate past bewildered diners just as another waiter comes out of the kitchen carrying another tray of food prepared by another excitable young chef.

"Turn back around!" I yell. "That food is tainted!"

"It is not!" squeaks ten-year-old Heavenlii Bryant (favorite recipe: beef bourguignon).

The new waiter looks unsure. Heavenlii tries to push me off the board. I dump Wackman's tray onto Heavenlii's plates and then skate past her into Parmesan Marmoset's kitchen.

The heat hits me like a shovel to the face. A boiling-hot shovel. Rivulets of perspiration dribble into my eyes.

Six little kids in white uniforms slave over stoves as the head chef, a big man with a bushy red beard, barks orders at them: "Watch your heat! Turn it over! Plate it! Too crusty! Give it another two minutes!"

Two cameramen follow the contestants' every move. I scan the scared, sweaty faces of the cooks. Only one looks calm and centered. A boy with an egg-shaped head works on his eggplant parmesan dish, while checking on the progress of his fellow contestants and murmuring encouragement. Nelson Geiger.

"A little more seasoning, maybe?" he suggests as he sprinkles a thimbleful of seasoning over another contestant's spaghetti and meatballs. Whatever he's putting on that plate, I'm guessing it's going have the same effect as Gigi Paredes's Portuguese paella.

"What's on the menu, Nelson?" I shout, my voice cutting over the yelling of the head chef. "Is it mole?"

"Mole?" repeats the red-bearded head chef. "You think we serve mole here?"

"I don't know," I tell him. "I've never eaten here. But I know you have a mole working undercover in your kitchen."

I skate past the other Little Chefs toward Nelson Geiger. "Stand back, kid cooks, this is a setup. Your talents are being used to make customers puke."

I snatch up a stainless steel whisk from the kitchen

worktop and point it in the direction of my number one suspect.

"This Little Chef you know as Dermot—he's not who he seems. Dermot is, in fact, Nelson Geiger, son of the guy who owns the Tastes Like Steak chain!"

Young Geiger glances up from his parmesan. I'll give him this—he has a perfect poker face. No stress. No fear. No anger. Only the slight hint of a smile.

"Come on, guys," he says, looking around the kitchen. "This is a classic TV stunt. I know you're not naive enough to fall for such nonsense."

I see from the expression on the head chef's face that he buys Geiger's lie. I need to think fast.

"Try this seasoning, Chef," I quickly say. I grab the plate of spaghetti and meatballs the contestant was preparing and hold it out to the man. (There's a loose Band-Aid half-buried in one of the meatballs. I don't see this kid as a potential winner.) "See if you think it enhances the flavors of these dishes. Or if it's poison."

Geiger pipes up. "We've worked too hard to have her to keep us from cooking the meals of our lives."

Red Beard looks from Geiger to me to the cameramen. Finally, he reaches out his hand. I roll toward him with the tainted pasta.

"Chef, this is a waste of our time," declares Geiger. *Now* I'm starting to see a little sweat on his brow. *Now* I see a tiny twitch at the side of his eye. "We've got customers out there waiting."

"They can wait another minute," says the head chef. He wraps a few strands of spaghetti around his fork. His mouth opens. The fork travels between his teeth.

Nelson Geiger's cool vanishes. I see panic seize him. He was not prepared for this.

"Stop!" he yells.

Geiger grabs the fork from the head chef and throws it at me.

I roll to the side. The fork shoots straight past me. I hear a voice from behind me yelp, "Ow! My hand!" I don't think that Band-Aid kid is cut out for kitchen work.

"I don't believe this," mutters Red Beard.

"You're no Little Chef," shouts Heavenlii Bryant. "You're a big cheat and a huge liar."

"Tastes Like Steak?" sneers Nate Wackman. "Tastes Like *Fake*!"

Geiger's shoulders sag at this barrage of disapproval. He lowers his head and hugs himself. Despite his evil intentions, I find myself feeling bad for the boy. This huge heart of mine is probably a weakness in my line of work. Besides, I'm betting Geiger Senior is the real brains behind this scheme.

"Hey," I say to Red Beard. "Let's not make this any

harder for Nelson than it has to be. Is there somewhere private we can go and talk about how we're going to handle this?"

The man nods and pushes Geiger from the kitchen. I follow him on the board.

As I roll away, I turn back to the stunned contestants. "I know this is a cruel blow, but you're all really talented cooks and I bet you'll all become famous chefs." I take a last parting glance at the Band-Aid kid. "Well, most of you."

The chef pushes young Geiger into the walk-in freezer. He ushers me in and closes the door. I hop off my board and approach the unhappy Geiger.

"This isn't your fault," I tell him in my sweetest, most sympathetic voice. "You're a pawn in someone else's game . . ." I glance at the frozen fish products in the open freezer box nearest to me and can't help adding, "Or should I say . . . a prawn?" He doesn't laugh. I continue, "You didn't come up with this plan alone."

Geiger finally looks up at me. "No," he says. "He helped."

He?

I whirl around to see Red Beard swinging a gargantuan frozen swordfish straight at my head. Quick as a flash, I lift my ring and shoot Red at the frozen monster.

He blasts straight through the fish and smacks Red Beard between the eyes.

"Go fish!" I shout at the evil chef as he clutches his forehead.

Everything goes black. Well, black and slightly smelling of onions. Someone just dropped a sack over my head!

Geiger! That little brat and Red Beard are partners in crime!

If I don't find a way out of this, I'm toast!

CHAPTER THREE

Big Chef, Little Chef

The frozen swordfish put me to sleep long enough for Nelson Geiger and the diabolical head chef of Parmesan Marmoset tie me up inside the smelly black onion bag, then smuggle me out of the restaurant and into the back of a van. Which is where I am now. Stuck inside a smelly sack. Sweaty, uncomfortable, scared, headachy, but awake. Every time the van comes to a halt or judders around a corner, I'm thrown across the metal floor. I can see through the lining enough to note the Tastes Like Steak logo plastered on packs of frozen meat. I'm guessing they're taking me to the big boss.

"I can't wait to meet Martin Geiger," I shout through the sack.

"Shut up!" yells Nelson from the front of the van.

"You must be so desperate for his approval to agree to this," I continue. "And you, Chef, what did he offer you? More money? A better job?"

"Shut up!" roars the voice of the older man. He pulls the van across lanes of traffic, causing the sack to roll into a frozen steak package that jabs me in the eye. It stings, but I'm a seasoned spy and I'm used to such hardships. Frozen meat is not going stop me from my mission of making these two fast-food conspirators question themselves.

"You're not really a super-loyal guy, are you, Chef?" I go on. "Do you think your new boss is ever going to really trust you? I know I wouldn't."

The radio starts to play. Drowning me out is not an option.

"Hey, Nelson?" I shout at the top of my voice. "My mom knows your mom. Vidina, right? I bet she'll really be thrilled that you had me assaulted and abducted. 'Cause she doesn't know about any of this, does she? Probably not going to be great for you when she finds out."

"Shut up about my mom," he yelps back at me.

What's my plan here? Do I keep needling and niggling

away at them until they see the error of their ways and let me go? Or will I only succeed in making them even madder? I'm stuck in a sack, so it's not like I've got anything better to do.

"Another thing," I shout over the radio. "Who do you think I am? How did I even find out Nelson was making people sick? Who do you think I work for? Because I work for *someone* . . ."

I let that *someone* hang in the air. If they weren't scared before, I bet they are now.

Suddenly, I hear glass shatter.

"The windshield!" shouts Nelson.

The van starts weaving left and right. I'm being thrown about like socks inside a washing machine. The van screeches to a halt. A door opens. I hear a scream, then another scream, and then silence.

I tear and claw at the lining of the sack, hoping to rip enough of a hole that I can unpick the ropes keeping me imprisoned.

The door of the van opens.

I feel a tug at the bottom of the sack. I'm dragged across the floor and out of the van. Am I being re-kidnapped?

"Hello?" I yell.

"Hello yourself," says a young male voice.

The sack hits the ground.

"Ouch!" I exclaim.

"Boo-hoo," says the voice.

I feel the top of the sack loosen and try to push myself out. My legs are unsteady, and my eyes take a moment to get used to my surroundings. It's dark, and I'm in the middle of a field. I look in the back of the van and gasp in surprise. Nelson Geiger and Red Beard are frozen inside blocks of ice. They look like life-size ice cubes. I turn around and see a boy who looks like he's maybe a year older than me tossing a snowball up and down in his hand.

"Nano-snowball?" I say.

"Obviously" is his reply.

"How does it work?" I ask.

"You wouldn't understand."

Wow. This guy thinks he's cooler than the round white weapon he bounces in his hand. He drops the snowball on the ground, and it immediately evaporates. Next, he pulls out a phone and sends a text while paying me approximately zero attention. I take a step closer to him.

"I don't think you're here to kill me or abduct me, so I'm guessing you saved me?"

He gives the smallest and most disinterested of shrugs.

"I guess I should thank you."

Not even a shrug this time. I get up in his face and push my hand out to be shaken.

"I'm Bridget Wilder."

His barely open eyes take me in and dismiss me in a single blink.

"And you are?" I demand.

"A better agent than you'll ever be."

CHAPTER FOUR

I Hate Adam Pacific

His name is Adam Pacific. He speaks fourteen languages. He can lip-read from thirty yards away. He is skilled in over twenty-nine martial arts disciplines, six of which he created himself. He can break and reset every bone in his body. He can hold his breath for eight minutes. He can slow his heartbeat down to the point where he is considered medically dead. He can turn a docile parakeet into a deadly predator with a single command. He can remove a bullet from his body and stitch the wound without the aid of anesthetic. He's been buried alive in a safe filled with snakes, thrown out of a plane without the aid of a parachute, and submerged in shark-infested waters inside a cage with a faulty lock.

Adam Pacific tells me all this within two minutes of meeting him. In the same two minutes, he also calls me a gimmick and labels me an embarrassment to the good name of teen spies the world over.

I stare at this kid with his baseball cap tilted to the side of his head, his unblemished olive skin, his leather wristbands, silver chain, and barbed wire tattoo on the back of his hand.

"Me, a gimmick?" I snap. "You're calling *me* a gimmick?"

"How's school?" Adam Pacific replies with an unpleasant smile. "What are you wearing to the winter formal? Are you having baked corn dogs for lunch? Is drama club everything you dreamed it would be?"

I mirror his unpleasant smile with an even more insincere grin of my own. "I get that you're attempting to rile me with those schoolgirl taunts," I say. "You probably don't know who you're talking to. So let me educate you. I'm the spy who took on Edward Dominion, the posh guy who ran the Forties. He doesn't run anything anymore. Neither does his daughter, Vanessa. Ever heard of Section 23? I tore that playhouse down, son. You know Doom Patrol? Scary band of thugs? They watch their mouths around me 'cause I'm liable to smack them. That's what I do. I'm Bridget Wilder. Ask about me."

"I have," says Adam Pacific. "You're a gimmick."

"*You're* a gimmick" is the best response I can come up with.

He yawns in my face and then goes back to his phone.

I'm standing in a deserted field with a two frozen corrupt chefs of varying sizes and all I can think about is coming up with an insult stinging enough to wipe the self-satisfied smirk off the face of this guy who thinks he's *so* much better than me.

My boiling rage is interrupted by the roar of a vehicle driving into the field. A black jeep with darkened windows hurtles toward us.

"Here comes the fat man," mutters Adam, not moving his gaze from the phone.

The jeep stops, the doors open, and Carter Strike climbs out. My bio-dad now divides his time between the Forties headquarters in New York and his cluttered condo in nearby Suntop Hills. Two other men, junior agents, head straight for the Tastes Like Steak van. One of them points what looks like a car key at the nano ice cubes. Both cubes melt. The agent herds the shivering, confused Nelson and the head chef into the back of the van. The other jumps in the driver's seat and pulls the van out of the field. Bye, guys.

As Strike passes Adam, the kid holds up a fist. Strike bumps it like they're bros and then walks up to me.

"Great job, Bridget," he says. "You noticed your mistake, and you corrected it. You can't teach that. Thanks to you, we now have a valuable asset in the fast-food world, and you know what that means . . ."

"Free food from Tastes Like Steak for life."

"You're the best." He grins.

Adam lets out a loud fake cough.

"You are, too," Strike calls over to him. "Mr. Sensitive."

"I'll be in the jeep while you and the gimmick play happy family," says Adam. With that, he slouches his way to the waiting vehicle.

"Who . . . ?" I start to say.

"Wait," Strike replies.

He watches Adam get into the jeep and slam the passenger door.

"Okay," says Strike.

". . . is that jerk?" I shout. "That rude, obnoxious, arrogant, ignorant . . ."

"Remember Charlie Pacific?" Strike says.

I will not be stopped. ". . . ill-mannered, foul-smelling, grotesque, wretched . . ."

"Buddy of mine," he continues. "We worked together in the field back in the day. He saved my life more times than I can remember."

"How many times did he try to kill you?" I immediately say.

"Three," says Strike. He gives me a sidelong grin that makes me forget how mad I am at Adam Pacific. *We so get each other.*

"What about him?" I say.

"He's dead," Strike replies. "Or he's being held captive in North Korea. Same thing."

"Sorry" is all I can muster.

"He had an inkling his days were numbered," Strike continues. "The last few times he went out on a job, he'd call me and say, 'If anything happens to me, I want you to watch out for Adam.'" Strike looks directly at me. "His son."

I feel my stomach churn. *This could be me.* My biological parents are in charge of the Forties, an organization that employs criminals to catch other criminals. Any random work day could be their last.

My intense dislike of Adam doesn't immediately melt away. But I feel like I understand the cool-dude facade he must feel he needs to wear as armor at all times. I'm compassionate like that.

"You're still the Forties' number one go-to agent when it comes to dealing with younger suspects," Strike goes on. "But Adam doesn't have any other family, so I made the decision to recruit him."

"And you want me to watch out for him." I nod. "Be his mentor. His point person. His handler. Help him heal."

There's a sudden honk from the jeep. Adam blasts the horn a couple more times. Strike waves in the direction of the blacked-out windows. Then he scratches the back of his head, rubs his chin, and tugs at his earlobe. *He does not look directly at me.*

"You don't want me to be his mentor, point person, and handler?" I ask.

"It's not that," Strike mumbles, again *not looking directly at me.* "Adam totally surpassed all my expectations today. He tracked down the Tastes Like Steak van, took control of the situation, and saved you."

I stand with my hands on my hips, glaring at him. "Unnecessary. I beat impossible odds all the time."

"I know, I know," Strike says, his eyes now searching the ground. "It's just that . . . here's the thing: Adam doesn't have anyone, he doesn't have a family, he doesn't go to school . . . whereas you . . ."

I let out a gasp of pure shock. "You're dumping me

for that jerk because I have a family and I go to school?"

He reaches for my hand. I snatch it away and stomp furiously across the field.

"There's no dumping," Strike assures me as he walks by my side. "No one's being replaced. It's just that . . ."

I stop walking and jab a finger at him.

"It's just *what*? Just that it's so much more convenient with sideways-baseball-cap, barbed-wire-tattoo cool dude because he doesn't have to come up with a web of lies to tell his family, friends, and principal. Whereas with Bridget, everything's so *complicated*. There are so many people in her life. She always has to come up with all these stories, and alibis, and fake identities. Almost like she's some kind of *spy*!"

That little tirade leaves me breathless. "Fine." I sigh. "I understand. It makes sense. Dale Tookey told me I couldn't be half a spy. You're telling me the same thing."

"What's the story with you and Dale?" Strike asks. "I heard you and he weren't . . ."

"Not appropriate!" I bark. "Stick to the subject at hand."

Strike winces. "You're my go-to," he repeats. "The OG of tween spies. The GOAT. But you're only one person, Bridget. An awesome butt-kicker without equal, but sadly they only made one of you. So I thought—we thought, Irina and I—the best use of your talents would be to save you for the *special* missions, the ones that need that Bridget Wilder magic. . . ."

I'm being handled here. I'm being flattered and manipulated by a master. I know it and Strike knows it, but it's still nice to hear.

"Go on," I say, fighting the urge to smile.

"For the grunt work, the meat-and-potatoes stuff, the unrewarding day-to-day grind, we have Adam . . ."

Strike shoves a thumb in the direction of the black jeep.

"He gets the dirty jobs?" I ask.

"He's like a supermarket shelf-stocker." Strike nods. His shoulders sag with relief that our spat is at an end.

I run a leisurely hand through my hair, feeling cool and superior.

"Like a guy with a plastic bag picking up dog poop!" I chirp. My brain crackles with images of Adam Pacific engaged in degrading menial work.

"Exactly!" Strike laughs along with me.

With bright smiles on both our faces, we walk—I actually *skip!*—toward the black jeep.

The passenger door opens. Adam leans out.

"Yo, Biggie," he bawls at Strike. "Shake a leg. I'm going to be late for the stupid L4E job."

Adam Pacific might as well have hit me in the face with a nano-snowball. My smile freezes. My eyes fix on Strike's suddenly nervous face.

"What?" is all I am able to say.

CHAPTER FIVE

L4E

Ruth Etting is my favorite singer. I discovered her by accident on one of those YouTube searches that's supposed to last two minutes but eats up three hours because you keep losing yourself in more and more clips. She was a legit big deal in the 1920s and has this *wah-wah* singing voice that I find an absolute delight.

I sing Ruth Etting's praises to make the point that Bridget Wilder is no mindless, slack-jawed, trend-following sucker. I'm suspicious of mass popularity. Whatever my peers are wearing, listening to, drinking, watching, following, or playing, I'm likely doing the opposite.

Except when it comes to L4E.

That's Live4Eva to the uninitiated. Five ordinary guys from Glasgow, Scotland, who met when they were all acting in the British TV show *Zoo Crew*, about the lives and loves of young apprentice zookeepers. Their soaring popularity inspired a manager to form them into a boy band. Boy bands are *not* my thing. The screaming senseless girls who scrawl the names of boy band members on their arms and send shrieking selfies of themselves to their favorite's Instagram account are not my thing. Spending hours refreshing some scruffy British singer's Twitter feed in the hope he might have retweeted a birthday greeting is not my thing.

Except when it comes to L4E.

They're not the best singers in the world. They might not even have been the best singers in the *Zoo Crew* zoo. They're not the most talented dancers. Their thick Glaswegian—yes, that's a word—accents can be hard to understand. Their concert merchandise is insanely expensive and completely defective. The tour T-shirt I bought shrank to the size of a postage stamp the first time it was washed.

But I don't care about any of that. The first time I saw those five guys—Cadzo, Benj, Lim, Kecks, and Beano—I knew I was doomed to be one of those senseless screaming girls. I knew I'd be writing Cadzo's name on my arm. I knew I'd try my hand at cooking Benj's favorite fast food: deep-fried Mars Bar, a hometown favorite. (I *do not* recommend it, unless you want to know what drowning in chocolate-flavored quicksand tastes like.) I knew I'd be sending pictures of me with and without glasses to Lim's Instagram to see which one he liked best, and I knew I'd be spending September 28 waiting to see if Beano retweeted my birthday greetings. What can I say? It's like they reached out of the computer screen where I first saw them singing "No Cage (Is Big Enough to Stop Me Loving You)" and chose *me* to be their numero uno fan.

So you can perhaps understand how loud my heart is pounding and how hard it is for me to keep a lid on my simmering emotions as I climb into the back of the jeep. I lean forward so my mouth is level with Strike's ear and whisper, "What L4E job is he talking about?"

"I'm going on tour with them, Gimmick," Adam Pacific says, turning to look back at me as if I'm a cockroach that crawled into the vehicle. "Their manager heard rumors that some of their security crew are planning to abduct the stupid band and hold them for ransom. They need someone undercover who can weed out the bad seeds. Kind of a waste of my talents, but I get to go to Madrid, Berlin, Bangkok . . ."

"Stockholm, Antwerp, London, Manchester," I breathe. I've memorized their tour dates.

"And I get to fly on a private jet and stay in five-star hotels, and I probably get a huge allowance. . . ."

I tune out his annoying voice and try to form words of my own.

"What . . . but . . . no . . . wait . . . I . . . Cadzo" are the best I can do.

"That's the most sense you've made since I met you," cackles Pacific.

Strike shoots me a worried glance in the rearview. "Are you okay? Were you grazed by particles of the nano-snowball?"

I let out a gasp of outrage. "How can you be so oblivious?"

"I—" Strike starts to say.

"Don't you think I should have been the first *and only* choice for this job? Don't you know how much I love L4E? Don't you know the idea of this jerk going on tour with them is killing me?"

Pacific hoots with laughter. "Congratulations, Strike," he gurgles. "She's an *amazing* spy. Totally professional. Perfect for any job."

Strike looks uncomfortable. "I didn't know you liked them."

"Take a knife and stick it in my heart!" I yell.

"Can I volunteer for that job, too?" says Adam.

"How can you not know?" I'm getting louder, and I can tell even from the back of Strike's head that he doesn't know how to cope with me when I'm like this but *I can't stop.* "Look at my arm!"

I roll up my sleeve and shove my wrist under Strike's nose so he can see the words *Cadzo Army* written in thick black Magic Marker.

"Does that wash off?" he asks.

I'm never doing another job for you ever!

"Does Irina know I'm being treated like this?" I shout in his ear. *Irina!* Why didn't I think of her sooner? She always takes my side over Strike's. I let out a sigh of relief. The situation is about to turn in my favor. I snap a finger at Strike.

"Phone!" I demand.

He passes me his phone. I find my biological mother listed simply as *Chechnya.* I touch the call button. *Be cool,* I tell myself. *Make your case calmly and rationally. Convince her you're the best person for the job.*

I hear Irina inhale. Before she even has time to utter a syllable, I start speaking.

"Strike's giving the L4E job to that jerkface Pacific, and it's not fair because I love them and I know all their songs and what their favorite food is and where they like to go on vacation and when all their birthdays are and I'd do an amazing job and I'd totally save them and I want it so much and I can't believe Strike didn't even think of me but you always have my back and you're the best ever and we're such good friends so can I?"

"I should have left her in the sack," I hear the jerkface Pacific say from the front seat.

"She's not always like this," I hear Strike reply.

"Bridget?" says Irina.

"Yes," I gasp. "Sorry. Hi."

"What's wrong? Why are you calling on Strike's phone? Did a war break out? You sound hysterical."

I manage to restrain myself from telling her that this is *much* more important than a war—though it absolutely is—and I repeat what I previously said, but at a slower pace and with a few sentence breaks.

"Well," says Irina. "I certainly understand why this is means so much to you. When I was a little girl growing up in Chechnya, there was a folk group whose name translates as We Ask Only for Crumbs of Bread, Yet You Feed Us Flies, and their songs made my gray world burst with color."

"They sound great!" I exclaim.

"But I don't think your other mother would approve

of you going on tour with a boy band, and your other mother has *so much more* experience in raising a child than I do."

My heart shatters into a thousand pieces. When my actual mom, Nancy Wilder of Reindeer Crescent, Sacramento, met Carter Strike for the first time, she was all smiles, warm welcomes, and dinner invitations. He's a chubby, affable guy who knows how to make people believe they've known him all their life. Strike fits easily into a family situation. Irina Ouspenskaya, with her black leather ensemble, mascara-smudged eyes, and faint hint of an East European accent, does not.

Mom continually brings up how *interesting* Irina is, and what a *free spirit* she seems. For her part, Irina keeps talking about what an *effective* authority figure Mom must be and how important it is for me to have someone in my life who's not afraid to seem *boring*. I get the feeling neither of them are saying what they really mean.

"She raised you, she put in the years," says Irina. "I will not be accused of disrespecting her."

I don't have an ally in this miscarriage of justice.

"Are you still there?" I hear her ask.

I end the call. And my dreams.

CHAPTER SIX

One of Our Fun Mother/Daughter Talks

"This is going to get so many likes," laughs Carter Strike. He's standing in my hallway, taking a selfie with my mom. They're pretending to be fighting over who gets to keep the Businesswoman of the Year figurine.

After we deposited the awful Pacific at a private airfield so he could go off and suck at the job that I was born to do, Strike and I came up with this plan to charm the pants off the Wilders—*especially* Mom—so my disappearance from the awards show doesn't evolve into a national emergency.

I didn't say a word when he brought me back home, I just hung back and watched as Strike reminded my dad of the hike the two of them were supposed to go on. "You're my fitness guru," he told Jeff Wilder, who rarely leaves his comfortable chair. "I'm relying on you to get me buff and cut like you." I watched as he congratulated Natalie on her success as head choreographer of the Reindeer Crescent Cheerminators and gave Ryan a link to a site that features bootlegs of the underground Mexican wrestling pay-per-views to which he's now addicted. I watched as he admired Mom's award and took the blame for my absence from the rest of the presentation.

This is the story he tells her: "By an incredible coincidence, I was at a meeting in the Three Trees Hotel, and I bumped into Bridget as I was leaving for my next appointment. Being the well-brought-up girl she is, she insisted on walking me to my car. When we got to the parking garage, I found out I'd locked my keys inside the car . . ." The saga continues with incredible twists and turns—malfunctioning phones, stray dogs, open manhole covers—that make him look like a chump and me seem like a smart, kind, and resourceful young person. He ends by pointing a finger at me and saying, "You did a good job with this one."

"I guess I did," Mom agrees, glancing in my direction.

I strike a half-flattered, half-embarrassed pose. Mom makes Strike produce his car keys before she lets him leave, and extracts a promise that he and Irina will show up for a family dinner in the near future.

Mom and I wave to Strike as he heads down our driveway. I let out a sigh of relief. All in all, not a bad day for young spy Bridget Wilder. An attempt to bring down a fast-food chain foiled by my sharp eye and quick thinking. My mother's suspicions put to rest by a clever mixture of outright lies, self-deprecation, and making my family feel important.

I head upstairs.

"Bridget," Mom calls out. "Can you help me with something in the office?"

Haven't I done enough? I feel like moaning "Do I have to?" but after the incredible portrait Strike painted of me as everybody's dream daughter, I have a lot to live up to. I shuffle into the small room Mom and Dad both use for their files and paperwork. Mom comes in after me and closes the door. I look at the pictures pinned to the wall. There's the portrait of the stick-figure Wilder family as rendered by five-year-old me. There's my drawing of our house with the windows made to look like eyes and a smiley face. There are some of Natalie's vivid, colorful illustrations of rainbows and mermaids. (Ryan was also a prolific drawer. Mom and Dad paid him to stop.)

Mom goes over to her desk, sits down, and looks at me.

"Did you and Carter rehearse that?" she says.

I wasn't expecting this.

"What?" is my quick reply.

"Did you tell him what to say to us? Nice, personal, complimentary things to take our minds off where you went after you left the conference room?"

Mom takes a pencil from the desk and taps it off her knee.

"Do you think I didn't know you were bored?" she asks me. "I know you thought the ceremony was stupid. The speeches went on too long, there were too many awards. Do you think *I* wasn't aware of that?"

"If you knew that, why did you make us sit through it?" I demand.

"Because it was important to me," Mom says, staring at me. "I started a business, and it's regarded as enough of a success that I got an award for it. That means something to me, and I hoped it would mean something to you. I hoped you'd be a little bit proud . . ."

"I was," I protest. "I am."

Mom leans forward in her chair, her face flushed. The pencil tapping becomes more rapid.

"Instead, I get lies," she says. "If you'd come out and

told me, 'I was bored so I went to hang out with my cooler parent,' I'd . . . I wouldn't have been happy, but it would have been less insulting than what I got. Coincidence. Lost keys. Really, Bridget?"

I feel my face redden. I don't know how to dig myself out of this.

"I get it." Mom sighs. "Carter's like a big, goofy kid. And *Irina*"—Mom draws her name out for maximum effect—"wears a lot of leather and looks like a vampire. They're fun. They're cool. I'm the boring, strict mom. But they're not *here*. They only see snapshots of your life. They get to dip in and out and act like they're your grown-up friends."

Keeping my mouth shut is physically painful. I want to tell Mom what I told Adam Pacific: that I've brought down criminal organizations, that I'm an in-demand spy, that Strike and Irina think of me as an equal. But I can't say any of these things. I lean against the wooden bookcase with my hands shoved into my pockets and my right heel balanced on my left toe. If it sounds awkward and uncomfortable, that's exactly how I'm feeling right now.

"The Bridget that Carter Strike describes?" Mom goes on. "The one who's so amazing? I wish I knew that girl. But I don't anymore." Mom squeezes her pencil tight. "The Bridget I know is thoughtless, selfish, and irresponsible."

"I'm not," I protest. "Things just got away from me today. I shouldn't have . . ." I trail off. What am I going to say?

"And lying comes *so* easily to you." She shudders. Mom closes her eyes for a second and then she stands up.

"Believe it or not, I don't enjoy having these kinds of conversations, Bridget. I want to trust you. I want to think the best of you. I want to know the Bridget that Carter Strike knows . . ."

You really don't, I think.

"But we're not going to have another day like today," she says. "You're grounded until further notice. If Joanna wants to see you, she can come here. If Carter and *Irina* want to spend time with you, they can come and do it here under my supervision."

Mom approaches me. She reaches out and takes my face in her hands.

"I know it feels extreme and unfair, but what you did to me today was extreme and unfair."

I blink back a tear. Mom does, too.

I hear a voice in my head. *Tell her everything. Put it all out in the open. Tell her you're a spy.*

It would make life so much easier.

I hear another voice in my head. *You can never, ever tell her. Ever. She could not handle it. Not for a moment.*

"I'll be better," I promise her. For the first time today, I'm not lying.

CHAPTER SEVEN

NJ

"I like T-shirt," Joanna suddenly says in the middle of me pouring out my woes about Adam Pacific and Strike and Irina and L4E and being grounded.

Up until a few months ago, the only time I expected to hear the words *I like* emerging from the mouth of my friend Joanna Conquest were in sentences that would end ". . . to see posters of missing pets" or ". . . the sound people make when they choke on sunflower seeds." But then she lived in Brooklyn with relatives for a few months while her grandmother, Big Log, was in the hospital, and she evolved into a happy, friendly, caring, positive person.

I'd even say fun. Big Log's health took an unexpected turn for the better, which obviously was a huge relief to all of us. But it meant Joanna had to leave the family she had grown to love and return to Reindeer Crescent.

Our friendship resumed as before. We walk to school every morning. Most evenings, Joanna comes over to my house after Big Log has settled in to watch her nightly diet of blood-spattered true crime TV shows. I share secrets from my spy life (only Joanna and my older brother, Ryan, are aware of my double existence). She grumbles about our fellow students at Reindeer Crescent Middle School. But that's where the problem lies. I don't think she really means it anymore.

Joanna—or the version of her I now think of as Old Joanna, OJ for short—used to wholeheartedly hate every kid in school, every teacher, and every parent. Since she's been back, her hatred feels halfhearted. It's like she's marooned in limbo where she goes through the motions of being OJ, but she's really NJ—New Joanna!—a happy, fun, caring person, or she would be but she's too scared to fully evolve. Do I say any of this to her? I do not. Instigating any kind of discussion about my theories regarding OJ or NJ would culminate in her regarding me as an untrustworthy enemy.

"I like T-shirt" might be a sign that she's aware of her own predicament.

I give Joanna my full attention. She's sitting on the end of my bed, painting her toenails yellow with Magic Marker. I stretch out from the top of the bed and poke in her in the back with my big toe.

"You like a T-shirt?"

"T-shirt," she repeats. "You know, Marlon Moats?"

It takes me a second. I *do* know Marlon Moats. Popular guy. Eighth grader. Plays soccer. Greets friends by shouting, "Yup, yup!" Wears a white T-shirt every day. Presumably a fresh one.

"Hence, T-shirt," I say out loud.

"He's nice, and he's got these long arms. I have conversations with him in my head."

"About what?"

"That's private," she mutters.

NJ! A total New Joanna transformation right before my eyes.

I wait to see if there are going to be further stunning revelations. NJ says nothing else. Opening up *that* much must have been agony for her. I poke her in the back again. "Turn around," I say. She does. Her face is as red as her toes are yellow.

"How are you planning to proceed?" I ask. "Are you going to tell him? Are you going to tell someone who knows him? Are you going to send him an intriguing message? Or are you just going to obsess over him? That can be better than an actual face-to-face meeting." I hold up the customized L4E case of my new Forties phone as evidence.

"Do your spy thing," says NJ, almost shyly. "Find out about him for me."

"We can do that right now!" I exclaim. "We'll go on his Instagram and his Twitter, we'll . . ."

She shakes her head no. "Too easy," she says. "I don't want to know what everyone else knows. I need an advantage." Joanna is nodding excitedly and clapping her hands at me like I'm a puppy ready to perform tricks for her amusement. "I need intel no one except someone who really understands T-shirt would know. Find out the stuff he keeps secret. Get inside his computer. Get inside his house. That kind of thing is like breathing to you."

Um. I get what she's asking me to do. But honestly? It feels creepy and invasive.

NJ senses my hesitation. She is not pleased. Again, in front of my eyes, I see her revert to OJ. That angry face. Those blotchy cheeks and tiny, accusing eyes I've missed so much.

"I never ask you for anything," she shouts. "And this one time I do, you slam the door in my face."

"There was no door slamming," I protest.

She climbs off my bed and stomps furiously around the room.

"It's because Dale Tookey broke up with you," she says, glaring at me. "You don't think I should have a boyfriend because then you'd feel abandoned."

Sigh. Dale Tookey, the hacker-slash-double-agent who accompanied me during the action-packed climaxes of my two biggest spy missions. The boy I kissed three times and danced with once. The boy who was always on super-secret assignments. The boy who emailed me out of the blue to let me know he was seeing a hacker who referred to herself as Ur5ula. (Replacing letters of the alphabet with numbers. Nothing pre10tious about that, Ur5ula.) The boy I try not to think about because when I do there's a small ache that won't go away.

"But it's not like someone else won't catch the Bridget cold," says Joanna.

"The what?"

"The sun always shines in Reindeer Crescent," she explains. "It never rains. The temperature never falls below sixty. And yet people wake up with scratchy throats. They can't breathe. They're hot and sweaty and their heads are sore. There's no reason for it. Just like there was no reason for Dale Tookey or my cousin in Brooklyn to like you. But they did. They caught . . ."

"The Bridget cold." I nod. "I get it." It's *sort* of a compliment, I suppose.

"And so will someone else," Joanna goes on.

Will they, though? Now that D—— T————'s out of the picture, I wonder if I'll ever have scratchy, sore, sweaty feelings for anyone ever again. I've learned you can't trust spies, and all you have to offer non-spies are lies. That's a pretty bleak future.

Joanna's voice turns quiet. "I'm a harder disease to catch. I need help to become contagious."

How can I say no to *that*?

I get off the bed and approach her. "Okay," I say, my voice low. "I'm not going to help you exploit tragic family deaths or weird religious beliefs, but I'll do a little digging."

"Bridget," she whispers, her face aglow with something I think might be gratitude. Is NJ going to hug me? *I think she's going to hug me! We've never hugged.*

Joanna moves toward me.

A loud, piercing shriek from my little sister's room causes me to spring to alert. I shove NJ out of my way and go flying out the door.

"Keep that hug for me," I yell. "I'll be back for it another time."

CHAPTER EIGHT

Say Hello to the Face of Say Hello

My first panicked jumble of thoughts are: *Someone is retaliating for something I did. Or it's a preemptive attack. Or it's someone coming back from the dead.* When you're a spy you make *a lot* of enemies, and the people who hate you most tend to get revenge by hurting those closest to you.

I kick open Natalie's door and raise my ring finger, ready to launch Red.

Natalie is sitting on her bed, eyes wet with tears, struggling to catch her breath and trying to form words. I rush over to her.

"Oh my God" is all she can say.

"What happened?"

"The principal." She gulps. "The first lady. The school. The campaign about phones. Me."

She's making no sense, or she's making as much sense as I do when I talk about L4E.

Ryan ambles into Natalie's room. "I hear screaming. I see crying." He rubs his hands together. "You found the dead pigeon I hid in your room. Classic prank."

"No," sniffs Natalie. "Jocelyn Brennan, our first lady . . ."

"She found the pigeon?" asks Ryan.

"Shut *up!*" snaps Natalie. She focuses on me. "You know her big cause? Her Say Hello campaign?"

"Um, I *think* I do," I lie.

Natalie shakes her head at me. "What galaxy do you live in? You know we're electing a new president next month?" She looks over at Ryan. He's pretending to clean his ears with one of Natalie's cheer choreography awards.

"I knew about the president," he brags. "You might be making the other thing up, though."

Natalie narrows her eyes at us both. "You're *so* stupid. It's an important nationwide campaign aimed at getting kids to stop isolating themselves by staring at their phones all day and interact with the people around them."

"Couldn't she have done something more controversial, like remember which is your left hand and which is your right?" snorts Ryan.

"Jocelyn Brennan is my role model," responds Natalie. "She's a strong, smart, kind, caring, concerned woman who's spent the last three months spreading her message to schools across America. And in two days she's coming to Reindeer Crescent, and the face of her campaign is going to be *me!*"

I know enough to say, "Natalie, that's amazing."

"I know, right?" She beams. "What they told me is, Mrs. Brennan and her daughter, Jamie . . ."

"The clumsy one?" Ryan smiles. "She's hilarious."

". . . will talk to the school in the assembly hall. Mrs. Brennan will tell Jamie how important it is that we all engage with one another in a face-to-face way, and then she'll say, 'I asked a student right here in Reindeer Crescent to see if she could spend a day without using her phone.' And then I'll come out. *I'm that student!* The White House people showed her a bunch of pictures of kids from our school, and she picked me!"

"Natalie, that's amazing!" I say again. It isn't, really. This is just another example of how luck-filled Natalie's life has always been and will always continue to be. She'll probably grow up to be president. (I only hope I'm not the spy who has to uncover the dirty secrets that bring her down.)

It's a half hour later, and the Natalie news has gone viral throughout the Wilder household. In our crowded living room, Mom is FaceTiming with members of the family she hasn't spoken to in years. She's singled out the parents with overachieving children to let them know that Natalie has just reached a height that their offspring, however gifted, will never equal. The Say Hello girl herself, ironically, has not looked up from her phone in the past thirty minutes. Her fingers are a blur as she texts everyone in her wide circle.

Joanna and Ryan, who developed a weird, unexpected friendship when he sort of chaperoned my visit to New York, are trading amused barbs about the campaign. My father leans back in his leather chair and delivers a lecture about the presidential race. "Chester Brennan is a doofus, but he's not the worst president we've ever had," Dad tells me. "He's doing his best, even if his best is only adequate."

I perch on the arm of his chair and pretend to take notes on my phone.

"This is great stuff, Mr. Wilder," I tell him. "Tell me more."

"His weakness is foreign policy," Dad goes on. "This whole mess with Trezekhastan. We shouldn't get caught up in this stupid fight between them and Sabopapo."

"Savlostavia," I say. "And it's not Trezekhastan's fault . . ."

I stop myself midsentence. I have no idea who is actually to blame for the long-running war between the two Eastern European nations. But I do know when I was in New York, I saved the son of the Trezekhastan secretary of state from being assassinated by the evil, vile, heartless, malicious Vanessa Dominion. (She is completely irrelevant to me. I don't dwell on her, and I *never* wake up screaming from nightmares in which she calls me "peanut.") The secretary's son reached out to the Forties to thank me, and we follow each other on Trezekh.chat, his country's heavily censored version of social media. We're sort of friends.

Dad, meanwhile, continues his current affairs commentary.

"It's this independent candidate, Morgan Font, I don't trust. He's a billionaire who thinks he can run the country like he runs his internet retail corporation. He might tell you he works for us, but deep down he thinks we work for him. If a guy like that rises to a position of power, we're all in trouble. You think there's too much snooping into our personal business now? If this Morgan Font has his way, we'll be under surveillance every second of every day. We won't know who to trust. Someone under our own roof could be a spy!"

I jump off the arm of Dad's chair, grab Joanna, and yank her out of the living room.

CHAPTER NINE

OK Cupid

Later that night, while T-shirt (aka Marlon Moats) sleeps, I remotely access his laptop. I poke around his private files to find something useful so Joanna can weasel her way into his life. It's a scarily easy process. D——— T———— showed me how to do it. (If I wanted, I could access and control *his* computer and find out personal details about Ur5ula. Except he's probably set up all sorts of locks and tripwires and trapdoors to prevent a rookie like me from sneaking in. Not that I've ever tried, so I wouldn't know.)

Do I feel guilty about invading Marlon Moats's

privacy? Extremely. I would hate to have someone do this to me. But I saw the way Joanna's face lit up when I agreed to do this illegal act for her. I didn't know her face was capable of lighting up like that, and I want to see it again. So I'm looking through pictures of T-shirt's black lab, Ambrose; the soccer websites he's bookmarked; his iTunes playlists—nothing by Ruth Etting or L4E, so of no interest to me—and the list of foreign countries he wants to visit.

That last item is good intel; that's something Joanna can slip into a conversation with T-shirt.

I go through his calendar for the coming month. He seems to have a lot of afternoon appointments with a Dr. Klee, including one after school tomorrow. I do a quick search and discover that Dr. Klee is a local dentist. T-shirt has gleamingly white, immaculately healthy teeth. I wonder why he needs to see the dentist so often. *Another* topic he and Joanna have in common; she's always pulling and twisting at her last remaining baby tooth. This is starting to look like a match made in heaven.

Encouraged, I start to hunt through T-shirt's download files and come across a hidden bunch of pictures. *Uh-oh.* On the one hand, I know I shouldn't do this. On the other, NJ's face lighting up. I double-click and find myself gazing at two young people in love. T-shirt and . . . my old non-friend, Nola Milligan. My classmates Casey Breakbush and Kelly Beach, who are Nola's two slim, pretty, popular best friends, don't particularly like me, but they also don't out and out detest me. Nola, for some reason, does. I did not know she and T-shirt were a thing. It must have happened when Joanna was in New York, so *she* wouldn't have known, either. Problem teeth and an interest in traveling abroad might not be enough to increase Joanna's chances of finding a soul mate in T-shirt. Feeling let down and little embarrassed about how snoopy I've just been, I log out of T-shirt's computer and crawl into bed, where I mentally rehearse what I'm going to tell Joanna when she starts pummeling me with questions tomorrow.

"I'm making progress" and "I'm definitely on the right track," were what I told her this morning on our way to school. Now, though, it looks like the odds of making a love connection might be a little more in Joanna's favor than I previously thought.

But let me back up a bit.

The lunch bell rang, and I walked out of class behind Casey, Kelly, and Nola, who were conversing breathlessly in high-pitched yippy-yappy voices about the first lady's impending visit and how unfair it was that one of them hadn't been selected to be the face of the Say Hello campaign. They trotted into the hallway and bumped into a group of lean, tan, rowdy guys from the soccer team, including T-shirt. Casey and Kelly immediately got all giggly and hair-tossy around the soccer dudes. *Nola Milligan did not.* T-shirt smiled at her, displaying those gleaming white, seemingly perfect teeth, and she barely gave him the time of day. The sides of her mouth twitched, and at no point did her eyes meet his. Nola greets *me* with more warmth than that. I also noticed she made a point of hanging a few feet back from her two best friends in the world, with whom she is normally unable to function without constantly touching. But not today. Today, Nola hung back and she looked uncomfortable.

Hmm.

With no motive other than wanting to see my friend's face light up, I approach a slim, pretty, popular girl who openly dislikes me.

"Hi, Nola," I say, falling into step with her.

"And now my day's complete," sighs Nola without looking at me. "I just stepped in a steaming pile of Bridget Wilder."

"You keep getting funnier," I respond. "But seriously, can I talk to you for a minute?"

"Do you need me to give you a list of all the things

that are awful about you?" she asks. "'Cause that's going to need a lot more than a minute."

"Another time, perhaps," I say. Notice how I'm not letting her rattle me? Rest assured, I'm rattled inside. She's a skilled rattler. "I need some advice. It's about Marlon Moats."

That cool, *we don't breathe the same air* manner Nola wears like expensive perfume evaporates. She turns to face me. Her eyes dart to Casey, Kelly, and the soccer dudes, and then back to me.

"What?" she demands, her voice low and tense. "Why ask me?"

"Someone I know likes him . . . ," I begin.

A mocking smile appears on Nola's pretty face. "*You?* Seriously?" She lets out a harsh laugh. "I wouldn't wish him on my worst enemy. So you have my blessing."

"It's *not* me," I retort. "It's a friend of mine. You don't know her; she goes to another school. She likes him, or thinks she does, but if there's something you know about him, something you think *she* should know . . ."

Nola sucks her lower lip into her mouth. She looks torn. I can see she does not enjoy my company. But I can also see she's bursting to talk to *someone*. Nola grabs my elbow. "All right," she mutters. "Two minutes. No more."

She hustles me along the corridor and pushes me into the girls' toilet.

"She's having a bout of explosive diarrhea!" Nola shouts at the other inhabitants. "Get out now or you'll wear her stink all day." A handful of grossed-out girls flee the toilet. I give her an admiring look. That was a spy-worthy lie, even though it will no doubt end in my class-clown nemesis Brendan Chew labeling me Poopy Wilder, or worse.

Nola regards herself in the mirror. She concentrates on retouching her makeup and doesn't look at me.

"I liked him," Nola suddenly says. "I liked how he was all into me. I liked how we looked so good together it would make people jealous."

"That's a lovely sentiment," I say.

"But . . ." She pauses while applying lip liner. "He was like two different people. There was this one time, we were at the Yogurt Hut? A fly was buzzing around our table. I kept swatting it away and it kept flying back, and I did *this* . . ."

Still focused on the bathroom mirror, Nola snatches out her finger and thumb.

". . . and I *caught* it!" she exclaims. "I have amazing reflexes. And before I knew what I was doing, I squished it."

In the mirror, Nola rubs her thumb and finger

together. She then screws up her face in distaste.

"Gross, I know. It just happened. I ran to the toilet to wash my hands and when I got back Marlon was gone. He didn't answer my calls or my texts. I saw him at school the next day, and he walked right past me like I was invisible. *You* know what that's like."

Even when she's opening up to me, Nola still finds ways to jab at my weak spots.

"Then that night, he's waiting outside my house, and before I can say anything, he's like 'I am *so* disappointed in you. Don't you know all life is precious?' I'm like *whaaat?* You walked out on me because I killed a fly? Um, *bye?*"

Nola goes back to her reflection. She applies an extra coating of smudge-proof eyeliner.

"So then . . . ?" I prompt.

"So then, *obviously*, the calls and texts start flooding in. *Please. I'm so sorry. I think about you all the time.* I figure he's paid his penance. One last chance. And then he starts in on me about seeing his dentist."

"Dr. Klee?" I blurt out.

Nola shoots me a sharp look. "Stalkerish," she mutters.

"My friend wanted me to check him out, so . . ." I trail off. Nola's not buying it, but she wants to talk. So I shut up.

"Dr. Klee." She nods. "Dr. Klee this, Dr. Klee that. Dr. Klee's a genius. He'll fix your smile, outside *and* *inside*. What does that even mean? First, I don't need my smile fixed."

"It's good as new," I agree. "Like it's never been used." (Come on. I'm allowed to get *one* jab in.)

"So I tell him it sounds like you're into Dr. Klee a lot more than you're into me. And he doesn't argue. I started to talk to Casey and Kelly about it, but they *love* hanging out with the soccer guys, and if they have my back over how weird Marlon is, then no more soccer guys."

Just for a minute, I see the hurt in Nola's face. She realized what she was worth to her friends, and it wasn't as much as she hoped.

"Thanks for opening up to me," I say. "Anytime you want to talk."

Nola grimaces. "You'll be the first person I think of. If everyone else on earth is dead."

With that one last jab, she walks out of the bathroom, leaving me alone to put together the pieces of what she just told me.

I start to think about flies and dentists. Then I hear Brendan Chew's voice from out in the hallway. "Bridget Wilder's got diarrhea. *Landslide!*"

CHAPTER TEN

Open Wide

"Amassing data," I tell Joanna after school. But I don't tell her anything else because I have an urgent appointment with T-shirt's dentist. Dr. Klee's office is about six blocks away, situated on the second floor of Reindeer Crescent Medical Center. The big white building has a huge poster hanging outside as a greeting that features a happy, smiling doctor and an equally inviting nurse. The words *We'll Take Great Care of You* hang over their heads. Those words and the smiling medical faces do not seem to be encouraging the crimson-faced, trembling eight-year-old girl in the plaid kilt who has frozen to the spot outside the entrance to the medical center and refuses to budge another inch.

"*Please,*" hisses the girl's flustered mother. "We talked about this. You have to go in."

The girl digs her heels into the ground, folds her arms around herself, and shakes her head. I feel you, boo. This was me a few years ago. This is me *now*. I fear the dentist and his tools of torture, especially that Waterpik. I feel like I'm drowning when liquid starts blasting into my mouth. But I'm not going to tell her that. Instead, I approach the unhappy girl and her exasperated mother.

"Hi." I smile sympathetically. "I know it's none of my business, but, honestly, you don't have to be scared. This will be over faster than you think, and it doesn't hurt at all."

The girl looks up at me, her eyes shining with tears. "R-really?"

The mother looks relieved and also annoyed that I got through to her daughter in seconds.

I touch the girl's arm. "I'm early for my appointment, I'll sit with you if you want."

The girl nods.

And *that's* how I get to spy on T-shirt and Dr. Klee without anyone asking why I'm hanging out in a dentist's office where I don't have an appointment.

By an incredible stroke of luck, T-shirt is disappearing into the dentist's exam room just as I walk into the reception area with my new best friend. I sit with the scared-stiff girl and focus all my attention on the wall just above the receptionist's head. I touch the left arm of my glasses and feel the slightest of vibrations. Soon, I'll be able to see straight through the wall and into Dr. Klee's exam room.

Oh, I'm sorry. Didn't I mention I NOW HAVE X-RAY GLASSES! The geniuses at the Forties' Research and Development department made them for me. I can see through wood, stone, and steel. You can surround yourself with solid concrete, but you can't hide from Bridget Wilder. Well . . . that's not entirely accurate. You actually *can* hide from me any time other than the SIX SECONDS the glasses are active. After that, it takes them another eight hours to recharge.

That's probably why the Research and Development guys were so happy to let me have them. But six seconds is better than no seconds. So, while my little scared friend squeezes my hand and attempts to stay calm, I allow a little time to elapse. By my estimation, T-shirt will have been examined by the dental hygienist. I see the receptionist dart a quizzical look my way so I engage in conversation with my weepy companion for a few moments. Then I let my finger stray back to the leg of my glasses.

The white wall behind the receptionist melts away. I see straight through the small hallway that connects the reception desk and the exam room. I see Dr. Klee, a thin spindly guy with slicked-back hair. There's no dental assistant with him. T-shirt's eyes are closed and his mouth hangs open. Dr. Klee isn't examining him. The dentist is leaning over him, beaming a thin metal flashlight into his eyes, and talking to him.

The white reception walls reappear, barring my view. I let out a moan of frustration.

"Are you scared?" gasps the girl by my side who I'd completely forgotten about.

I jump to my feet. The girl gets up with me. "You'll be fine," I say, shaking her off. "It hardly hurts at all."

I hurry out of the dentist's office, trying to make sense of what I just witnessed.

My phone has access to the Forties' massive bulging criminal archive. I search for Dr. Klee. Nothing. I take a screenshot of his photo from his office website and download it to the archive's facial recognition technology.

By the time it makes a match, I have already walked home, watched three clips of Rose Murphy, a squeaky-voiced singer from the twenties recommended to me by

YouTube because of my Ruth Etting love, eaten a sandwich, and—worst of all—been wounded by a message from Adam Pacific. "Have fun at school today?" it said. Attached to the message was a picture of Pacific lounging in a dressing room with Cadzo, Lim, and Beano! Did I mention I hate him? Luckily, my phone distracted me from the Pacific injustice by making a *ding* sound to tell me the information I needed had been found.

The dentist in Reindeer Crescent Medical Center may call himself Martin Klee, but that's not the name on the criminal records the archive dug up. When he lived in Florida five years ago, he was known as Wyngarde Nacht, *Insect Activist!*

That is correct: our local dentist used to devote his life to protecting ants, worms, caterpillars, beetles, flies, and every other creepy-crawly you never think twice about stepping on. Except in Wyngarde Nacht's mind, that made you no different than a murderer. Our dentist used to break into supermarkets and destroy their stock of bug repellent. His home was filled with beehives, ant colonies, and spiderwebs the size of curtains. He was eventually arrested for repeatedly harassing a Florida politician for not doing enough to protect insects. Wyngarde Nacht was a drooling, babbling nutcase who, at one point, went out in public wearing a beard of live bees.

Dr. Martin Klee is something else. But what? And what is T-shirt doing making repeated visits to his office?

Luckily, I'm still grounded, so I have plenty of time to sit in my room and think through all the possible angles of this strange situation. I fixate on the image of Klee/Nacht on my phone and wonder what's going on in his bizarre insect-infested mind.

"What's happening with the T-shirt investigation?" says Joanna, pushing my closed door open and making herself at home in my room, as she does most nights. I go to click the image of the dentist from my phone. But then I stop. If Nola Milligan hadn't talked to me, I would never have found out about the dentist's former identity. It gets lonely keeping all this stuff to yourself. Maybe Joanna will see T-shirt in a new light if I tell her everything. Maybe she'll stop idealizing him and realize he's just as flawed as the rest of us.

I have to be careful, though. New Joanna has *feelings* now. Sensitivities. She has a heart, and that heart can be broken. I have to baby-step her through the truth about T-shirt. I reach for a box of tissues as I talk, just in case I have to deal with a tsunami of tears.

"*That*'s his type? Nola *Milligan*?" are her first words after I've told her the strange story of my trip to the dentist. "So over him."

Oh. Okay then.

"But that thing he said when Ebola Milligan murdered the fly, 'All life is precious.' Do you think the crazy dentist has been converting T-shirt to the cause of insect activism?"

I . . . would have made that connection eventually. I'm a little put out that Joanna made it instantly.

"What's the plan?" she says, sitting on the end of my bed, her face all eager.

"*My* plan," I reply, emphasizing the *my* part, "is to find out from T-shirt what Klee's been filling his head with."

"Right, but what if he doesn't know?" argues Joanna. "What if . . ." She gnaws on a fingernail, working the problem around in her head. "What if he's under the power of suggestion? What if there's something lodged in his subconscious. Like, the dentist told him to go free a bunch of bees from their beehives or something?"

I struggle to keep up with her. "And he doesn't know it until someone coughs three times or says 'submarine' or something equally random?"

"Maybe." She nods.

Can I admit to being a little bit jealous here? Spying is *my* thing. New Joanna shouldn't be that good at it. Or maybe I'm just bad? Maybe I really am a gimmick like

Adam Pacific said. God, seeing that picture of him with Cadzo and the boys really dented my self-confidence.

"We need to get back into the dentist's office," says Joanna. "And I know how."

She sticks half of her hand into her mouth.

"What are you doing?"

"Ah ja be a mu" is what I think she says.

Then a thin sliver of blood trickles down her chin.

"Ack!" I exclaim.

Joanna pulls her hand out of her mouth, and clutched between thumb and forefinger is her last baby tooth. She points to my phone and says something that sounds like *Make an appointment for me.* She gives me an excited nod, while blood continues to dribble out of her mouth.

I look at Joanna in disbelief.

"Have some tissues," I say, passing her a handful from the box I brought to mop up her heartbroken tears.

T-shirt. Nola Milligan. Dr. Klee. New Joanna. No one's exactly who they seem to be anymore.

What's going on?

CHAPTER ELEVEN

Spider Man

"You're a smart young person," says Dr. Klee. "The first lady is visiting your school today, but you chose to come here rather than waste your morning on phony promises and hot air, which means I can give your cavities the attention they deserve."

Joanna was fizzing over with excitement about her big plan to uncover the truth about Dr. Klee. So much so that on the way to the dentist's office she began spontaneously singing a theme song dedicated to the mission.

"Here come the spy twins on another adventure, here come the spy twins coming to your town."

Her catchy chorus runs through my head as I sit back in the dentist's chair with a bib around my neck staring up at the spindly Dr. Klee. Yes, even though Joanna yanked out her own baby tooth with her own hand, I couldn't put her in the path of potential danger. Instead, I've put myself in the path of unexpected dental work. (Luckily, Dr. Klee offers free consultations for first-time patients.) But I have a plan, and Joanna's out in the reception area, ready to put *her* part of the plan into operation should things go hinky on my end.

Before Dr. Klee can start stabbing and scraping inside my mouth, I raise a hand to scratch my nose, at the same time giving him a clear view of the spider tattoo that temporarily occupies the back of my hand.

"You know, that's the St. Andrews cross spider," announces Dr. Klee. "Indigenous to Australia."

"So called because of the cross he forms in the center of his web," I retort knowledgably. "His distinguishing feature is his yellow-and-brown-striped abdomen." (Exchanging spider trivia was a private little joke between me and D——— T————. I'm sure he and Ur5ula have their own secret jokes. Not that I care.)

The expression on Klee's face is somewhere between surprised and suspicious.

"Ah, we have a young arachnologist in our midst," he says, testing me.

"I wouldn't say I'm a spider expert," I volley back. "Not when there's so many other species out there."

Klee's big eyes and droopy mouth turn sorrowful. "Unfortunately, there are less and less. Our bees are facing extinction, and that's just the start. The leaf beetle. The stone fly! They're vanishing before our eyes, and no one seems to care."

"I care," I pipe up, though, honestly, I'd never heard of the stone fly until Klee brought it up, and I'm pretty sure I'll be able to survive its sad loss. "If enough of us raise our voices, we can still save insects in peril."

Klee gives me a sad smile. "To the people in power, we don't matter any more than the black-backed meadow ant." His face darkens. "But they might not feel that way when something happens to one of their own."

"One of their own what?" I ask.

"Enough talk," says Klee. "Let's take a look in there." I open my mouth. He holds up a penlight and moves it toward my open mouth. As soon as the thin metal flashlight gets close, I involuntarily shut my mouth.

"Don't be scared," says Klee in a low, smooth voice. "Eeeverything's fiiine. Nooothing to worry about. Truuust me. Thaaat's riiight."

The drone of his voice causes my fear to fade. I open my mouth. He pushes the flashlight toward me and moves it slowly in a semicircle. "You're doing greeeaaat," he intones. "Niiice and wiiide for me. Gooood girl."

The exam room seems to get hotter. The chair vibrates ever so slightly. I feel myself start to drift away. It's like I'm not in Klee's office anymore. I'm floating in warm blue water, the sun caressing my face.

"Concentrate on the sound of my voice. Nothing but my voice. Save the insects by any means necessary. Just my voice, Bridget. That's gooood."

And then, like a shark causing the calm sea to ripple, I hear Joanna in my head: *What if he's under the power of suggestion? What if there's something lodged in his subconscious?*

My eyes spring open. That's what Klee's doing to me! He's planting a suggestion, just like he must have done with T-shirt.

"Clooose your eeeyyyes. Let yourself floooaaat away."

What does he want with me? What suggestion is he trying to implant into my subconscious mind? Did he say something about saving the insects by any means necessary? I not only open my eyes, I touch my X-ray glasses. I have six brief seconds to search Klee's exam room for clues. The room turns transparent. I see dental records, scary metal instruments, and, on the top of a medical cabinet shelf, I see a row of plastic vials. Each one contains a winged insect. There's a space in the middle. One vial is missing. My six seconds come to an end. The exam room returns to normal.

"Alllmooost done," Klee purrs. "A feeewww moments more."

My mind unclouds. Fresh thoughts pour in. T-shirt's frequent visits. One missing insect. "They might not feel that way when something happens to *one of their own*."

I shoot out an arm and grab for the nearest dental instrument lying in the metal tray at the side of the chair. As I shove it into Klee's face, I see that I'm clutching my old enemy, the Waterpik. I spray it in his open mouth. He starts gurgling and choking. *Now you know how I feel!*

I give him another spray in the eyes, and then, faster than lightning, I jump up on the dentist's chair, kick out, and slam my foot into the still-choking Klee's shoulder. He staggers backward, falling onto a footstool. I rush at him, holding the Waterpik out at his soaking face.

"What did you tell T-shirt to do?"

"HEEELP!" Klee starts to screech.

From outside the exam room, I hear far louder screams. The other spy twin, Joanna Conquest, has just swung into action. By action, I mean that she pretended to sneeze and, at the same time, bit into a packet of ketchup, to give the impression that blood is pouring from her mouth, thus distracting the dental staff from responding to Klee's cries for help.

"Marlon Moats!" I yell over the dentist's screams. "You planted a suggestion in his head."

"HEEELLLPPP MEEE!!!" Klee continues to screech.

I run to the medical cabinet, wrench the door open, and reach up to the top shelf. I grab a plastic vial with what looks like a wasp inside it.

"Don't touch that!" Klee gasps.

I start to unscrew the top.

"No," begs Klee. "It's not ready."

"For what?" I snarl, brandishing the Waterpik and the insect vial in his wet, twitchy face. "Tell me everything, Klee. Or should I say Nacht?"

He shrinks at the mention of his real name.

"It's a common household fly implanted with the stinger of a tarantula hawk wasp. It's been kept unconscious until the body accepts its new part, and then I'll get one of my army to use it as a weapon."

I stare at him in horror. No wonder people are scared to visit the dentist!

"Can't you see?" he wails. "This has to be done. It's the only way to get the insects the attention they deserve."

"Is Marlon Moats part of your insect resistance?" I

demand. "Does he have the missing bug vial? What sort of hybrid monster is in it?"

"A wasp implanted with the stinger of the Japanese giant hornet," Klee says proudly.

"Who are you using it against?"

Klee gives me a defiant look. "It's too late," he says. "You can't stop him. It won't hurt her. She'll be paralyzed. And if they want the antidote, they'll have to do what I say."

I start to ask, "Who'll be paralyzed?" But I already know. "It's the first lady, isn't it? You sent T-shirt to unleash one of your creatures on Jocelyn Brennan?"

"By any means necessary!" Klee yells.

I suddenly feel faint. "My little sister's going to be on that stage alongside the first lady."

I want to rip Klee to screaming shreds, but I can't waste another second. So I give him a final blast of Waterpik to the face and then I charge out of his exam room.

At the start of my spy career, I saved Natalie from being drugged and abducted by the evil, psychotic head of Section 23. Now I'm rescuing her from being stung by a mutant insect.

Best big sister EVER!

CHAPTER TWELVE

The Sting

"*Faster, Uber driver!*" Joanna and I both scream at Jesse, whose only crime was his promptness in picking us up the second we fled the Reindeer Crescent Medical Center. Big Log got Joanna an Uber account in case of emergencies. She probably didn't think we'd be using it to rush to our school to stop a hypnotically suggested soccer player from letting a wasp fitted with the stinger of the deadly Japanese giant hornet attack the first lady of the United States of America, *or* my sister, Natalie, the face of the Say Hello campaign. But if this doesn't qualify as an emergency, I don't know what does.

Jesse flinches as we scream at him, and he drives his little blue Mini Cooper toward our school as fast as it is capable of going on an unusually busy weekday morning. I texted Strike and Irina the shocking details of Klee's scheme and tipped off the local police that the dentist was a threat to the first lady. If Jesse can't get us to the school on time, at least I know I've alerted reinforcements.

"You think T-shirt was under suggestion when he dated Nola?" Joanna asks, breaking my concentration. "She has insectoid features."

I give Joanna a pained look. Her face is still smeared with ketchup.

"Just trying to keep things light," she says. "We'll get there in time to save the most important woman on the planet. And also Jocelyn Brennan."

I laugh out loud. Joanna, it turns out, is fun to have around on spy missions.

She breaks into our catchy theme song. "Here come the spy twins on another adventure, here come the spy twins coming to your town. . . ." I join in for a reprise of the chorus.

"Uh-oh," says Jesse.

I stop singing as I see the reason for his *uh-oh*.

A police car signals us to pull over. Maybe they got Klee to confess? Maybe they want me to help them catch

T-shirt? Maybe I'll get to ride in the cop car with the siren wailing!

Jesse stops his Mini Cooper and rolls down his window.

A uniformed cop leans inside and looks back at us. "Bridget Wilder?" he says.

"Did you get Klee to talk?" I ask, sounding brisk and businesslike, as if we're fellow law enforcers.

"Step out of the car please, miss," says the cop.

I'm getting a ride in the police car!

I climb out. The cop peers down at me. "Dr. Klee made a complaint against you. He says you assaulted him, disrupted his place of business, and caused him emotional distress."

My mouth opens and closes. "He what . . . I what . . . he what?"

"His receptionist saw you get into this car. I need you to come with me to the precinct."

"You're taking Klee's side?" I yelp. "Didn't you get my tip? He's a threat to . . ."

This is pointless. Whatever I say next will make me sound like a hysterical nut job. I nod sadly, lower my head, chew on my lip, and put my hand in my pocket. I pull out a tissue to dab my eyes.

The officer is kind enough to wait for me to gather

my emotions. This is a mistake on his part because, as I reached into my pocket, I also pulled out Klee's vial. I pop the lid and yell, "You're free, you monster, now *attack!*"

Nothing happens.

I shake the vial, and a dead fly falls to the ground.

"Klee!" I howl in frustration.

"Get in the car," growls the officer. He takes a step toward me and then freezes to the spot. His face reddens, and he lets out a scream of pain.

The officer hops up and down on one foot. I stare at him in confusion, and then I realize what just happened. He stood on the dead fly's transplanted stinger, which, obviously, was long and sharp enough to pierce the leather of his cop shoes. Klee's reign of terror has claimed its first victim! I'm not sticking around to let him sting anyone else.

"Call nine-one-one," I yell at Joanna. "That cop's been stung by a tarantula hawk wasp. He has a one in five chance of survival if treated quickly."

"One in *five?*" yells the cop. I probably shouldn't have said that out loud. He yanks his shoe off and hops to his car to call for assistance.

"What are you going to do?" says Joanna.

"Run!" I shout over my shoulder as I take off toward the school.

CHAPTER THIRTEEN

VIP

WELCOME FIRST LADY blare the signs and banners decorating the outside of Reindeer Crescent Middle School. A few camera crews, some local news, some national, are lined up outside the front entrance. Breathless from my mad dash to save the day—how fondly I think back to the time I wore nanosneakers and ran like the wind—I slink around behind the school where the food supply truck delivers the fresh slop for the cafeteria. I'm hoping to avoid the black suits, dark glasses, and headphones of the Secret Service agents scoping out the area. After almost getting arrested, I figured I needed to be inconspicuous.

As I make my way toward the kitchen, the door opens and a girl, wearing a white apron and a kitchen worker cap pulled down over her eyes, comes running out. I try to step aside before we collide, but she, of course, steps aside at the exact same moment, and we bang into each other. My forehead makes contact with her cap. I see a pair of panicked eyes.

"Move," she gasps and shoves past me, pulling the cap back down.

"Rude," I fire back.

I run into the kitchen and through the empty cafeteria. As I approach the assembly hall, I hear a mass of voices, some shouting, some laughing, some arguing, some yawning. This is a hall filed with bored, impatient middle school kids. The first lady's visit has not started yet. I'm not too late to save the day.

"She's here," crows Brendan Chew, his screechy voice cutting above the drone. "The *worst* lady!"

Every head in the school auditorium swivels to look my way. I feel my face go red. Grateful for the distraction from the boredom, the student body erupts in cheers. Vice Principal Tom Scattering stomps up to me. "Stop trying to make this about you," he grumps. "Find a seat and stay out of trouble."

I exhale loudly to signify my disgust at the unjust way I'm being treated. Then I squeeze past the long, sprawling legs of three sixth-grade guys who don't even move to let me past, and sit down in the one empty chair in the middle of the second-to-last row.

I look around for signs of T-shirt. Four rows ahead of me, I see the soccer guys sitting with Casey, Kelly, and Nola. I do not see their teammate, Marlon Moats. My phone dings. A text with a photo attached. *Please don't be from Adam Pacific.* It's from Adam Pacific. It reads "Another boring day." *Don't click on the picture.* I click on the picture. Pacific riding a water scooter in what looks like Hawaii with Cadzo and Kecks. I let out a loud groan.

Our principal, Mr. Piedmont, walks onto the auditorium stage. A mass of boos greets him. He is visibly nervous, pulling out a handkerchief to mop his glistening forehead. Gradually, the noise lessens.

"It is my pleasure to introduce to you," booms Piedmont. "That she made the time in her busy schedule to single out Reindeer Crescent. Not only an honor, but an opportunity to learn and be inspired by a public figure with not only a conscience but also a conscience."

Laughter fills the auditorium. Piedmont blinks in confusion. There is no connection between his brain and the words that are flopping out of his mouth. I glance at the auditorium exit, where Tom Scattering is doing a poor job at hiding his embarrassment. Piedmont attempts to wind up his incredible introduction. "And so without further ado, let me thank her for her time and dedication, the president of . . . the *first lady* of the United States of America, Mrs. Jocelyn Brennan."

Two Secret Service agents stand on both ends of the stage. At the same moment, a blinding light fills the auditorium, causing the assembled students to utter a collective gasp. That blinding light is the combination of confidence, friendliness, and charisma exuded by Jocelyn Brennan. She has a lot of blond hair, a lot of white teeth, and only two eyes, but they're big enough to make even the slobby sixth graders who wouldn't move their legs to let me past feel as if she were gazing straight at them. Even though I can't look away from her, I am aware of those three slobs sitting up a little straighter in their seats.

She's casually dressed in a blue denim jacket opened to reveal a white sweatshirt emblazoned with the words *Say Hello*.

Mrs. Brennan lets us drink her in, then she raises the microphone to her lips and says, "Hello."

She lets out a laugh like a gurgling stream, as if she's just said the funniest thing in the world. The three sixth-grade slobs laugh and clap, and not in a mean way. The first lady won them over with just one word.

"First, I want to thank Principal Piedmont for letting

me come visit your beautiful school. I only wish my daughter, Jamie, could have been here today, but, poor thing, she's a little under the weather. I'll tell her y'all said hello, though."

Massive applause erupts from the student body. Jocelyn Brennan knows how to stay on message. Addressing us in her Texan twang, she continues. "I guess Jamie's heard my little talk about a hundred times too many." She impersonates a sullen teen voice. "*I get it, Mom. I spend too long on the phone.*' How many times have y'all heard that one? But I'm not talking about the cost of the calls you make. I'm here today to talk about another kind of cost. A human cost. Let me bring out someone you probably all know. A student here at Reindeer Crescent and someone that I'm excited to get to know. Say hello to Natalie Wilder."

I feel a swell of pride. My little sister, who has maybe never looked prettier, steps out on stage, smiling shyly but clearly relishing every moment.

At this point, I'm not really listening to what's being said. We all get the idea: stop living your life through apps and Instagram. I'm just watching Natalie interact with the first lady, charming, confident, and completely unfazed. I'm so wrapped up with what's happening on the stage that I fail to notice Marlon Moats is now sitting with the rest of his soccer teammates.

How did I miss that? When did that happen?

I move my focus from the stage to the back of Moats's head. He will not make a move that I will not see. I will be ready for him.

Mrs. Brennan talks to Natalie some more and then closes with some stuff about us being the next generation of leaders, and blah-blah-blah. Piedmont gestures needlessly for us to show our appreciation. Every student is up on their feet applauding. I keep my eyes trained on T-shirt, ready for him to make his move.

The applause continues. Mrs. Brennan hugs Natalie and gets my sister to put her number in the first lady's phone.

I smell flowers and, sure enough, Vice Principal Tom Scattering is walking up the aisle toward the stage, clutching a bouquet of red roses.

I look back at T-shirt. He stops applauding, reaches across his row, and hands Nola Milligan a single red rose. I didn't see Marlon enter the assembly hall. I didn't see where Veep Scattering got the bouquet. My spy senses kick in: *Klee's insect resistance protects its own. The suggestion he planted in T-shirt's mind must have included the command to find someone to take the fall for him.*

That bouquet that is making its way ever closer to the

stage—to the first lady, and to Natalie—contains a wasp with the lethal stinger of a Japanese giant hornet.

I jump to my feet, and once again those slobs will not move their legs to let me past.

"Mr. Scattering!" I yell. "Drop the bouquet. There's a mutant wasp/hornet thing inside!"

Applause, cheers, and loud declarations of *Hello!* echo around the assembly hall. No one hears me.

"Get the first lady off the stage!" I scream.

Again, no one pays attention.

I stumble my way out of my row, hold up my palm, and, with a squeeze, demagnetize Red.

The unleashed nanomarble hurtles toward the vice principal, striking him on the ankle.

Scattering's leg gives way. He falls to the ground, and, as his arms flail in the air, the bouquet flies from his open hand.

The assembly hall erupts with laughter.

Up on the stage, the Secret Service agents attempt to hustle the first lady out of the nearest exit. I see her gesture for them to step back. With a concerned look on her face, she starts to climb down from the stage. "How could I leave without saying hello to my beautiful bouquet?" she asks us.

Mrs. Brennan's graciousness sends the students into

an even louder frenzy of applause.

Her life is literally in my hands at this moment.

I run to the back of the assembly hall, detach the fire extinguisher, and charge toward the stage.

"Stop right there," snarls a Secret Service agent, putting himself in front of me. I lower the fire extinguisher and raise my hand. I squeeze my ring, and Red bounces off his forehead, knocking him on his back. I grab the fire extinguisher, hop over the Secret Service agent's body, and head for the stage.

As I run, I discharge the extinguisher, and a huge white jet of foam sprays out in front of me.

Just as the first lady reaches to pick up the fallen bouquet, the foam hits her full in the face.

Mission accomplished! It's only when I try to switch off the fire extinguisher that I realize two things:

1. Everyone is staring at me in shock, disbelief, and, in some cases, open hatred.
2. I do not know how to shut the fire extinguisher off.

White jets of foam splatter onto the dark suits of the Secret Service agents, who charge off the stage toward me. Principal Piedmont slips on the foam and flaps around on the floor like a goldfish dumped out of its bowl.

I let the fire extinguisher fall to the ground. I glance at the enraged faces of my fellow students. For a second, I catch a glimpse of Brendan Chew. He is *seething* with jealousy. Just before the Secret Service agents reach me, I look back at the stage. Natalie stands alone, staring straight at me. She is *furious*.

I feel the hands of the Secret Service around my arms. They walk me out of the assembly hall. I stare straight ahead, ignoring the glares of my fellow students. A breathless Joanna enters the hall as I am being led out. Our eyes meet.

"Did I miss anything?" she asks.

CHAPTER FOURTEEN

Consequences

I got suspended from school for a week. Mom and Dad had to come to Principal Piedmont's office and collect me. It wasn't a great meeting. The principal read out the list of my alleged crimes. "Assaulting a dentist, wounding a police officer's foot and avoiding arrest, knocking over a Secret Service agent, and dousing the first lady of the United States in foam."

"Yeah, okay, when you put it like that, it sounds bad," I said.

I heard my dad laugh and, for a second, felt a burst of optimism. Then I saw his face. It wasn't the right kind of laugh. It was the "I have to laugh because otherwise I might punch a hole in the wall" kind of laugh.

"Is it true, Bridget?" asked Mom, her face pale. "Everything he said?"

I shifted in my seat. "Yes, but . . . there were reasons . . ."

And that's when I trailed off and fixated on the floor.

"I thought we talked about your lying," Mom said.

I obviously wasn't that good of a liar because there was no way for me to lie my way out of this.

"I'm *so* sorry, Mr. Piedmont," I heard Mom say. "I've always known Bridget was a little bit envious of Natalie. She's such an accomplished girl. She's popular, and she gets a lot of attention. The things that come easy to her are harder for Bridget. I understand she gets jealous. But for her to act out like this . . ."

I felt my face burn. "I'm not *jealous*," I snapped. "I was trying to save her."

I heard Dad's non-laugh again.

"Is that what Carter Strike told you to say?" Mom responded. "Or did that come from *Irina*?"

"God, Mom," I said. "Stop saying her name like that. If anyone's jealous, you are."

And the meeting went downhill from there.

Neither of them said a word to me on the way home. Natalie hasn't spoken to me. She won't even look at me.

I don't think she'll ever forgive me. How could I tell her why I ruined her big day? I'd rather she think I was crippled with jealousy than have her find out she was in danger of being paralyzed by the sting of a mutant insect. Ryan actually had my back. "She's following in my footsteps," he told our grim-faced parents. "But I wear big shoes. Give her a break." There was no break to be given. My after-school grounding now became an all-day grounding. No phone. No computer. No contact with the outside world. Not even Joanna. How could I argue with that?

So here I am, lying in bed on the first full day of my week-long banishment from Reindeer Crescent Middle School and my ostracism from the Wilder family. Normally at this time, I would be trying to get into the bathroom after Natalie but before Ryan. (It smells nice after her, less so after him.) Today, there's no reason to get out of bed.

"Get out of bed," says Mom. She walks into my room with a tense look on her face.

"Why?" I yawn. "What's the point?"

"The point is, the director of the Secret Service is downstairs in our living room, and she wants to see you. So get out of bed, get dressed, and get downstairs *now*."

Mom hasn't had her first cup of coffee of the day. She

hasn't washed her face or brushed her hair. She's flustered, nervous, and mad at me.

"Why?" Am I going to get in trouble for using Red to knock that agent out?

"Do I look like I know why?" Mom barks. "Who knows what other disasters you've been responsible for."

"Mom . . . ," I start. I want to say something about how this isn't in any way my fault, but because of the huge teetering mountain of lies I've told her to successfully maintain my secret spy life, I'm lost for words.

"Don't keep the Secret Service waiting," she says.

A tall woman wearing a tailored gray suit with closely cropped silver hair and thick black glasses stands in the middle of the Wilder living room.

"Adina Roots," she says as Mom and Dad lead me into the room. The director of the Secret Service gives me a quick up-and-down look, as I'm sure she's done to many suspects over the years.

"She's always been a good girl," says Mom, who looks increasingly nervous. "She's never been in any trouble."

"We used to *wish* she would get in some trouble," Dad chuckles. Mom shoots him an enraged *shut up* death-glare.

"She recently came into contact with her biological

mother," says Mom. "I think she might be a bad influence."

"*Mom!*" I moan.

"Bridget's not in any trouble," says Adina Roots of
the Secret Service. "But we need to get a more complete
picture of why the events leading to yesterday's incident
occurred. I'd like, with your permission, to interview
Bridget about the events leading up to her attack on the
first lady. . . ."

"It was so not an attack," I interrupt.

"Bridget!" cautions Mom.

"I'd like to evaluate your daughter's psychological
state so we can get a better understanding of what drove
her to do what she did, and so we can prevent anything
similar occurring in the future."

I start to get nervous. "What's happening here?"

"Director Roots," Dad starts to say. "This seems like
an overreaction."

"We all want what's best for Bridget, don't we?"
says Roots. "Nobody wants to see her get into any more
trouble."

Mom and Dad look at each other. "What will the
evaluation entail?" asks Mom.

"I'd like to bring Bridget into our local office for
questioning," replies Roots.

"Wait, the Secret Service has an office in Reindeer Crescent?" says Dad.

"We're everywhere," replies Roots. "I have a car outside. I will take Bridget to the office. One or both of you need to follow in your own vehicle and pick up your daughter at the end of the session, which I do not expect to exceed ninety minutes. Any questions?"

"I've got a question," I pipe up. "How's the agent I hit in the head? I'd like to apologize to him, if that's possible."

"Of course," says Roots. "Maybe the sound of your voice will wake him from his coma."

Mom, Dad, and I all gasp in unison.

"He's quite fine," the director tells us. "That was Secret Service humor. We're known for it."

A Secret Service agent stands by the back passenger door of a black SUV parked outside our house. The agent opens the door as Adina Roots and I approach. I look over my shoulder at Mom, who is climbing into our Jeep Compass.

"It's okay," she calls to me. "I'll be right behind you."

I give her a half-smile that I hope gets across that I'm scared and I'm sorry she got dragged into my mess, but I'll be okay. Then I slide into the vehicle.

"Why would your mother throw me under the bus like that?" demands Irina, who is sitting in the back of the car with Strike, pointing to the listening device in her ear.

CHAPTER FIFTEEN

Career Opportunities

"Irina?" I say, aghast. "Strike? Why are you in the back of the Secret Service vehicle?"

"We're both mothers, both professional women," rages Irina as the SUV pulls away from my house. "We should be supporting each other. Instead, she undermines me and benigns my character every chance she gets."

"*Maligns* is the word you're looking for," says Strike.

"That's right, take her side," snaps Irina.

"What are you doing here?" I ask my biological parents a second time. "Why didn't you come into the house?"

"And be called a bad influence to my face?" sniffs Irina. "No, thank you very much."

Adina Roots shakes her head at Strike and Irina. "The CIA really put its trust in you two to run an entire department?"

"*I* run it," declares Irina. "*He* eats tortilla chips and plays video games."

"So delusional." Strike sighs.

Roots gives up talking to my birth parents and addresses her remarks to me. "I'm going to be truthful with you, Bridget. The Secret Service is underfunded and understaffed. We don't have the best public profile. Mistakes that shouldn't happen keep happening. I've worked with Strike in the past . . ."

"And yet she's still speaking to him," mutters Irina.

". . . and when he forwarded me your text about the attack on the first lady, I should have given it top priority. But I didn't."

I don't know exactly what's happening in this SUV, but I do know that I'm being treated with respect and taken seriously.

Roots goes on, "I didn't because, at the same moment I received your warning, the first daughter went missing."

"She wasn't under the weather like Mrs. Brennan said?" I ask.

"Jamie Brennan has a habit of disappearing from public engagements," replies Roots. "I had to make a decision whether to concentrate on getting her back or preparing for a mutant insect attack. I made the wrong call. Fortunately for this country, for the president and the first lady, you were there. You acted quickly and smartly. You did great work, Bridget."

"She always does great work." Strike smiles.

"She gets that from me," says Irina. "Maybe a bit from him."

Adina Roots looks at me over the tip of her thick glasses. "The Secret Service cannot afford a repeat of that situation. But as we get closer to Election Day, Jamie will be called on to make more public appearances, and no matter how many times she promises to accept her responsibilities, she will find some way to sneak away."

I inhale sharply. The girl who banged into me when I tried to get into the Reindeer Crescent school kitchen. The one with the cap pulled down over her eyes. I'll bet that was Jamie Brennan making her escape.

"We've managed to locate her and bring her back in one piece," Roots tells me. "We won't always be that lucky, and I no longer have the time or the manpower to devote to tracking her down."

"Which is where you come in," says Strike.

I get a little thrilled shiver. I feel a big mission coming up.

"You want me to be her bodyguard?" I ask.

"We want you to be *her*," Adina Roots replies.

"I . . . what now?"

Irina opens her black leather handbag and pulls out a white plastic circle. She fits it over her face. It's a nano-mask. A device that allows the wearer to assume another person's face. One of the pre-CIA Forties' most diabolical creations. In a split second, Irina's pale, severe features disappear and are replaced by those of my mother.

"I don't like this *Irina*, she's a bad influence," she screeches in a voice that sounds nothing like my mom. "How can someone as young as that, who dresses as cool as that, be a good mother? I am a very judgmental person."

"Okay, you made your point," says Strike.

Irina touches a finger to her chin. My mother's face vanishes in a hail of static and the plastic circle slips off her face. Irina passes it to me.

"You want me to wear the nanomask and become Jamie Brennan?" I ask.

"For public engagements," says Roots. "For the purposes of smiling, shaking hands, and posing in pictures. All the tasks Jamie finds so arduous."

"The week you've been suspended from school coincides with the West Coast leg of the president's reelection campaign," Strike tells me. "If you say yes, we can integrate you into the Brennan family almost immediately."

"Wait," I say. "They're okay with this? Jamie Brennan's okay with this?"

"Jamie's *thrilled*," grimaces Roots. "The president and the first lady are not in love with the idea, but they understand that it makes protecting them that much easier, and they want the world to see them as a happy, functional family, which your presence would accomplish."

I squirm around in my seat and look back at my mom's car, which is following behind us. I smell more lies in my immediate future. When you want to paint a picture of a happy, functional family, call Bridget Wilder.

"What do I tell *my* family?" I ask.

"After your psych evaluation, we're going to recommend that you spend your free week at the Secret Service foundation for at-risk youth, where we will endeavor to instill direction and motivation in you," says Roots.

"There's no Secret Service foundation," Strike assures me. "It's a total lie."

"But we have documentation and websites, and we'll Photoshop you into pictures and edit you into videos."

Irina smiles. "It'll be like you're there."

"Can I have a minute to think about it?" I ask.

"Of course." Roots nods. "Unfortunately, I don't have much more than a minute."

This is crazy. Lies on top of lies on top of lies. I look out the window as we drive through the streets of my hometown. I don't think I have the talent to assume someone else's identity for an entire week. I've never worn a nanomask before and don't relish the prospect of hiding under it for an extended period of time. But given the choice of being locked at up at home with no internet and no human contact but *a lot* of disappointment, or passing myself off as the daughter of the most powerful man in the world . . .

I hear Joanna's voice in my head singing: "Here come the spy twins on another adventure, here come the spy twins coming to your town . . ."

Would she say no to a job this big and this insane? I think she would not. And neither will I.

"Okay," I say.

"Thank you, Bridget," says Roots, breathing an actual sigh of relief.

"We'll be monitoring you every step of the way," Strike assures me. "If you feel you're in over your head, we'll be ready to jump in and help you."

"I have a question," I say.

They all look at me.

"There isn't really a Secret Service office in Reindeer Crescent, is there?"

Roots smiles. "We rented a space in the mall. We'll use the ninety minutes of your supposed interview to start orienting you to every aspect of Jamie Brennan's life."

"Plus we'll have breakfast," says Strike, looking happy at the prospect.

"That's basically all he cares about," Irina tells Roots.

I tune out my bickering birth parents and ponder the choice I've just made. Can I really pull this off?

"I know you can do it," says Adina Roots. "Just one thing, though."

She reaches toward me and pushes up the sleeve of my hoodie. The Magic Marker words *Cadzo Army* still run from my wrist to my elbow.

"You'll have to wash that off."

CHAPTER SIXTEEN

She's Leaving Home

"Who would have put money on you going to juvenile detention before me?" Ryan laughs. He walks with me as I head down the driveway of our house and roll my wheeled suitcase toward the government vehicle that's taking me to the nonexistent Secret Service foundation dedicated to setting troubled young people like myself on the road to a brighter future.

Mom and Dad don't say much. Adina Roots did a good job convincing them that I'd benefit from spending time among other at-risk youths, and they agreed a week stuck at home would be a waste of time. But now that

I'm actually leaving, they're both looking a little shell-shocked.

"This is all happening so fast," says Mom. "Maybe it's a mistake. Maybe we should talk to some other parents with kids who went to the foundation, see how the experience was for them."

"She doesn't need to go to some government brainwashing center," Dad says. "What if I took a few days off work? I'm a great motivator. I can talk to Bridget, set her back on the right track."

I feel sick with guilt.

Ryan takes the wheeled suitcase from my hand and rolls it toward the trunk of the vehicle. He bangs the top of the trunk for the driver to open and turns back to face our parents.

"First of all," he says, pointing a finger at himself. "This is Exhibit A in the case against Dad being a great motivator. Second, if she doesn't go, it'll be on her record that she sprayed the first lady and refused to take the Secret Service up on their generous offer of help. Yes, it'll be hard to get by without Bridget's happy face and winning personality, but we'll have to do our best to cope for the week she's gone."

The trunk opens, and Ryan throws my suitcase inside. He turns and walks past me, giving me the slightest of punches on the shoulder.

"Thank you," I whisper.

Dad hugs me. "This is nothing," he says. "This is a bump in your road, and your road is going to take you to awesome places."

"You *are* a great motivator," I tell him, and hug him back.

Mom pulls me close to her. "I didn't mean what I said about you being jealous of Natalie. This is all my fault. I don't let you know enough how special you are to me."

My throat swells, and my eyes get teary. "Mom, I know," I try to say.

She keeps hold of me. "When you get back, we'll spend more time together, just you and me."

I wait for her to let me go. This is the part of being a spy I'm never going to be okay with. I open the passenger door and get in.

"Let's go," I tell the Secret Service employee behind the wheel.

He starts the car. There's a series of loud bangs on my window.

It's Natalie.

"Wait," I yell at the driver. I jump out, and she throws her arms around me.

"I'm *so* mad at you," she gasps into my ear. "But I don't want you to be sent away."

"I know I messed up your big day, but I'll find a way

to make it up to you," I promise her.

"Just don't get in any more trouble," she replies.

I'm sitting on a toilet in the back of a Scandinavian delicatessen named Knudsen's, somewhere in San Francisco. My head is buzzing with all the information I've accumulated about Jamie Brennan in the two hours since I left Reindeer Crescent under a cloud of lies and tears. Adina Roots sent me an app packed with biographical details, family photos, press clippings, and TV interviews. In a perfect world, I would have had weeks to prepare. I would have watched videos of the way Jamie Brennan moves, the time she takes between answering questions, how loudly she laughs, and how many times she chews her food. I would be familiar with the little body language giveaways that signal if she's happy, sad, or lying. But I didn't have weeks. I had yesterday and the car ride to San Francisco and the twenty minutes I've been in Knudsen's toilet, changing out of my jeans and sweatshirt into the sort of floral shift dress Jamie favors.

This is all the stuff I've managed to memorize about Jamie Brennan: her upbringing in Westlake, a suburb of Fort Worth, Texas. Her childhood love of horse riding. Her favorite subjects in school. Her pets. Her best friend, Molly Costigan-Cohen. Her taste in fashion. The countries she hopes to visit. The books that inspire her. Her ambitions for the future, and the food she likes to eat.

I also know about the moment it all went wrong for Jamie. I remember Ryan referring to her as "the clumsy one," but I never really gave that too much thought until I saw the YouTube clip that had hundreds of millions of views. The clip where Jamie Brennan fell.

Six weeks after her father had been elected president, Jamie and her parents attended an awards ceremony. Jamie, who had proved very popular with the voters in the months running up to the election, had been chosen to introduce a children's choir. Sitting on the toilet in the back of Knudsen's, I replay the clip I've been watching on repeat since yesterday.

I see Jamie looking happy and confident as she walks onto the stage. I see her acknowledge the cheers and applause from the audience, and then I see her trip over a microphone lead and tumble off the stage. The drop is only about three feet, but as she falls she lets out an ear-piercing *AAAHHHRRRGGG!* of shock and terror. She isn't hurt, but she's ferociously, agonizingly embarrassed. Her mother, First Lady Jocelyn Brennan, goes rushing up to her fallen child to help her. The appearance of her mother, who, it should be said, looks *incredible*, has the effect of making Jamie even more embarrassed. She shakes First Lady Brennan off, backs away from her, and *falls over again*, this time grazing her knee. Jocelyn gasps and goes running to her daughter. Jamie pulls herself to her feet, runs away, and *falls over one more time!* The clip ends with the choir bursting into song as Jamie lies on the ground, motionless and sobbing.

What would I do if something that horrific happened to me in a public setting? Leave town. Change my name. Get a new face. Never speak or make eye contact with anyone ever again. Jamie didn't have that option. Her trilogy of falls inspired the unfortunate hashtag *#triple-tripper*, a million YouTube parodies, even more millions of memes, and some cruel TV sketches. Even now that it's almost four years later, I can see exactly why Jamie Brennan is no fan of appearing in public. Enduring something like that can scar a person for life. I'm still cringing about being kidnapped in an onion sack in the fridge of Parmesan Marmoset, and only two people saw that. So, even though I've been thrown into this mission, I feel a kind of kinship with Jamie Brennan. I want to do right by her. I want to remove the *#tripletripper* stigma from her name. I want to rehabilitate her public image and, in doing so, maybe give her the confidence to step back into the spotlight on her own, without falling over.

"Almost time to put your new face on," I hear Irina's voice murmur in my earpiece. "You ready?"

I get up from the toilet and approach the mirror. I lift the round piece of plastic to my face.

The nanomask was in my bedroom all last night. I held it in my hand. I lifted it up to my face. But I never put it on. Stupid, I know. I should have taken the time to get used to wearing it instead of leaving it to the very last minute, but I was afraid it would attach itself to my face and I'd never be able to remove it. Or that maybe it would burn my real face off and I'd be forced to wear it for life to hide the hideous scars underneath. But those are the fears of a scared little girl, not an experienced spy about to embark on the most important mission of her career.

"Don't forget to take off your glasses," says Irina.

"I hadn't forgotten," I reply. (I totally had.)

My glasses come off. A shiver rolls over me. The nanomask molds itself to my face. I don't feel a thing. I also can't see anything except a blurred outline of my reflection and then, magically, the nanomask adjusts my vision. My reflection comes into focus. I say *my* reflection, but what I mean is the pretty face of Jamie Brennan comes into focus. I stare at her perfect skin, dazzling white teeth, and dimpled cheeks. I can't believe criminals invented this technology and kept it secret. The Forties

could make billions selling this to people who are insecure about their looks.

"You're staring at yourself, aren't you?" says Irina.

"I'm not," I lie. "I'm just . . . adjusting the wig."

The wig goes on. It's a jet-black pixie cut. The final
touch is a smart white blazer. That is one stylish, well-
put-together young lady looking back at me in the mirror.

"Jamie Brennan, first daughter of the United States.
Very pleased to make your acquaintance," I tell my reflec-
tion. The words emerge from the mouth of the mask in
Jamie's soft Texan accent.

My phone emits a little digital whistle. The signal for
me to emerge from the bathroom and become a whole
new person. There's that shiver again. This is the biggest job yet in my short spy career, and I'm suddenly *very*
aware of the pressure on me.

"Showtime," says Irina.

"Wish me luck," I say.

"You don't need it."

I take a breath and then push open the bathroom door.
Suddenly I'm thrust into a babble of loud raised voices.
The staff and customers of Knudsen's are yelling and
shoving one another in order to show their support of the
first lady. They bark her name and shove their phones in
her direction. Jocelyn Brennan remains serene amid the

chaos. She looks around and gives me that thousand-watt smile.

"Jamie," she sings out. "At last. Come and say hello to everyone here at Knudsen's."

I freeze as every phone in the packed delicatessen is pointed at me.

"Look over here," shouts a customer.

"Wave to my uncle in Monterey," demands another.

First Lady Brennan makes a beckoning gesture, and I pick up my pace, anxious to launch into my role as the new, improved, reliable, relatable version of Jamie Brennan.

I concentrate on smiling and waving for the phones that are recording my every movement. I'm also trying to maintain eye contact with Jocelyn Brennan. I don't immediately see the waitress backing away from the table to my left, carrying an armful of dishes.

Luckily, my birth mother is monitoring my movements.

"Bridget," I hear Irina shout. "Veer right!"

My whip-fast reflexes enable me to sidestep out of her path inches before we collide. Unfortunately, I slam straight into a frazzled, breathless mother carrying a red-faced, shrieking baby.

"He's going to be sick," bawls the mother, just as the baby unleashes a powerful blast of milky puke.

"Pivot to your side," Irina yells in my ear. I leap sideways to avoid being splattered and instead hurtle into the open doors of a display case crammed with basketball-size doughnuts topped with whipped cream. I am immediately overcome by a tidal wave of strange sensations. My hands sink into the doughnuts, my face is splattered in whipped cream, and I breathe in sugar frosting.

"Bridget . . . um . . ." I hear Irina in my ear. She has no advice to give me.

I peel myself off the display case, and *that* is when I slip on the puke and hit the ground butt-first.

"Hold on to your wig!" Irina finally shouts.

CHAPTER SEVENTEEN

Great First Impression

Luckily, the first lady was amazing. She's the definition of grace under pressure. While her campaign staff—none of whom have high enough security clearances to be entrusted with the secret of my true identity—freaked out, she picked me up and dusted me off. She smoothed out my clothes and escorted me away from Knudsen's and into her huge luxury campaign coach.

Her smile was radiant as we passed the bulging, astounded eyes of the Knudsen's staff and customers.

"You know what?" she told the crowds of staring faces. "No one's perfect. What matters is how we deal with the little setbacks that life throws in our way, and if I know my daughter, she's going to be laughing about this real soon. Won't we, hon?"

She gives me an encouraging nod. I feel relief wash over me. This might not be a disaster. I smile and roll my eyes at the crowd.

"That's my girl," says First Lady Brennan. "And her father and I, we'll be laughing right along with her."

But now that I have emerged, cleaned up and wearing unsplattered clothes, from the toilet of the Brennan campaign coach, Jocelyn Brennan is not laughing. She stares at her laptop, occasionally shaking her head in disbelief. The dozen or so men and women who work for her are glued to their phones, and they are not laughing, either.

"It's everywhere," mutters a tense-looking woman.

"It's gone viral in places that don't even have the internet," moans a balding guy.

"We're down an eighteenth of a point in the polls," frets a man wearing a baseball cap with the words *Stat Hat*.

"Jamie," the first lady says. "Let's step into my office."

The big-screen TV at the front of the bus shows a slow-motion replay of Jamie Brennan staggering back from the display cabinet, face covered in whipped cream, and losing her footing on the baby puke. The news anchors watching the footage find it hilarious. I smile, too, at the hilarious slapstick before I remember I'm looking at myself. My dumb, clumsy self.

"My daughter, *Jamie!*" First Lady Brennan says sharply. Right. That's me.

"My office," she says. I follow her to the back of the bus and close the door behind me.

The first lady's office is dominated by a very big, very comfortable looking double bed that I would very much like to crawl into right now. I fight the impulse and stand by the closed door as Jocelyn Brennan sits at her desk and stares at me. It's a long, hard stare devoid of any warmth. I shift awkwardly from foot to foot. The stare is punctuated by the vibrating of her phone, which she ignores.

"Your sister was so sweet and charming," says the first lady. "When Adina Roots told me that you were exceptional, that you were an experienced agent, I found it hard to believe, but then, I thought, why not? This is a nation of overachievers. Why wouldn't both sisters excel in their own chosen fields?"

"I'm adopted," I retort.

"I'm not surprised." First Lady Brennan scowls.

Gesturing to my face, she snaps, "Take that thing off. It's eerie."

I touch a finger under my chin, and the nanomask

slides off. I remove the wig. The first lady does not look impressed by what lies underneath.

She lets out a weary sigh and rubs her eyes. "This is my fault," she says. "Why would I agree to let you pass as my daughter? You soaked me with a fire extinguisher the first time we met. This was a terrible idea from beginning to end."

She picks up her phone. "I'll arrange to have you sent home. It's too close to the election for me to ask for Director Roots's resignation, but if your antics today haven't kept us out of office, I'll take her job away."

The first lady starts to make the call.

I have saved the world twice. I have brought two huge criminal organizations to their knees. I'm not going to be sent home because of a doughnut and a puking baby. I may have to live with the fact that my mother thinks I'm a screw-up, but I'm not having the first lady of the United States of America treating me like that.

"Wait," I say. "Let me fix this."

"Do you have a time machine?" she asks, her finger hovering on *call*.

I shrug off the first lady's attempt at sarcasm. I want her to understand who she's dealing with here.

"There's a fund-raiser ball in Santa Barbara tonight, right?"

"You'll be able to watch the highlights on CNN," replies Jocelyn Brennan.

"Let me go to the ball," I beg, and I immediately wince as I hear how that comes out. "Not like Cinderella. Like a spy. Like a smart spy with a plan to undo the damage she did."

There's fire in my eyes and a firmness to my tone that takes First Lady Brennan by surprise. I venture further. "You asked why the director of the Secret Service would recommend me. Because she knows my reputation. I've saved lives. I've stopped wars. I protected you from a paralyzing sting by a mutant insect. Yes, I slipped on baby puke and fell over, but you know what else I do?"

I give the first lady of the United States my own long, cold stare. She blinks at me in confusion.

"What?" she says in a quiet voice.

"I get back up."

"What does that mean?" asks First Lady Brennan.

Oh. I hoped my forceful delivery would be enough to restore her shaken faith in me, thus giving me time to come up with a plan. I guess not.

I begin to pace the length of her velvet-carpeted office. Long strides, shoulders back, head high: a professional deep in thought. "It means," I tell her, "that I'm going to put on that mask and that wig. I'm going to make some phone calls to some powerful people who you don't know and you don't need to know. And, by the time you've done your hair and put on your party dress, I'm going to do something that will get the name Jamie Brennan trending for all the right reasons."

Jocelyn Brennan's big eyes are even bigger. "What are you . . . ?" she begins.

"Leave it up to me," I tell her. "I'm Bridget Wilder, and I'm a spy."

Her face softens. She chews on her lower lip and then gives me a nod.

"Okay," says the first lady. "We all make mistakes. But you can't afford to make another one."

"I've got this," I brag, my hands on my hips, looking her straight in the eye.

The first lady gets to her feet and points a finger at me. "Then you shall go to the ball."

CHAPTER EIGHTEEN

POTUS

It might seem like being a spy has done wonders for my previously nonexistent social life. I get to meet interesting people and go to parties. But the interesting people usually want to kill me, and the parties are never that much fun. Tonight, I'm going to a party with the president. I've been in the penthouse suite of the super-posh Hidden Willows hotel in super-posh Santa Barbara for the past two hours. I spent a fraction of that time putting on my nice white party dress in preparation for tonight's fund-raising event, and the rest avoiding the disapproving glances of the campaign staff, who clearly blame me for the president slipping another twenty-ninth of a point in the polls.

"What's she going to do for an encore?" I hear the tense-looking woman whisper.

"I liked her better when we couldn't find her," moans the balding man.

Doesn't really put you in a party state of mind, does it?

First Lady Brennan—or FLB, as I now think of her—emerges from her room at seven o'clock, looking like a seven-foot-tall goddess with her big hair piled up, her high heels, and her sparkly silver dress.

"Doesn't Jamie look adorable?" she demands of her staff, who make mumbling *yes* noises but don't look very enthusiastic.

FLB pulls me close to her as if she's going to give me a motherly hug.

"I'm going to take you to meet the president," she says softly. "He's a very busy man with a lot on his mind. He's been briefed by Director Roots about who you are and what function you'll be serving while you're with us."

Okay. Time out. I'm meeting the president. I haven't even been a spy for very long, and I'm meeting the most powerful man in the world. I think I'm allowed to feel a little bit proud of myself. Not bad for a gimmick, huh, Adam Dumbface Pacific?

"Try to act normal, and don't break anything," hisses FLB.

FLB marches across the eight spacious rooms that make up the penthouse suite. I trot along at her side. We stop at a closed door flanked by two Secret Service agents. FLB gives me an appraising look up and down. She grabs my wrists and peers at my arms.

"They teach you to wash yourself where you come from?"

I follow her gaze to my forearm. There are very, very faint marks where the words *Cadzo Army* used to be.

"Get her a jacket," she orders one of the Secret Service guys. She nods at the other one, who opens the door.

Inside, the president sits with his feet up on a huge desk, watching a football game on his laptop. A crushed Diet Coke can sits alongside him.

FLB coughs loudly. The president looks up and an expression of guilt flashes across his face. Then he grins and swings his feet off the desk. As he stands up, I see he has the size and build of the college athlete he used to be. But he doesn't seem all arrogant and into himself like the middle school athletes I know. He seems nice.

"Here're my girls looking all pretty," he drawls, walking across the huge room toward us.

"Mr. President, this is Bridget Wilder," says the first

lady. "*Agent* Bridget Wilder, on special assignment from the CIA."

The president's grin fades. He stops in the middle of the room.

FLB gives me a nudge.

"Mr. President, this is an honor and a privilege," I declare, attempting to summon up the kind of sincerity Natalie would bring to such an important moment. "For you to put your trust in me is something I do not take lightly, and I want you to know—"

"Joss," he interrupts, looking over my head at his wife. "It's kind of creeping me out. Can we switch it off? Is there a chip or something?"

"Chester," FLB says with a tight smile. "Bridget is an experienced agent who . . ."

"I'll have one of the tech guys mute it," says the president, reaching into his pocket for the phone I clearly see sitting on his desk. He checks his jacket and pants and then throws up his hands in frustration.

"I *hate* machines," he shouts, and then gives me an apologetic look. "No offense."

Wait, *what*? Why would he say that? Unless . . .

Does the president think I'm a robot?

"Mr. President, I'm not a robot," I say.

"He knows you're not a robot," the first lady assures me.

The bemused expression on the president's face does not convince me of this.

I touch a finger under my chin, and the nanomask comes off.

The president lets out a cry of shock, and Secret Service agents burst into the room, guns out.

"It's fine," says FLB. "Return to your posts."

The two agents leave. The president stares at me. All of a sudden, he breaks into a smile and holds out his hand.

"Can I see that real quick?"

I look at FLB. She shrugs. I hand the nanomask to the president. "How come I don't have one of these?" he says.

"We'll get you one," the first lady tells him. "Now, we should head downstairs to the fund-raiser."

"How's it work?" he asks me.

"You know Shazam?" I say.

"The music gizmo? What, you just hold it up to a film of the person whose face you want to steal?"

"It has a facial recognition chip and enough memory for a hundred thousand faces," I tell him excitedly. "You select the person you want to be, and it turns you into him or her."

"What's it feel like when you put it on?"

"Scary," I admit. "Claustrophobic, at first. But you get used to it so fast, you forget you're wearing it."

"Chet," the first lady interrupts. "You can talk to Agent Wilder about the clever toy at the ball."

"Who's Bridget again?" asks the president. Then he breaks into that big grin and punches me on the shoulder. "Just kidding."

"He's always kidding," says the first lady, with a tight smile.

Secret Service agents open the door. Time to go.

I walk with the presidential party. As we're escorted to the elevator—with me now hiding my hideously disfigured arms inside a blue jacket—President Brennan leans in close and says, "I like it when people underestimate me. That way, they don't see me coming."

I gape at him. "You just summed up my entire existence."

The president laughs out loud. "I think you and me are going to get along fine, Bridget Wilder."

"You'll get along even better if you refrain from calling her Bridget Wilder when we're in a public place," says the first lady.

"Consider my wrist slapped," the president replies, giving me a wink like we're friends.

The elevator doors open. FLB pulls me back and leans down. "He's easy," she says. "You've got a lot more people to win over. Don't mess it up."

No pressure there.

She hustles me into the elevator, and I look at my reflection in the closing door. I am standing in between the president and the first lady. We are surrounded by Secret Service agents and campaign staff.

President Brennan touches my shoulder. He leans down and talks quietly. "You're already doing better than Jamie. Usually, she gets halfway to where we're going and either says she's got a headache or she needs to pee real bad, and that's the last we see of her."

The elevator reaches the ground floor. The doors open, and I see the cameras and the crowds of people in the hotel lobby craning their necks to get a closer view.

I suddenly need to pee real bad.

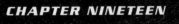

CHAPTER NINETEEN

Shake It Off

Think of the most expensive, most exclusive, most impressive hotel you've ever visited. Now think of the litter box where your cat poops. *That's* how Santa Barbara's Hidden Willows Resort and Spa compares to your dream hotel. I wish I were able to enjoy my luxurious surroundings, but ever since I made my way out of the elevator and walked with the presidential party through the hotel into an outdoor restaurant that overlooked the calmest, bluest bay, every eye has been on me. I'm not being self-obsessed when I say that. Everyone in Hidden Willows, from the super-rich guests to the hotel manager to the guy who cleans the toilets, has been shooting me judgmental side-eyes. *She slipped in baby puke. What will she do to ruin this beautiful evening?*

All that is required of me is to stand with the Brennans at the restaurant balcony and be a silent smiling presence as guests are ushered toward them. I'm close enough to hear the first lady whisper their names in the president's ear and to watch him call out each name with a delighted laugh as if each one were a long-lost friend, though it's obvious he has no idea who they are and will forget them the moment the fifteen-second encounter ends.

After a half hour—it seems *much* longer—every hand is finally shaken. We get to sit down at our table, but the first family's duties are far from over. Before we get to enjoy our dinner and then dance to the band that is noodling away politely in the background, there are speeches to be given praising the president, and, more important, Chester Brennan has to let the rich guests know that he needs them to keep pumping money into his campaign. It's going to be a long, boring night.

I excuse myself from the table.

"Make sure she doesn't get lost in the bathroom," the president yells. "It's been known to happen."

Two Secret Service agents follow a few paces behind

me as I weave my way through the restaurant.

Just then, a waitress backs away from a table, carrying an armful of dishes. My whip-fast reactions enable me to sidestep out of her path inches before we collide. That's when I *almost* slam straight into a frazzled, breathless mother carrying a shrieking baby.

I hear a collective gasp from the assembled guests. *She's done it again!* The phones brandished in my direction bathe me, the three of us, in a shimmering spotlight.

The drummer of the band starts knocking out a beat that I feel in my gut.

The mother, the waitress, and I all start shaking our hips in unison.

The mother throws her baby over her shoulder. One of the Secret Service guys catches it.

The waitress throws her dishes over *her* shoulder. The other Secret Service guy catches *most* of them.

The rest of the band starts playing in as funky a fashion as they are capable.

I look around the restaurant and see mouths hanging open in confusion and horror.

The mother tears off her blouse to reveal a Reindeer Crescent Cheerminators uniform underneath.

The waitress does the same.

They do cartwheels behind me as I continue shaking my hips.

And then . . .

Six more Cheerminators dance their way through the tables and take up position behind me and the other two girls. The cheerleaders standing right behind me clasp their hands together. I walk backward and *very carefully* step onto their hands. As the music swells and the band really starts to cut loose, I am lifted into the air, and I step onto the shoulders of the Cheerminator behind me and point my fingers skyward. Okay, me and cheerleaders? We've had our differences over the years. But I've got to admit, being perched high on the apex of this Cheerminator pyramid—it's kind of a thrill.

From my vantage point, I can see that the guests in the restaurant are on their feet, clapping along almost in time to the beat. They laugh and make loud whooping noises. The loudest yelling comes from the president, who punches the air and throws his head around like he's at an actual concert. I catch the first lady's eye. She gives me a nod of approval and, for the first time since I've met her, a genuine smile. Even the Secret Service agents who were *not* thrilled about being coerced into this performance have little smiles on their faces. The guy who caught the plastic baby doll is tossing it from hand to hand in time to the music.

The Cheerminators take up position behind the girl who holds me on her shoulders. I mouth a silent prayer and let myself fall backward. I keep my eyes tightly shut until I feel the hands of the Cheerminators catch me. The band stops playing, and we hit our final position, with big beaming smiles and arms stretched up to heaven.

The applause is *deafening*.

The cheerleader who played the waitress looks like she's going to *explode* with happiness and excitement.

She sees me looking at her and goes to hug me, but she stops before making contact.

"Is it okay?" she says.

I grab my little sister and squeeze her tight. "I told you I was going to make it up to you," I *want* to tell Natalie, but if she knew who she was hugging her head would explode.

"Oh my God!" shrieks the Cheerminator who carried the plastic baby. "It's everywhere already!"

She holds up her phone, and the clip of Jamie Brennan's dance routine is an instant sensation. Did I imagine when I hatched my insane plan six hours earlier that I would salvage Jamie's disastrous public image and reboot her as a live wire with a sense of humor who owned her mistakes and came back a hundred times stronger? Let's say I had hope.

When I got the first lady to call Natalie and say, "I have my daughter, Jamie, here. She'd like to ask you something," I had no idea what was going to happen. But then I heard the calm in Natalie's voice. She was totally unfazed that the first lady had called her. It did not throw her that she was talking to the first daughter and being asked to throw a dance routine together with a few hours' notice. It was not a stunning surprise to her that she and her team would be whisked from Reindeer Crescent on a private plane to Santa Barbara to perform in front of a completely unsuspecting audience. When you're Natalie Wilder, that's just what you expect from life. She was given a ridiculous mission, and she rose to the occasion.

The president is actually standing up on the table. "Play it again!" he yells at the band.

The guests also take up the chant. "Play it again!"

Even the two Secret Service guys are mouthing, "Play it again!"

The band, who probably never gets a chance to play anything other than soft background music, seizes the opportunity to make noise.

I turn to Natalie, who is on her phone. "Mom, Mom!" she screams. "Did you see it? It's on YouTube . . . yeah, Jamie's cool, she's nice. Mom, *no* . . ."

Natalie looks at me with a pained expression on her face. "I'm *so* sorry, it's my *mom*. She wants to say hi."

Mom? Talking to her is not a smart idea, but I'm

having an amazing night because of Natalie. And I want to hear my mom's voice.

I take the phone. "Hi?" I say.

"Miss Brennan?" I hear Mom's breathless voice. "I just want to thank you so, *so* much for giving Natalie such an incredible opportunity. That was so brave of you, and it was so much fun, and so awesome to watch. . . ."

"I know!" I shout back. "It was all Natalie, she pulled it out of nowhere. I just did what she told me. You know me, I'm just about coordinated enough to move my hips, she had to work around me. But it turned out great. Did Dad see it?"

"I'm sorry," Mom says. "I didn't quite catch that. Are you asking me if my father was watching?"

"Yes. No. Sorry," I yammer. "So loud here. I should go."

"It's wonderful to talk to you," says Mom. "Thank you again for thinking of Natalie."

And, because I can't help myself, I say, "I only wish I had the chance to meet your other daughter."

There's a silence. It stretches two, maybe three seconds.

"Dancing's not really her thing," my mother replies. "She hasn't really found her thing yet."

It's funny how your mood can change in a moment.

How you can go from feeling total euphoria to not feeling so good about yourself. I hand the phone back to Natalie.

"There's my girl!" shrieks Jocelyn Brennan, who rushes toward my sister and scoops her up in a hug.

"Talk to my mother," demands Natalie. "She'll die."

"And there's *my* girl," booms the president. He grabs me by the hand and drags me out in front of the band, where he starts throwing himself around to the beat. The fund-raiser guests join him and attempt to copy his unique dance moves.

"Who are you and what have you done with my daughter?" He laughs. "I'm so proud of you tonight, Jamie."

Wait, *what*?

"You know I'm not Jamie, right, Mr. President?" I say, moving closer to him.

"Sure, sure." He nods. "I'm just putting on a show." He doesn't seem like he's putting on a show, though. He seems like he's having fun with the daughter he wishes he had. I look across the restaurant and see Natalie and the first lady taking selfies. And then I think about the two or three seconds it took my mother to think of *anything* to say about me.

Because all I do is lie. Even my face is a lie.

The band is too loud and there are too many people,

and I feel like I'm about to start crying.

"I need to go to the bathroom," I tell the president. "For real this time."

I don't need to go the bathroom. I just need to be myself and *not* wear this mask.

Secret Service agents clear a path through the congratulating crowds. None of their love is for me. No one here knows me.

Right now, I feel like no one *anywhere* really knows me.

CHAPTER TWENTY

Officially Obsessed

Morgan Font, the independent candidate who is President Brennan's closest rival, looks like a raven. He has dark hair that begins in a little clump at the center of his forehead and then fans out into a cresting wave. His eyes are eerily far apart and his beak-like nose comes to a sharp point. His mouth is talking about me.

"No, I didn't watch the first daughter dancing, but I'm happy for her that she gets to live such a perfect life. She'll never know what the children of my constituents know: what it's like to walk through a metal detector before they can get into school. What it's like to come home in the afternoon and not know whether there's going to be electricity or gas. What it's like to be scared to play in the streets. What it's like . . ."

Click.

I aim the remote control at the TV and flip channels to see if I'm being talked about in a more positive fashion.

Click.

"We're officially obsessed with Jamie Brennan. Who knew the first daughter had those moves?"

Click.

"President Chester Brennan surged three whole points in the polls this morning, and some folks are saying it's all because of the viral video of his dancing daughter."

Click.

"Yesterday, she was the girl who hid from the cameras, but what a difference a day makes! Today Jamie Brennan is *hot-hot-hot.* We've heard the White House is seriously considering an offer from *Dancing with the Stars.*"

Click.

"Join us after the break when the Sacramento cheerleader who taught Jamie Brennan to dance will show us the steps that caused a sensation."

Click.

Here's my old friend Morgan Font again. He's

standing on a stage in front of a curtain emblazoned with a big red, white, and blue striped F. Font is surrounded by gloomy-looking kids wearing black T-shirts emblazoned with the words *Font Force*.

"When I built the Font Foundation, here in Washington, DC," he says, "it was to give these children a place to gather, to play sports, to enrich their minds, and to plant the seeds for a future. A future where they'll contribute more to the world than just dancing."

Ugh.

Click.

I switch off the TV and sink back into the pillows of my huge California-king-size bed in my huge bedroom in my even huger hotel room. I roll on my side and look at the nanomask, which sits on the other pillow. That round piece of plastic has made me invisibly famous. Invisible fame is a strange sensation to describe. It's like being the voice of a beloved animated character. Or a rapper's ghostwriter. Or an action star's stunt person. The world loves what you do, but no one knows you do it.

My phone receives a text. It's from the first lady.

Get up. Get dressed. Got a surprise for you.

I hate surprises.

In my experience, a surprise is a smile that hides a slap in the face.

"Surprise! You're getting to spend two whole weeks with Grandma!"

"Surprise! We didn't get you the puppy you wanted. That would be too much work for you. We got you a cactus instead!"

I wash, dress, and wait in the living room for the Secret Service double-knock that is our agreed-on code for me to don my mask. The knock comes. Time for me to hide behind a popular face again.

Jocelyn Brennan bounces into the room and almost blinds me with her insanely radiant smile. She's in a *very* good mood.

"*Three* points!" are her first words to me. She grabs me by the shoulders and shakes me. "Three points. That Morgan Font can kiss my you-know-what. I knew bringing you in was a good idea."

I step back a few paces before her enthusiastic shaking makes me nauseous.

"So this surprise?" I say.

"You're going to love it." She laughs and gestures for me to follow her out of my room.

We walk the length of Hidden Willows' top floor, the entirety of which has been taken over by the presidential party. Jocelyn, looking lovely and youthful in blue jeans and a white T-shirt, repeats "Three points" to herself as we reach the door at the end of the hallway.

She turns to look at me.

"Mmm," she murmurs. "Mask on? Mask off? Just for fun, let's keep it on."

I slip my glasses over the mask.

FLB double-knocks on the door.

I touch my X-ray glasses. The door turns transparent. Inside, I see Jamie Brennan sitting on the arm of a chair, putting on a sneaker. The door becomes solid again.

I gasp. "Your daughter's *here*?"

The first lady looks shocked. "How did you know that?"

"Spy," I say.

A Secret Service agent opens the door and then steps aside.

"Go in," urges Mrs. Brennan. "You two have a lot to talk about."

I step into the doorway, and a sneaker hits me in the face.

CHAPTER TWENTY-ONE

First Daughter

If my glasses had more than six seconds of X-ray capability, I would have seen that Jamie Brennan was taking off her sneaker. Didn't I say I hated surprises?

The impact of the hurled shoe knocks the nanomask from my face. I scramble on the ground to pick it up and examine it for damage.

Behind me, I hear FLB's voice. There's a pleading tone to it. "Jamie, honey, we talked about this. We agreed you'd meet with Bridget and you two would get to know each other, and when you felt comfortable, we'd transition you back into the public eye."

"I never agreed to anything!" Jamie shrieks. *"You're a liar. You've been lying so long you don't know what's real anymore."*

"Jamie, baby," the first lady begs.

"Get out, I hate you!" yells Jamie.

I see FLB beat a tearful retreat from Jamie's room. I go to follow. FLB shakes her head and mouths "please" at me. One of the Secret Service agents closes the door, and now I am stuck in a lavish hotel suite with a furious girl who detests me and has a shoe she has yet to throw.

Jamie lies facedown on the white couch, her fingers trailing back and forward in the carpet. She no longer acknowledges my presence. This is not the kind of situation in which I thrive. I never know the right things to say when people are upset. The only thing I can think of to do is to throw Jamie's mother under the bus.

"I didn't know about this, either," I say to the back of Jamie's head. "She didn't tell me she was going to put us together."

"Shut up!" spits Jamie as she springs up from the couch, her face red and blotchy. "You've made things worse."

She kicks the cushions off the couch and onto the floor and falls on top of them, all the while staring at me with seething hatred. "I only made it through the last four years because I knew my dad's popularity was going down the drain. He didn't fix the economy. He didn't address climate change. He sent troops to Trezekhastan. There was no way he was going to get reelected. And then what happens?"

She jumps up from the cushions and comes stomping toward me. Is this going to get physical? Am I going to have to throw down with the first daughter?

"Three points," she snarls, stopping a few inches from my face. "He's up three points. You did your stupid dance, and now he's going to get reelected, and I'm stuck with the dumb jock and the pageant queen for another four years of living in that big house with those Secret Service goons."

She pauses for breath. I feel scalded by her anger.

"I did my best to stay off the radar." Jamie sighs. "The internet had almost forgotten I was the girl who fell over. But now . . ." She adopts a high-pitched screech. *Do your dance like the puppet you are.*" Jamie moves her hips and lurches into a miserable, mocking impression of my world-famous dance moves.

I wince in sympathy. Jamie Brennan wants no part of being a public figure, and I just shoved her back into the spotlight.

"And what's *your* story, anyway?" she demands, her

expression contorted with dislike. "How much must you hate who you are to hide behind someone else's face? And who becomes a spy at, what are you, thirteen? What kind of hole in your life are you desperately trying to fill?"

I've been insulted and talked down to by criminal masterminds, but they didn't make it *sting* like this girl.

Jamie gives me a vicious grin. "Oh, wait. I've seen your sister. Jocelyn *adores* her, and is it just me or does she look nothing like you? So, okay, I get it. You're a ghost. You don't exist. But you really think being me is going to make you feel better about being you?"

Do not kick the first daughter in the face, I tell myself. *No matter how good it will feel.*

Jamie gives me a contemptuous head-to-toe gaze. "It must be nice to pass for one of the pretty girls," she sneers. "Even if it's only for a few days."

And then . . . her face changes. The hate fades away. Jamie inhales sharply. Her eyes widen, and her mouth opens. She grabs at my wrist. I try to pull away, but she has a surprisingly strong grip. The first daughter looks up at me with an expression of pure astonishment.

"What did they say?"

I don't understand.

Jamie squeezes my wrist. Tight enough to break the skin.

Her voice is hoarse. "What did those marks on your arm say?"

What is it with these Brennan women and their insanely good eyesight? I scrubbed the Magic Marker words away a dozen times. I look down at my arm. There are tiny remnants, barely visible to the human eye.

"Did they say . . . ?" She trails off, her eyes shining with hope.

"*Cadzo Army.*" I nod.

Jamie Brennan lets out a loud, piercing, sustained shriek.

The Secret Service agents burst into the suite, guns drawn.

"Get out," says Jamie, not even bothering to look at them. "I'm hanging out with my friend."

Friend?

All hail the healing power of L4E! Ten minutes ago, Jamie Brennan *hated* me. Now we sit on the cushions she threw onto the floor, gazing at her iPad. We watch an old interview where the boys are celebrating their first hit song. "How does it feel?" the interviewer is asking them.

"Dinnae pay nae mind tae seein' us on ra boax, wur jist like youse, so we are," Cadzo is saying. "Schemies and manky weans frae up a close. See aw this? Nae idea."

Cadzo looks at the rest of the band.

"Aye," they chorus. "Nae idea."

Cadzo continues, "But we'd be glaikit if we didny gie it laldy frae noo on, so we would."

Jamie pauses the clip and stares at me. "What do you think he's saying?"

I tap my bottom lip. "Obviously, I've given this a great deal of thought," I tell her. "I think he's telling us that even though we might have seen them on TV, L4E are no different from any of us, they're normal kids who grew up in a normal environment. They never expected this sort of success. But now that it's happened, they're going to pursue it to the best of their ability."

"*Wow*," Jamie breathes. "I have watched that a hundred times and it just sounded like they were grunting and swallowing things." She beams at me. "You're like the Cadzo Whisperer." Jamie picks up her iPad and starts scrolling down L4E's YouTube channel for more interviews that I can translate. Suddenly, she stops and moves her cushion closer to mine with a mischievous smile on her face. Lowering her voice, she says, "What's your L4E fantasy?"

I feel myself blush because I never expected to be asked that question . . . and because I don't even have to think about the answer.

"Okay, I'm at the airport lounge and the flight's over-booked. They say, we're looking for someone to give up their seat so we can take off on time. You'll get an upgrade on the next available flight."

"Is this a fantasy about air travel?" asks Jamie. "Because that is not what I want to hear."

"Shh," I command her. "I volunteer to give up my seat because I am a good person. I have to wait hours for the next plane, but I get my upgrade to first class. I board the plane, and the only other people in the cabin are . . ."

"*L4EEEE!*" squeals Jamie. "Who do you sit next to?"

"Kecks." I've played this scenario out in my head so many times and I never thought I'd tell anyone. The thought of confessing this to Joanna—even NJ—is like a nightmare. She'd laugh in my face for fifteen minutes. But here I am pouring it all out to the president's daughter, who is nodding and saying, "Uh-huh."

"But the others get jealous," I go on. "Beano keeps leaning over and trying to talk to me. Lim wants me to hear this new song he's written . . ."

"He's totally making that up to impress you." Jamie laughs. "Lim's never written a song in his life."

"The only one who doesn't bother me is Cadzo. Eventually, I get up to go to the bathroom and, as I pass him, his hand touches mine. I stop. He looks up at me and says—I can't do the accent—'People think they know me, but they don't understand who I really am. There's something different about you . . . something that makes me think you're the only one who gets me.'"

"Oh my God!" shrieks Jamie. "Hall of fame fantasy. Mine is weak by comparison."

"Tell me anyway."

Jamie curls up on the cushion like a cat and folds her arms under her chin. "They play a concert for me. Just me. I'm the only one in the audience. I'm right in the middle of the front row. They're all looking at me. They dedicate every song to me. *My name* is in the lyrics. Every time they're about to sing *girl*, they change it to *Jamie*. And Cadzo's got the orange hair."

"The 'Zohawk'?" I splutter. "The controversial shaved-at-the-sides look that split the Cadzo Army down the middle?"

"I liked it," she pouts.

"It's your fantasy." I shrug.

Jamie gives me this long look, and then she lets out a groan of pain.

"What is it?" I say, concerned.

"I *like* you," she moans. "I should hate you. I'm entitled to hate you. Why can't I just hate you?"

I smile at her. "You caught the Bridget cold. It's going

around. There's no known cure."

Jamie rolls off the cushion onto the carpet and looks up at the ceiling. "You're weird," she says. "You're like my friend from home. . . ."

"Molly Costigan-Cohen," I blurt out.

"Oh, of course you checked up on me," says Jamie. "Yeah, MC-C. I haven't seen her in *sooo* long. I mean, I see her on Instagram and Snapchat. She's got all new friends. I don't know what it'll be like going back to Westlake and starting my life over, but . . ."

Jamie sits up and hugs her knees to her chest. She looks at me with moistening eyes. "I really want Morgan Font to win. I really want to go home."

"You know I'm only here for a week, right?" I tell her. "You have to take over when I'm done."

"Are you asking if I'm I going to take advantage of the goodwill you built for me or if I'm going to run away again?" she says.

"What's your gut feeling?" I ask.

Right away, Jamie says, "Do you have a backup mask? We could swap. You could stay on as me. I could go back to your life and pretend to be you."

"You're the first person *ever* to want my life over theirs."

I give her a quick guided tour of Bridget Wilder's

amazing non-spy life. Being overshadowed by Ryan and Natalie. My bumpy friendship with Joanna. And the thing with my mom.

"I can't risk her ever finding out what I do," I tell Jamie. "So I end up lying all the time, and she treats me like I'm this big disappointment."

"That's too bad," Jamie sympathizes. "But you're only disappointing one person. I'm letting down the entire nation."

"That's not true," I say.

"It *is!*" she insists. "The campaign staff have the numbers to back it up. *Jamie, you don't poll likable enough. You're not warm and friendly like your mother. You don't have her big, open personality.* They're right, I don't! So stop dragging me to events where I'm going to get compared to her. Stop acting so shocked when I run away."

"I had the exact same experience," I almost shout. "My mom dragged me to this boring event that I ended up running away from due to spy business, but I didn't want to be there and she should have known that."

"Right!" Jamie shouts back. "People come to see her. They don't want to see me."

"They do now," I correct her. "They're officially obsessed with you. Except no one knows it's really me. Which is the job I signed up for. But still . . ."

"You want to be noticed." She nods. "You're good at something, and you can't tell the people you most want to tell."

It's so easy with her. I don't want to stop talking. I tell her about the wonders of Reindeer Crescent Middle School, with special emphasis on Brendan Chew.

"Wait," says Jamie. "You let someone called Brendan Chew call you Midget Wilder? Why didn't you call him Brendan Poo?"

"I . . ." I don't have an answer.

"It's *so* obvious!" she yelps. "You might be a better me, but I'd make a way better you."

This isn't the healing power of L4E anymore. This is two girls in a hotel room getting to know each other.

I'm still aware of a distant throb in my nose from where Jamie's sneaker hit me, but I feel something for this girl I didn't expect to feel.

I let out a groan of pain.

"What is it?" she asks.

"I think I just caught the Jamie cold."

CHAPTER TWENTY-TWO

Home

*P*eople think they know me, but they don't understand who I really am. There's something different about you, something that makes me think you're the only one who gets me.

That's my good-bye text from Jamie. My time with the first family is officially over. Their West Coast campaign is finished. First thing tomorrow, they fly back to the White House for a grueling week that starts with the president taking part in his first live televised debate at Georgetown University and continues with the entire family answering approximately a million questions, posing for a billion photographs, and shaking hands till all the feeling in their fingers has gone. These parts I will not miss. But I can't lie, I am going to feel a little bit empty without my fake family.

The president is, as my dad said, a doofus, but he's a lovable one. FLB can be scary if she doesn't like you, but I think she came around. And Jamie may forget we were friends the second I'm gone, but the best part of my week with the Brennans was the time I spent hanging out with her.

Sure, our friendship was L4E based, but it grew beyond our mutual love of Cadzo. We had sleepovers in my room where we rehearsed new dance steps for her to bust out in public, and I attempted to introduce her to the musical delights of Ruth Etting. ("That sounds like a toilet being flushed" was her verdict.)

Toward the end of my stay, we made a pact.

"You try not being a disappointment to your mom," I said, holding out a pinkie to her. "And I'll try not being one to mine." We hooked our pinkies together and swore that we'd make the effort to make our lives more bearable.

I didn't just know a New Joanna, I now knew a New Jamie, too. Not long after our pinkie swear, I saw her asking the campaign staff about what she should wear to the following day's big events, the Celebrate America's Families afternoon affair at the White House, and the evening's televised presidential debate with Morgan Font. I can't deny I felt a swell of pride knowing I helped coax Jamie out of her shell.

I look around my swanky Los Angeles hotel room. It's hard to imagine, after this week of five-star accommodations, that tomorrow morning I'll be back in Reindeer Crescent. Back home with my real family. As soon as I begin to think about my family, a word springs into my head: *lies*.

I need to memorize a long list of credible lies about my time in the Secret Service motivational foundation for troubled youths. Strike and Irina have sent me files filled with fake information about my week: where I slept, what I ate, what the other kids were like. There's no way Mom and Dad are going to be satisfied with one-word answers and vague shrugs. I have to be a walking commercial for the benefits of a place that doesn't exist. I kick off my shoes, crawl onto my bed, and start studying.

"Bridget . . . Bridget, wake up . . ."

I hear my name. I feel a hand on my shoulder. I have a horrible dry taste in my mouth. Where am I?

"Bridget, it's Adina Roots. Please wake up."

I focus. I'm in my swanky Los Angeles hotel room, sprawled out fully clothed on the bed. I fell asleep rehearsing the lies I have to tell my family.

"What time is it?" I yawn.

"It's two thirty in the morning."

I sit up on the bed and stare at Secret Service Director Roots, who is standing over me flanked by two agents. A skinny, unshaven guy stands by the window, talking on his phone.

"What are you doing in my room?" I ask.

Roots pauses for a second. She glances over at the unshaven guy, and then looks back at me.

"Jamie's gone."

CHAPTER TWENTY-THREE

Gone Girl

"What do you mean gone?" I say.

Before Roots can reply, the skinny guy comes stomping up to my bed. "Disappeared. Vanished. Departed. Evaporated. That kind of gone."

"Bridget," Roots says, "this is White House Chief of Staff Hayes Oberman."

The skinny guy gives me a curt nod. "Great job, fake Jamie. Looks like you got the gig full-time."

Right off the bat, I don't like this guy. I don't like his bleary eyes or the way his hair sticks straight up from his head. I don't like the way he's furiously chewing gum, or that I can hear him breathe while he chews. I turn to Roots for an explanation.

"There was no sign of Jamie in her room. No one saw her leave. We've checked the hotel surveillance records. There's nothing. We've tried tracking her cell phone. It's still in her room. The LAPD are on high alert."

"Awesome timing," says Oberman. "Makes the first family look like they can't control their own daughter. Which is why she did it. Hurts the campaign at a time it doesn't need to be hurt."

"Jamie wouldn't do this," I am quick to say.

"Right," sneers Oberman. "It's *completely* out of character."

"It *is!*" I shoot back. "You don't know her like I do. She's changed."

I want to tell him about the sanctity of our pinkie swear, but *this* guy wouldn't get it.

"I'm the White House chief of staff," Oberman repeats. "I've spent every minute of the last four years dealing with the first family, the media, and the opposition. Putting out fires, averting disasters. Every minute. As opposed to your six days."

I sit up in bed. "I got to know Jamie better in twenty minutes of those six days than you did in four years," I snap. "And I'm telling you she's changed. She doesn't want to run away anymore. If she's gone, it's because . . ."

Oh my God.

"We have to accept the possibility Jamie's been taken." Roots nods.

"I've got every confidence in Director Roots and her team," declares Oberman. "But in the meantime, we need you . . ."

"Anything!" I am terrified for Jamie and also determined to do whatever I can to get her back.

"Just keep doing what you're already doing," says Roots. "Keep wearing the mask. Fly back to the White House with the president and the first lady. Show up to First Lady Brennan's Celebrate America's Families party and smile. Go to the debate and wave to the audience."

I can't hide my shock. I've barely processed Jamie's abduction and now *this*?

"I get it," I tell Roots and Oberman. "You don't want the country to panic. But the president and the first lady? Isn't it going to be impossible for them to keep pretending nothing's wrong?"

Oberman and Roots swap looks.

"Not if they don't know," mutters the chief of staff.

"You haven't told them?" I bawl.

Oberman lunges at me, shoving his hand over my

mouth. I rear back and kick his hand away. He howls in pain, as recipients of my kicks tend to do. Roots steps in between us, a warning look in her eyes.

"I need everybody to calm down right now," she says, her voice low and steady. "Mr. Oberman, explain your decision to Bridget."

Oberman rubs his hand and glares at me. "I don't need to explain myself to some kid who's half animal."

"*Mr. Oberman,*" repeats Roots, in a harsher tone than I've ever heard her use.

Oberman sighs and sits down on the end of my bed.

"This is a crucial time for us," he says. "The live debates start tomorrow. The president cannot afford to be distracted. He cannot afford to look weak."

"Worrying about his missing daughter won't make him weak," I protest. "It'll make him human."

"When we have a better handle on what we're dealing with," Oberman continues. "When we know who's got Jamie and what their demands are, or if it ends up that she just went on one of her adventures, *then* we inform the president and the first lady. But right now I need them to focus."

Oberman stops talking and rubs his eyes. "It's my job to make decisions like this. If it's the wrong one, I'll take responsibility for it."

"We know what we're asking, Bridget," Roots says. "We can't force you to do it. But we need you."

"What about *my* parents?" I ask. "They're expecting me to come home from Secret Service motivation camp tomorrow morning."

"Agent Strike is ready to put a backup plan into operation," says Roots. "Your parents will be informed that you volunteered to spend one more week at the camp."

"Because I was so awesome or so bad?" I ask. "Seriously, you better convince them I'm staying on because I'm such a shining example to all the other at-risk teens. Because otherwise they'll think the worst."

"You going to do it?" demands Oberman. "Y or N?"

"Have you checked all flights headed to Fort Worth?" I ask. "Have you been in contact with Molly Costigan-Cohen?"

"We'd be doing all that and a lot more if we knew we had a fake Jamie ready to go back to work," says Oberman.

I hug a hotel pillow to my chest and think about what I'm being asked to do.

Don't do it. This is a bad idea. It will cause pain and suffering. Mostly to you.

I find my thoughts wandering to the unpleasant subject of Adam Pacific. He wouldn't hesitate to say yes, but for him, it would be a chance to cover himself in glory. For me, it's because my friend might be in trouble. We bonded. We pinkie swore. We exchanged L4E fantasies. I can't let her down.

"Y," I reply.

CHAPTER TWENTY-FOUR

White House Party

You know how my first week under the Jamie mask was an undeniable triumph? My unexpected second attempt at passing as the president's offspring can officially be categorized as a disaster.

Here's the problem: when Mr. and Mrs. Brennan knew I was pretending to be their daughter on their West Coast tour, they were impressed by the way I grew into the part. Now that they don't know I'm not Jamie, they see me looking lost when I'm meant to be doing things they think they've seen me do a hundred times in the past.

This morning I flew from Los Angeles to Washington in Air Force One. Jamie Brennan has been in the president's private plane enough not to freak out when she sees that it's a big as a city street, and that it has its own gym, its own bedrooms, its own boardrooms and kitchens. Bridget Wilder didn't just freak out at the size of Air Force One, she did not know which cabin Jamie usually sits in, and she certainly didn't know Jamie was friendly enough with most of the flight crew and the kitchen staff that they had private jokes and pet names for her.

If I'd been briefed maybe I could have done a convincing job, but I came across as standoffish and ended up alienating everyone who tried to be nice to me.

The real Jamie Brennan has lived in the White House for the past four years. When she is driven into the building, she does not squeal, "Oh my God, I can't believe I'm in the actual White House!" like I did.

Luckily, the president laughed and said, "I still feel the same way, honey," but FLB gave me a suspicious squint. The real Jamie Brennan knows where her bedroom is located. I had to search Google for a layout of the White House to find out Jamie resides in the so-called Blue Bedroom on the west side of the second floor. (Mary Todd Lincoln stayed there after her husband, Abraham, was assassinated. Google again.) I should have breathed a sigh of relief when I was able to take refuge in the Blue Bedroom, but I actually felt like more of an intruder being in Jamie's room than I did wearing her face.

As I gaze around Jamie's spotless, beautifully decorated room with its vintage rocking horse, dollhouse, and chess board, I can only think *I should not be here.* The longer Jamie is missing, the more time I spend impersonating her, the more the Brennans are going to hate me when the truth comes out. This may be the chief of staff's insane plan, and Adina Roots may have gone along with it, but *I'm* the one betraying the Brennans the most. I'm the one letting them believe their daughter is safe.

I spend maybe five minutes standing dead still in the middle of Jamie's room. I don't want to touch anything. I don't want to sit down. I don't want to open any doors or look inside any drawers. Finally, I tell myself, *You can keep feeling guilty or you can act like a spy and look for clues.*

I do all the things I don't want to do. I look under her bedclothes and inside her closet. I take some of the pictures down from the wall—the official portraits she'd posed for and the ones she'd taken herself—and feel inside the frames. Nothing. No folded-up notes. No hidden hard drives. I open the top drawer of the mahogany dresser by her bed and take out a journal.

The friend in me freezes. *This is too far over the line.*

You shouldn't look inside. You wouldn't like it if someone invaded your privacy like this.

The spy in me ignores the friend. *If you were missing, you would want someone you trusted, someone you knew was amazing, to do anything she could do to find clues that could bring you home. So shut up!*

I open the journal and see a page filled with scratches. I stare for a second before I realize what I'm looking at. Four vertical slashes with a fifth diagonal slash through them. Repeated over and over. I turn the page. More vertical scratches with inky slashes through them. And the next page. And the next. This is how prisoners marked the passing days of their incarceration. I continue flipping through the pages, looking at the same slashes, and feeling just how unhappy Jamie must have been for these past four years.

I hear a knock on the door. I throw the journal back in the top drawer of the dresser.

"Hey, lady," said FLB. "Let's talk about what we're going to wear."

Wear? Wear where? I need time alone to look for clues.

"Just a minute," I call out.

Jocelyn Brennan opens the door and enters with her smile on full blast. "Remember, we're celebrating

America's families so we've got to make everyone feel comfortable and welcome. No showing off our fancy stuff." She opens Jamie's closet door and begins looking through the racks and shelves of clothes.

"Yeah, um, about that," I mumble. "I don't feel so good. My head hurts. Maybe I'll just stay in my room."

I see Jocelyn Brennan deflate in front of my eyes. She regards me with huge sad eyes.

"Jamie." She sighs. "I thought we were past this. I thought I had my daughter back. The last few days you were so happy and confident."

FLB comes up close to me and takes my hand. "I know having Bridget around took the pressure off you, but let me tell you something. I've spent time with Bridget Wilder, and she doesn't hold a candle to you. That mask she wore may have fooled the masses, but I always knew they were getting a second-rate version of Jamie Brennan."

What is it with moms and their amazing ability to make me feel bad about myself?

She reaches out to touch my wig. "You can't fake class," she said.

You'd know, I think but do not say.

I push her hand away, partly because I don't want her touching the wig, and partly because, even though

I know she's only trying to boost her daughter's fragile ego, being around her is making me annoyed and uncomfortable.

The first lady takes a step back and raises her palms in surrender. "Sorry I tried to get close to you. I'll know better in the future. Wear the green dress, it brings out your eyes. I'll expect you to be ready at seven tonight."

So, three hours later, having discovered exactly zero clues as to Jamie's location, here I am in the beautiful Rose Garden, smiling, shaking hands, trying to be normal, approachable, and not say anything horribly inappropriate. During a quick interlude between greeting guests, my personal phone vibrates. It's a text asking me if I need help with my math homework. I know I shouldn't click on it, but, of course, I do. Adam Pacific's smug face fills the screen. Behind him, L4E stand on a stage, gathered around a couple of microphones, rehearsing their harmonies. I let out a moan of pain.

"Jamie, I won't ask you again," says the first lady. "Put your phone away. Every time one of the press people sees you staring at it, there's another story undermining the Say Hello campaign."

With an effort, I pull my eyes away from the screen. Where was that filmed? The boys are supposed to be playing an arena in São Paulo today.

"Jamie, pay attention. The Meehan family from Covington County are approaching. They lost their home in a tornado."

"They should move in here," I say. "There's plenty of room."

"Keep your voice down," FLB retorts, her smile wide, but her eyes panicked. "That's exactly the sort of thing the press seizes onto."

Jocelyn stops berating me and greets the unfortunate Meehan family with warmth and sympathy.

"We're so pleased that you could come," she says. "You're what Celebrate America's Families is all about."

"Blown away to meet you" is how I greet the Meehan family patriarch. He gives me a *did I just hear right?* look. I can't believe I just said that. I don't know where it came from—maybe there was a file marked *Worst Possible Things to Say to Someone Who Lost Their Home in a Tornado* buried deep in my subconscious? I can feel the first lady's eyes boring holes of disbelief and horror into my skull.

I look out at the sea of tables with their exquisitely arranged centerpieces, and the families sitting around them pecking at their chicken dinners. White families, black families, Asian families, Latino families, gay families, single-parent families, blended families, all sorts of families mingle under the crabapple trees, their presence in the White House Rose Garden meant to prove to the nation that the Brennans are a normal, everyday family just like you or your neighbors. Except the Brennans have a spy masquerading as their daughter.

Just get through this, I tell myself. *Jamie will show up soon.*

"Do your dance," demands a middle-aged woman who has appeared in front of me and is brandishing her phone inches from my nose. "Thank you so much for coming," I say robotically, "and celebrating America's families with my family."

A Secret Service agent swiftly escorts the woman out of the garden. Jamie's prediction was right: my viral success *has* turned her into a dancing monkey, but I still wish she were here suffering rather than me.

The president, who had been occupied in the Oval Office rehearsing for his televised debate later tonight, joins us in line greeting the families selected to attend this event.

"You know you're doing great, right?" he whispers in my ear. "Picture perfect. America's favorite daughter."

I tell him my tornado blunder.

He lets out a hoot of laughter. "One time? I was

introduced to the crown prince of Denmark. He asked me what I thought of his country."

"What did you say?"

"Great, Dane!" He grins. "It just popped out."

"How did you get elected?" I laugh.

"Not a day goes by I don't ask myself that," says the president.

I feel a hand touch my arm. "Jamie," the first lady says. "There are some people here I think you'll want to meet."

I give the president a little wink. "Watch me make this next bunch fall in love with me," I tell him. I plaster on a smile every bit as wide and dazzling as Jocelyn Brennan's. I widen my eyes the way she does, and I turn to find myself looking at my mother.

"This is Nancy Wilder," says Mrs. Brennan. "From Reindeer Crescent. She's . . ."

"I'm Natalie's mom," she says. "We spoke on the phone."

I'm too surprised to form words. FLB beams at my distress. "I have my secret little ways. Surprised?"

All I can do is nod. The president takes my mother's hand and says, "We're happy to be sharing this celebration with you," as my father walks toward me. He gives me a quick, shy smile.

"Nice to meet you," he mumbles. Dad looks awkward and out of place. I know how he feels.

"They tell me you're the best manager in Pottery Barn," I say, trying to make him feel included.

He looks stunned. *"Really?"*

I hear a burst of mocking laughter. Ryan. "No, not really, *Dad,*" cackles my brother. "She has to say *something.*"

"I hear awesome things about you." I smile sweetly at Ryan, who has shown up for his big night at the White House wearing a Lucha Underground T-shirt, and has a half-eaten burrito shoved in his jacket pocket. (Good God, Mom, you let him out the house looking like *that?*) "They say you're the funniest guy in Reindeer Crescent."

"Really?" marvels Ryan.

"No, not really." I smirk. (Ha.)

Ryan examines me through narrowed eyes. He knows something's not quite right here. I want to send him some kind of signal that it's me. I want to get him alone and find out what my entire family is doing here. Pretending to be Jamie, looking for clues about her disappearance, and now finding the Wilders in the White House is freaking me out.

Natalie pushes him away and takes both my hands. "I can't believe we get to meet again. It's so great of the first lady to do this. The worldwide views on YouTube? Bananas! I've been on TV! If your dad gets elected, we should come up with a victory dance."

"That'll be my motivation," laughs the president, who greets Natalie with a warm hug.

"And this is Natalie's sister," I think I hear Mrs. Brennan say. But that can't be right. *I'm* Natalie's sister. Did I just say I was freaking out? That was before someone very familiar reached out to shake my hand.

"Hello, I'm Bridget Wilder," says a girl who has my face.

CHAPTER TWENTY-FIVE

Me Two

"I know you met my little sister and talked to my mother, but we've never had a chance to meet," says the girl with *my* face, wearing *my* clothes and *my* glasses, standing in line with *my* family, in *my* voice. "Imagine how shocked I was when I heard your mother was going to fly my whole family out here? On a private plane! What an amazing surprise!"

Reporters are everywhere. There are TV crews filming the Celebrate America's Families event. Actual American families are lined up in the Rose Garden waiting for their turn to meet the first family. I cannot cause a scene or act like anything out of the ordinary is happening.

"Thank you so much for coming," I say in a mild, polite voice. "And celebrating America's families with my family."

"Thank *you*," I see my face reply. "I'm very close with my family, so I love that we all get to share this amazing experience together. And then we all get to go home together."

Did I just see the corner of my mouth turn up? Did I see a mocking glint in my eyes? Whoever I'm looking at is sending me a message. *I'm a bomb planted inside your family, and you don't know when I'm going to go off.*

To my left, Mrs. Brennan is making polite conversation with a family who are all wearing gigantic Stetson hats. To my right, the president is actually talking to Ryan about his favorite *luchadores*. At this particular second, no one is paying any attention to me.

If I'm going to deal with this threat, I have to act *now*.

"You're hungry?" I say. "I'm so sorry. Let me take care of that."

The girl with my face looks confused.

"I didn't . . . ," she starts to say.

Moving like lightning, I snatch the burrito out of Ryan's jacket pocket and jam it straight into my clone's open mouth.

I see my face go red. I see myself double up. I spin the girl around, wrap my arms around her waist, and give her a sharp squeeze. The half-eaten burrito shoots out of her mouth. The girl gasps for breath. I turn to the shocked Brennans.

"She wolfed it down," I explain. "It was like she'd never seen food before."

My parents look shocked. Natalie looks embarrassed. Ryan chews on his lower lip as if he has a vague idea something in this scenario is not quite as it should be.

"Oh, Bridget," sighs my mother. She starts to make her way to the still-gasping girl.

"Please, Mrs. Wilder," I sing out. "Stay where you are. Enjoy the party. Let me help get Bridget cleaned up."

Mom looks at me like I'm an angel newly descended from heaven, and the girl with my face is something that should be kept in a cage.

"Come on, Bridget Wilder," I say brightly. "We can get to know each other better."

Two Secret Service agents follow behind me as I drag the coughing, spluttering girl up some steps and into the West Wing.

I keep an arm tight around her waist and hold on to her hand as I guide her toward the nearest restroom. She tries to pull away from me.

"Make a move and those Secret Service dudes will rip you up into little pieces," I warn her.

"They can try," coughs the girl with my face. "But if anyone knows what a formidable opponent I can be, it's you, peanut."

Vanessa?

CHAPTER TWENTY-SIX

Face 2 Face

Vanessa Dominion. My nemesis. My mortal enemy. My nightmare. The daughter of the evil ex-leader of the Forties. The cold-blooded chameleon who pretended to be Ryan's weird girlfriend, Abby. The snobby, English-accented brat who messed with my middle school reputation, hung me from a meat locker hook, and, on more than one occasion, shoved a gun in my face with intent to kill. *That* Vanessa Dominion. Back nestling like a viper inside my family and wearing *my* face!

I kick open the restroom door and shove her inside. She goes flailing across the black-and-white tiled floor, but manages to steady herself before hitting the nearest sink. I see the superior smirk forming across my face. I see my hand on my hip. That girl may look like me, but *that* is not Bridget Wilder.

The sight of her incenses me. I feel my phone vibrate again. I can't decide who I hate more at this moment, Vanessa Dominion or Adam Pacific. No, wait, I can. It's Vanessa. I raise my hands, ready for a fight.

"Fists down, First Daughter," says Vanessa as she leans back against the sink. "Nanomasks don't grow on trees."

"Take yours off," I command her. "I can't bear to look at it a second more."

"Imagine how *I* feel." She shudders. "Talk about a face only a mother could love. Except she's not that hot on you right now."

"Take it off!" I yell. My voice echoes around the restroom.

"Everything okay in there?" says a Secret Service agent from outside.

"Shh," whispers Vanessa. She makes a beckoning motion. I walk toward her. Do I trust her? Not a fake hair on her fake head, but I beat her before and I'll do it again.

"Count of three, we both de-mask and de-wig," she says.

We touch fingers under our chins. Both our faces vanish and turn to static. Both plastic circles fall away, revealing our true faces underneath. I breathe a sigh of relief to be free of Jamie's face, but my relief vanishes at the sight of Vanessa's porcelain complexion and shiny blond hair.

"You shouldn't have assaulted me with that burrito," she says, her annoyingly perfect English intonation replacing my somewhat high-pitched voice. "But I am also guilty of relishing the element of surprise a few moments too long. I underreacted and you overreacted. Call it even."

Why is this would-be assassin chatting casually to me like we're old friends?

"Who are you working for?" I demand. "If you've done anything to my family, if you've hurt Ryan . . ."

Vanessa shushes me again. "Stop barking like a demented seal and I'll endeavor to explain. My being here and wearing that Halloween mask you call a face was almost as much of a surprise to me as you. I didn't think I was ready, but when the first lady decided to fly the whole Wilder clan to DC, Mr. Strike had no option but to . . ."

"Wait, stop. Shut up." My head is spinning. "Mr. *Strike*? As in . . ."

Vanessa luxuriates in my ignorance. She could not look more smug or more satisfied.

I actually stamp my foot in frustration.

"Calm down." She laughs, which infuriates me further. "After my capture, Agent Strike came to see me at the CIA facility where I was being held and offered me the chance to redeem myself."

"He *what*?" I've talked to him ten, twenty, hundreds of times since we defeated the Dominions in New York. Not a word about redeeming Vanessa Dominion. Not. A. Word.

"He told me there may be a future in the Forties for someone with my skills. But he needed to believe that I could be capable of change. He wanted to be sure I was trustworthy. He suggested I make amends to those I hurt."

I feel my phone vibrate *again*. Adam Pacific. Another lost soul saved by the kindhearted Carter Strike.

"So that's what I'm doing here," Vanessa goes on. "Being nice to the Wilders. Being friendly to Ryan. Being of use. I don't know why Agent Strike wouldn't have given you advance warning, though."

I don't buy it. Not for a second. Nobody changes that much. My phone vibrates AGAIN! I decide to take out my mounting anger on Adam Pacific. I pull out my phone.

The caller is my not-ever-really-a-boyfriend, D———— T————.

The previous seventeen missed calls were also from him.

I click accept.

"Hello?" I breathe.

"Bridget?" says Dale Tookey. He sounds breathless and scared. "I think you're being set up for the kidnapping of Jamie Brennan."

CHAPTER TWENTY-SEVEN

Desperate Measures

The connection is terrible. Dale's voice fades in and out. "The CIA shut down the Forties," I think I hear him say. "Strike and Irina are in the box. They're sharing intel with the Secret Service and . . ."

"Stop, stop," I beg him. "Slow down. Back up. What's this about? Where are you? And . . . what sort of box?"

"They're being interrogated. They'll overpower their interrogators and escape, which will mean a nationwide manhunt."

"Why? What did they do? I don't understand what's happening here."

Vanessa leans toward me, shooting me a quizzical

look. I turn my back on her, which, I immediately realize, is a dumb thing to do. I turn back around. She goes to the mirror and pats her perfect hair into place.

Through the crackling line, I hear Dale's voice. "I don't have a ton of time. I'm bouncing this line off a disguised satellite, but the longer I talk to you, the more chance there is of someone hearing me."

Did Ur5ula help you locate the disguised satellite? I find myself thinking but do not say because I have my priorities straight.

"So be quick," I tell him.

"I've been doing freelance security work for Strike, listening in on any calls that have anything to do with the Forties. I intercepted a call this morning that said there were twenty-five minutes of surveillance footage missing from your Los Angeles hotel room last night."

I don't understand. But of course I say, "Uh-huh, go on, I'm listening."

The line crackles some more. Dale's voice gets louder. "After Jamie had been gone for a couple of hours, the FBI were contacted. They sent a forensic team to the hotel. They went to your room. They found stuff."

I feel the tips of my ears burning, which is a new, and not very nice, sensation.

"What sort of stuff?" I croak.

"Who is that?" Vanessa pipes up. "What's going on?"

I wave her away.

"Is that Vanessa?" I hear Dale say.

Everyone knows everything but me. I hate spies.

"Put her on speaker," he demands. "She can help."

"Really?" I say. "How? You don't buy that stuff about her trying to redeem herself."

"Are you talking about me?" Vanessa asks.

I touch the speaker icon.

"Yeah, actually, I do," says Dale's suddenly clear voice.

"Dale Tookey?" chirps Vanessa. "Lovely to hear your voice. How's Ur5ula?"

"Doing good," says Dale cheerfully. "We should all hang out again."

Okay, let's make a list of all the awesome things that have just happened.

1. I apparently am implicated in the kidnapping of the president's daughter.
2. My biological mother and father are being interrogated by the CIA and will more than likely become fugitives.
3. My nemesis, my ex-boyfriend, and his current girlfriend are besties.

"Sorry to interrupt," I say, with as much dignity as I can summon up. "You were saying something about the FBI forensic team?"

Vanessa's eyebrows shoot up.

"They found some of Jamie's hairs on your bed," he says.

"She slept over," I reply. "We're really good friends."

I give Vanessa a look that says *See, I have friends, too.* Petty, I know, but consider my position.

"That's not all," Dale goes on. "They found traces of fingernails attached to carpet strands. Like she'd been dragged out of your room against her will."

"That doesn't sound right," Vanessa breaks in. "Usually people can't wait to get away from Bridget."

Oh my God, I hate her so much!

"They found some dried blood," Dale continues. "And some wax residue from a scented candle that contained sedative qualities. They took what they found and factored in the missing twenty-five minutes from your room . . ."

"And they figured that was the time Bridget used to drug and overpower the first daughter!" gasps Vanessa. She leans in close to me. "Did you do it, peanut? You can tell Auntie V."

I push her away from me. "Of course I didn't do it."

"It doesn't matter if she did it or not," said Dale.

"I think it matters a little bit," I say. "And thanks for your unwavering support."

"The FBI found out the CIA was involved via the Forties, and then they found out the Forties had loaned you out to the Secret Service . . ."

Vanessa sticks her hand up in the air like she's trying to attract a teacher's attention. "Ooh! Ooh! Ooh! And now the CIA and the Secret Service look like fools for hiring some dopey thirteen-year-old girl from a department that no one even knows exists. . . ."

"And is filled with criminals," Dale adds.

"So now that the FBI suspects Bridget Wilder is part of a conspiracy to kidnap the president's daughter, the Secret Service and the CIA get a chance to make up for being so dumb by bringing you in," says Vanessa, looking even more pleased with herself than usual. "You're public enemy number one."

She gives me an impressed thumbs-up. I hear the sound of loud knocking on the door.

"We need you to come out right now." That Secret Service agent sounds a lot less friendly than the last time I heard his voice.

The door handle starts to turn.

Vanessa opens it. Two bodies slump to the ground.

"Bridget, what's going on?" Dale shouts.

Vanessa turns back around to face me. She's pointing the barrel of a gun at me.

Oh wait, it's not a gun. It's a small clear-plastic cylinder with a spray nozzle at the top. She hands it to me.

"Amends," she says.

"You just killed two Secret Service agents," I moan. "Not a great help in establishing my innocence."

"It's a perfume atomizer that sprays liquid amnesia," says Vanessa. "It's still in the test stages, as everything from the Forties tends to be." She gives me a smirk and a shake of her head. "Did you think it was a gun, you funny little dunce?"

"NO," I reply.

She gestures in the direction of the motionless Secret Service agents lying outside the bathroom door. "They'll be fine, but the previous hour will be a blank. You've got approximately ten squirts. Use them wisely."

"Thanks," I find myself saying to Vanessa Dominion. "Now I need you to do something else for me."

"Okay, but then you'll owe me," she says.

I pass her my nanomask. "Be me. Well, be me being Jamie."

Vanessa's mouth forms into an O shape.

"Bridget," I hear Dale say. "Is this a good idea?"

"Bye, Dale," trills Vanessa. "Give Ur5ula a kiss from me." She reaches out and ends the call.

A scary smile spreads across her face. "I always imagined myself marrying into the royal family. President's daughter is something of a step down, but I will embrace the challenge wholeheartedly."

Vanessa snatches the nanomask from my hand and fits it over her face. She adjusts the wig and gazes raptly in the bathroom mirror as her features change.

"Hi, y'all," she says in Jamie's Texan accent.

"She never says y'all," I inform her. "It's best if you just smile and say nothing."

"Whatever," says Vanessa. She's still caught up in her new reflection. I've probably made a gargantuan mistake, but desperate times call for desperate measures.

"Don't get too used to that face," I warn her as I head out of the bathroom. "I'm bringing the real one back."

"Where are you going?" she asks. "Do you have a plan?"

"I have parts of a plan," I admit. "I need to get my family out of here. If I'm a suspect, the people who suddenly showed up in the White House with me are also suspects. I've got to put them in a place where the FBI, the CIA, and the Secret Service can't find them, and then I've got to figure out who set me up, find the real

Jamie Brennan, bring her back, and clear my name."

"Good luck, peanut," says Vanessa.

As I open the bathroom door and step over the bodies of the two Secret Service agents, I hear Vanessa's voice.

"I'm going to be president."

The sound of her laughter echoing behind me is the scariest thing that's happened all day.

CHAPTER TWENTY-EIGHT

Asylum

I do not like or trust Vanessa Dominion, and I certainly don't believe that she is trying to redeem herself . . . BUT.

In her first moments pretending to be Jamie Brennan, she marches to the top of the West Wing steps, looks out at the Rose Garden, and addresses the assembled guests thusly:

"What better way to celebrate America's families than starting a conga line?"

I notice that she's wearing my Forever 21 gingham dress and I'm wearing her much more stylish green outfit. We forgot to change clothes! But she makes my thing look like a million dollars, and I'm fairly certain I make her designer dress seem like an old sack of potatoes.

She shimmies her way down the steps, shaking her hips and kicking her feet. The Rose Garden is immediately filled with applause and smiling faces. The spontaneous Jamie Brennan with her happy dancing feet is back!

Vanessa gestures to the president to join her conga line. He almost trips over the tables to dance with his daughter. A mad scramble of guests jostles to join him. She's too immersed in leading her followers around the Rose Garden for her to notice me giving her a grateful, admiring smile. That ice-hearted snob has just done two very clever things. She has made it impossible for the Secret Service to get anywhere near her, and she has given me the opportunity to slip away from the Rose Garden unnoticed, which I will do as soon as I have the rest of the Wilder family with me.

I see Ryan, now wearing a huge white Stetson hat, midway down the conga line. I charge toward him, grab him by the wrist, and drag him behind a tree.

"What's going on?" are his first words to me. "Is it spy action?"

I am mortified that Ryan showed up to the White

House in a Mexican wrestling T-shirt, but right now I could hug him. Having one member of my family I don't have to lie to, who knows most of my secrets and never needs explanations, is an amazing luxury.

"I can confirm it's spy action," I tell him. "Want in?"

Ryan's eyes widen. "You're cutting me in on the spy action?"

"If you think you can handle it," I say.

"What's the mission?" he asks.

I'm about to tell him, but I'm suddenly overcome by curiosity. I don't want to tell him that I've been impersonating Jamie or that she's missing and I *really* don't want to tell him that Vanessa wormed her way back into the Wilder family home, but there's something I need to ask him. "Hey, Ryan, did I . . . act weird, or weirder than usual, when I came back from Secret Service camp, or when we were on the plane? Did I do or say anything . . . ?"

Ryan looks surprised. Then he thinks about it a little more. (That narrowing of eyes and scratching his nose: that's the sign of Ryan in the act of thinking.) "Yeah. You were *really* weird, even for you."

I knew it. I *hate* her.

"What was that?" Ryan asks. "When you got home? The stuff you were saying to me?" He does an inaccurate impression of my voice, doing the squeaky thing everyone thinks is so funny, but adding a verge-of-tears tremble to it.

"'Thank you for giving me this second chance. I'm trying hard to redeem myself, and if I ever did anything to hurt you, I want you to know I'm sorry, that is not who I am now. I'm going to do my best to make it up to you.'" Ryan shakes his head at me. "Was that part of the mission? Were you undercover?"

I take a second to let *that* strange little picture sink in.

"Yeah, kind of," I say mysteriously. I can see he's hungry for more details. Instead, I poke a finger into his chest. "You know how you've devoted your whole life to pulling dumb, stupid, ridiculous pranks that bring shame and embarrassment on our family?"

Ryan nods.

I grin at him and say, "I want you to pull the dumbest, stupidest, most ridiculous prank *ever*!"

And right now, I could swear my brother has a little tear in his eye.

Ten minutes after I told Ryan exactly what I needed him to do, the conga line is *still* snaking its way around the length of the Rose Garden. *Everyone* is part of the dancing festivities. The first family, the guests, the press, the caterers. It's another massive win for Jamie Brennan. I run up the line until I catch sight of the flying feet and waving hands of my mother, my father, and my sister.

"Mom, Dad," I gasp. Dad tries to pull me in step with him. I evade his hands and act like I'm attempting to catch my breath.

"What have you done now?" says Natalie, who looks furious at the very sight of me.

"It's Ryan," I say.

"Oh God," my mother says, shuddering.

"He ran off," I tell them, hoping I look sufficiently terrified. "He . . . he said something about storming the Trezekhastan Embassy."

Mom, Dad, and Natalie react to this bizarre statement as if they were just punched in the face.

"He wouldn't," says Natalie. "Not tonight."

But she knows he would. And just to seal the deal, I add, "He said the best way to celebrate America's families was to confront the enemies of our freedom."

I grab Mom and Dad's wrists. "We've got to stop him," I yell at them. "Being arrested in Washington is a whole different deal than being arrested in Reindeer Crescent. We might never see him again."

For a second, relief floats across the faces of my family members. Then reality kicks in. The Wilders make a hurried exit from the Rose Garden while, behind us, the conga line goes on.

And now my barely-thought-through, totally-improvised plan to keep my family out of danger begins!

As far as Mom, Dad, and Natalie know, an Uber car just happened to be waiting outside the White House to transport us the three miles to Wisconsin Avenue, the location of the Trezekhastan Embassy. As far as they are concerned, the Trezekhastan ambassador turned out to be a gracious, polite and accommodating host who not only welcomed them into the embassy but insisted in feeding them, giving them a tour of the building, and lecturing them on the history and culture of Trezekhastan. As far as they know, Ryan has barricaded himself in the ambassador's office and is demanding to talk to the Trezekhastani prime minister.

But that's not what happened.

Even before Vanessa began her epic conga line, I frantically pondered ways to keep my family out of harm's way. Hiding them from the combined CIA, FBI, and Secret Service seemed like it was going to be a tall order, especially when I didn't know anyone in Washington. But my brain comes into its own in times of crisis. Sometimes it helps to say your problems out loud.

"You're right," I told myself. "You don't know anyone in Washington. But you know someone who owes you a big favor. You know the son of Trezekhastan's secretary of state, the boy whose life you saved from the hands of Vanessa Dominion back when she was still completely evil."

I kept up my one-sided conversation. "The Trezekhastan Embassy is here in Washington, and they grant asylum to refugees from countries that are enemies of Trezekhastan."

This thinking-out-loud thing was going great! I thought some more. "The CIA, the FBI, and the Secret Service cannot remove those refugees without lengthy negotiations with the Trezekhastan government."

I'm friends with the secretary's son on Trezekh.chat. I DM'd him and got him to talk to his father. I had him tell the embassy to treat the Wilders like refugees and keep them cooped up in there until I discovered who was out to get me.

Great thinking! Especially with Ryan in the embassy finding new ways to make a bad situation worse.

Getting out of the embassy without Mom and Dad noticing I was gone would be a no-brainer. After Secret Service camp and the burrito incident, Mom, Dad, and Natalie are *so* ready to believe the worst of me. All I have to do is fake being sick, hole up in the embassy toilet, and they'll leave me alone.

Was this really a good idea? It was about as good as

not telling the president and first lady that their daughter had been kidnapped, but is it the best I can come up with.

The first few stages of my plan seemed to work without a hiccup. Mom and Dad are confused and upset, but they are safe inside the embassy. I am sitting in the building's kitchen with Natalie, as one of the staff cooks us a Trezekhastani delicacy that looks like brown custard, and which will I imagine will give me a credible reason to spend a few hours in the bathroom.

Something that's been nagging at me for the past few hours simmers to the surface. I take out my phone and look at the last video attachment Adam Pacific sent me, the one where his big fat head partially obscures L4E rehearsing behind him. Their tour schedule is tattooed on my heart. They should be in an arena in Brazil. But that clip makes me think they're somewhere else.

"Oh my God. Seriously, Bridget," says Natalie. "Ryan might be starting a war, and you're drooling all over your silly boy band."

"They're not silly," I start to say. But arguing is useless. You can't make non-L4E people understand. I ignore my sister's disdain and freeze the clip at a moment when there's a little bit less Pacific head and a tiny bit more of the band.

When the Forties' Research and Development weirdos gave me my phone, they told me of its incredible zooming capabilities. Now is the time to put their claims to the test. I zoom past Pacific, and I see two distinct colors. One is orange, and one is blue. If I am correct, the orange is a strip of hair on top of Cadzo's head. The *Zohawk* is back!

What a coincidence that Jamie and I talked about the wildly divisive 'do a few days ago and now he's sporting it again. I zoom some more. The blue is the bottom of a big F. The same big F I saw on the news report where independent candidate Morgan Font stood on the stage of his Font Foundation surrounded by kids and talked trash about my beloved dance routine.

My spy senses kick in. Or maybe it's my L4E fan senses. Whatever it is, *something* has kicked in. The band is in Washington, DC. But why are they singing in front of the big F? And why is Cadzo wearing his hair in the style that tore social media apart?

I take a bite of the Trezekhastani delicacy. It's actually quite delicious, but I have questions that need answering, so I dry-heave after my first spoonful, and tell Natalie I have to make a run for the toilet. She gives me an exasperated look. Lately, I do nothing but embarrass and disappoint her. I feel bad about that, and also guilty that

I'm abandoning my family in unfamiliar surroundings, but I can live with guilt.

Somebody out there is messing with me. It's time I messed back.

CHAPTER TWENTY-NINE

The Big F

The Uber driver who picked the Wilders up at the White House takes me down Constitution Avenue. The car passes the Federal Reserve, the Lincoln Memorial, the National Archives, the Environmental Protection Agency, and lots of equally impressive buildings I should probably recognize. Maybe when I've returned Jamie safe and sound to the White House, her parents will be so grateful, they'll give me the keys to the city, and perhaps a parade in my honor. Or maybe they'll discover the true identity of the possibly reformed assassin I enlisted to take my place as their fake daughter and have me deported to

Trezekhastan. (And what if Vanessa is under deep cover? What if she's still in league with her criminal mastermind father, the distinguished Edward Dominion? I'm the one who put her within killing distance of the president and the first lady. My head is pounding with increasingly horrific worst-case scenarios.)

"This is the place," the driver says, freeing me from my nightmares.

The car drives up the southwest side of Constitution Avenue, coming to a halt on the other side of the road from an oval tower of black glass. In the middle of the tower is a metal red, white, and blue F.

This is the Font Foundation, the headquarters of Morgan Font's presidential campaign. A group of about thirty kids, some who look to be in their mid-teens, some younger, are gathered outside the front entrance wearing black-and-white T-shirts that read *Font Force*.

They hand pamphlets, stickers, and badges to passersby. Some of them chant: "We want Font." Catchy.

"My kid wears that shirt," says the driver. "He wants to volunteer for Font's campaign."

"What does he see in him?" I ask.

"I try to ask him," the driver replies. "He tells me I wouldn't get it. He says Font's real, that he listens to kids and understands them."

"That's amazing," I mutter. "*I* don't even understand kids."

I do, however, understand that if I can get the Font Force kids to accept me as a potential new recruit, I can gain access to the black glass tower.

I take my leave of the embassy car and hurry across the road to the Font Foundation.

A girl who looks to be about fifteen with intense, staring eyes approaches me, leaflet in hand. "A vote for Morgan Font matters," she says. "Because our future matters."

"It's the only thing that matters to me," I tell her, while staring back with equal intensity. "I'd like to help with the important work you're doing here."

"You can help by making sure your parents vote," says the Font Force girl, whose necklace identifies her as Hayley.

"Consider it done," I lie. "But right now, what can I do to spread awareness and build Font buzz?"

Starey Hayley reaches into her back pack and hands me a brown envelope.

"In here," she says. "You will find forms for your parents to read, declare their approval of you volunteering for the campaign, and sign."

Hayley holds out a pen with the red, white, and blue

F logo. "And here's a nice pen for them to write their names. Once that's done, bring it back and we'll give you and your parents free Font phones."

Free Font phones. I think I might have just uncovered a clue as to why Morgan Font is so popular with teens. But I already have a phone, and I don't have time to waste.

"But I'm here now," I insist. "Couldn't I just . . ."

"Come back with the signatures," says Hayley. "And we'll find something for you to do. That's how it works."

I could argue. I could appeal to the other volunteers. I could start a fight. But the last thing I need right now is to draw attention to myself.

"Okeydokey," I tell Starey Hayley, and I shove the envelope and the awesome free pen in my pocket.

I saunter away from the volunteers and then break into a sprint. My plan is to hang around outside one of the back exits of the tower, waiting for someone to leave, so I can fire my loyal nanomarble, Red, at the closing door, thus giving me the opportunity to sneak inside. I walk down a side street on the way to the back of the tower. My head is filled with important questions: *What if I bump into Cadzo? What do I say? Should I prepare something? Should I drop a Glasgow reference? Maybe something about local soccer teams: Do you think the Rangers will beat the Celtics? Or will that sound too rehearsed and not sincere?*

A loud banging breaks my feverish pileup of thoughts. Faint, frantic, wordless, muffled screaming accompanies the banging. I whirl around, prepared for an out-of-nowhere attack, but the side street is empty. The banging and muffled screaming continues. A few feet ahead of me is a gray Dumpster with a black lid. The Dumpster is shaking. Something inside is kicking it. Something inside is trying to express rage, fear, and frustration. My immediate reaction: some monster has abandoned a helpless animal. I creep closer to the Dumpster and touch my X-ray glasses.

The plastic Dumpster fades away. Inside, I see something abandoned and helpless. But it's not a pet. It's a person. A person whose hands are tied behind his back, whose ankles are bound together, and whose mouth is covered by pink sticky tape. My six seconds of X-ray vision end. The Dumpster returns. But the vision is seared into my mind.

Someone threw Adam Pacific out with the trash.

CHAPTER THIRTY

Dumped

How often does this happen? How often does someone who mocked you when you were in a vulnerable position find himself in the exact same vulnerable position, only now *you* get the chance to mock *him*? This is what I ask myself as I stand, arms folded, in the narrow street to the side of the Font Foundation, listening to the cries and kicks of Adam Pacific.

Except . . .

I know how it feels. It does not feel good to be powerless and exposed. I should be the better, more mature, more compassionate person.

I open the Dumpster lid and recoil from the stench. Holding my breath, I look down and see Adam Pacific's face. His expression goes through several stages:

1. Fear.
2. Relief.
3. Recognition.
4. Despair.

Seeing his face when he recognizes the person who has discovered him at his lowest moment, it makes me . . . shall we say, not quite as compassionate as I should be.

"Mmm mnnn urggg," I think he says beneath his gag.

"Hi, Adam," I trill. "What a surprise." I make a surprised face and put a finger to my lips. "Oh. Oh, wait, are you on secret spy work? Should I go? I'll go."

I start to lower the lid.

"MMMNNN! URRRGGGHHH!" is his reaction.

"So, how did you wind up in there?" I ask before continuing. "Doesn't matter. You probably want some help getting out, am I right?"

He nods at me.

"The fact that you want me to help you would suggest that I'm not a gimmick." I smile down at him. "Wouldn't you agree?"

He stares back at me, his eyes aflame with hate. But I am no stranger to hate-filled eyes. I've been death-glared by the first lady of the United States. Adam Pacific is a rookie by comparison.

"Well, obviously, I'm not going in there," I tell him, waving a hand across my nose. "Why don't you try to haul yourself upright. It shouldn't be a problem for someone with your many skills. Then I'll help pull you out."

Pacific flails around like a goldfish who's been scooped out of his bowl and is drowning on dry land. He thrashes and rolls and kicks and finally gets himself in a position where his chin is jammed against the side of the Dumpster. And then he bangs his chin into the Dumpster, using the impact to lever himself upright. That's something I haven't seen before.

Once he gets into a standing position, I try not to inhale while reaching into the Dumpster, pushing my hands under his armpits, and dragging him with all my strength over the top of the Dumpster and onto the ground.

I catch my breath while he twists and squirms on the ground. Nothing would give me greater pleasure than to leave him there for stray dogs to lick and hopefully pee on. But I remember that I should be better, more mature, and more compassionate. I kneel down and rip the sticky tape from his mouth.

"Aaarrgghh" is his reaction.

I push my palm over his mouth.

"Quiet," I hiss. "Don't attract attention. Act like a spy."

Those burning eyes of hate again.

"Wilder," he spits. "What are *you* doing here? School trip?"

"Oh, you don't know?" I say.

I do not get the upper hand in life a lot. But right at this minute, I know something Pacific does not. In fact, I know a whole *world* Pacific does not. So I tell him. The whole world. I was asked to be the president's fake daughter. The Forties is done. Strike and Irina are in a box. Jamie has probably been abducted. The CIA, FBI, and Secret Service all think I did it.

Pacific looks even more goldfishy now than he did a minute ago. I can actually see his brain rushing to keep up with the whirlwind of information I just laid on him.

"But," he finally says. "If you were pretending to be the president's daughter, and she's gone, and you're here, who's wearing the nanomask now?"

I make a disgruntled face. "Yeah, that might be a problem. I had to act fast. My family was right there in the White House. I picked probably the worst person to replace me. Have you heard of Vaness—"

His face brightens. "Vanessa Dominion?" he says before I even get her whole name out. "That's a great idea. She'll do an awesome job."

This is *outrageous*! Even Adam Pacific knows and likes Vanessa. I hate spies!

"No, she won't," I retort. "That's why I've got to get Jamie back to the White House before your friend Vanessa wreaks havoc."

"You want to give me a hand untying these?" Pacific whines, raising his roped ankles.

"I thought you escaped from a safe filled with snakes," I reply. "This should be easy for you."

I notice he's wearing an L4E T-shirt with the words *H8 ME* scrawled underneath the band logo.

"Nice T-shirt," I remark. He flinches, which means there is no way I am not going to ask the question he's probably dreading.

"So. How did you end up in the Dumpster?"

Pacific looks pained. "When you travel with a band, you become like a family. You play pranks on each other. No one takes it seriously. No one takes offense. It's my turn to get back at them. I'm already planning my revenge."

"I absolutely believe your very convincing story," I

tell him, my sarcasm levels turned to full volume. "What really happened?"

Pacific looks up and down the side street, hoping someone who isn't me will come to his aid.

I start to walk away. "Time's ticking, Pacific. I've got a president's daughter to find."

"I can find her faster than you," he growls.

"We'll never know," I say, as I pick up speed.

"Wait!" he shouts.

I stop.

"We were getting along okay," I hear him say. "And then . . ."

I walk back to Pacific. He's squirming on the ground, trying to loosen the ropes around his ankles and wrists, but he's only making them tighter. I bend down and start to untie his ankles. I'm good with knots.

"I started telling people I was Beano's brother," he mutters. "I wasn't the only one. Some of the security guys did it, too. You get in places for free. Stores beg you to wear their clothes and be seen with their headphones. I wasn't hurting anyone, but Beano found out, and the band turned on me."

I stop working on his knot and give him a disgusted look.

"I don't blame them," I say, proud of my boys for

defending their innocent fans standing up for the truth.

"It wasn't just that they stopped talking to me," he goes on. "They got mean. My bags would go missing. They stole my passport. They'd get me thrown off planes and kicked out of hotels."

I want to laugh but Pacific is a picture of misery, and if what he's saying is true, his punishment *far* outweighed his crime.

"I could have demolished all of them," he says quickly, as if he sensed my pity. "I could have taken the 4E out of their name. And the L."

"But you didn't," I say. "Because you didn't want to blow your cover. You were there to prevent them from getting abducted." See, I *am* a better, more mature, and more compassionate person.

"Right." He nods. "So I have to take it when they jump me from behind and do stuff like *this*." He holds up his bound wrists.

"What are you doing here?" I ask. "In Washington?"

"The management got a call from this Morgan Font guy, asking if the band would play a private show."

"But they already had an arena concert in Brazil," I point out.

"From what I heard, Font offered them so much money to cancel that gig and do his event, there was no way they could refuse."

"What event?"

"I don't know," he says. "They locked me in the bathroom for most of the flight. One thing I heard before they attacked me, though. Font had a demand. Cadzo had to shave the sides of his head."

Jamie's fantasy. Font's demand. Coincidence or coinci—I don't think so?

I spring to my feet and break into a run.

"Where are you going?" Pacific yells after me.

"Stay there!" I shout back, as if he had any choice. "I'm forming a plan."

CHAPTER THIRTY-ONE

Bad Samaritan

"**Y**ou *poor* thing," coos Starey Hayley to Adam Pacific. "I am *so* sorry this happened to you. What an awful, terrible experience. *This* is Chester Brennan's America. But you're in a safe place. We're going to get you cleaned up, find you some nice fresh clothes, and give you a hot drink, and we'll make sure you get home."

This is *exactly* how I hoped Hayley and the Font Force volunteers would react when I came scampering back to the entrance of the Font Foundation, shrieking about a poor kid who had been mugged, tied up, and chucked in a Dumpster *by supporters of President Brennan.*

No envelopes, no parental signatures, no special pens were required. The Font Force swooped down on Pacific, lifted him to his feet, and carried him into the reception area of the Font Foundation, while telling him how brave, strong, and special he was. How Morgan Font was going to make America a better place for him. To give Pacific credit, he played along, acting like a confused, possibly traumatized, victim. And because I was the caring, selfless, bighearted individual who discovered the shocking crime, I was also allowed into the black glass tower.

How can I best describe the interior of this building? If you think your house doesn't have enough American flags big enough to cover an entire wall, you might like it here. If you wish you lived in a huge dark gym hall where giant video screens all featuring a man who looks like a raven stare down at you, this is the place for you.

As the Font Force smothers Pacific with attention—which I bet he *hates*—I do what I do best. I disappear unnoticed into the bowels of the Font Foundation. Okay, bowels is inaccurate and a little gross. But I sneak away from the volunteers and tiptoe through the nearest door. I hurry through a corridor lined with framed photos commemorating Morgan Font's rise to extreme wealth and power. The corridor leads to a room with four Ping-Pong tables. A group of kids are sprawled on foam rubber bean bag chairs painted red, white, and blue. They're all engrossed in their phones.

"Font Force Michigan reports two hundred new volunteers," says one kid.

"Font Force Boston coming on strong," says another.

One of them looks up and eyes me with suspicion. I pull out my envelope and pen.

"I'm taking orders for pizza," I say.

The suspicion dims. The kids all look excited. They bark their toppings demands at me while I pretend to write them on the back of the envelope. My spy advice: when you venture into unknown territory, a potentially tense situation can be quickly defused by bringing up free pizza.

The same clever ruse allows me to weasel my way through the Font Foundation's recording studio, its library, and its gym. I now know that the majority of the volunteers prefer plain to pepperoni, but I'm no closer to finding the answers I seek.

Then I smell something.

Something *disgusting*. Something sort of familiar. Something disgustingly familiar.

Something like . . . *deep-fried Mars Bar*. Benj's favorite fast food. The monstrosity I once tried to cook. There is no reason anyone in America should be deep-frying chocolate unless they're making it for someone who rates it as his favorite fast food.

Which means that . . .

Benj is here.

Which means that . . .

L4E is here.

Which means that . . .

Jamie might be here.

Which means that . . .

L4E is here!!!! (Sorry, I had to go back to that one again.)

I follow the rancid smell down a flight of stairs that leads me into the Font Foundation kitchen. It's empty, but the smell of deep-fried chocolate fills the air. I look down and see chocolate stains on the ground. I follow the stains out of the kitchen and down another corridor. As I walk, I feel vibrations under my feet. I hear a muffled sound growing increasingly loud.

I hear music. I hear L4E!

Don't freak out. You're on a mission. An important mission. Which you can't remember right now. Keep it together.

I turn a corner, and the sound of the music overwhelms me. To my right, there is a sign on the wall. It reads FONT FOUNDATION CONCERT HALL. The arrow under the sign points straight ahead. I break into a run. As I pick up speed, the music fills my head. I see two metal doors. Once I push them open, I'm going to see L4E live and in person.

All I have to do is get past the two huge security guards who bar the doors and look at me with eyes filled with menace. Both men crack their knuckles. I crack mine.

Just in case.

CHAPTER THIRTY-TWO

Scream

"No entry," yells one of the guards over the roar of the music.

"This is private," barks the other. "You shouldn't be here."

"Who wants pizza?" I shout back.

"Who authorized you to come down here?" demands the first guard.

"Where's your Font Force T-shirt?" bawls his colleague. (Okay, so not *everyone* loves free pizza.)

These two guys are colossal lumps of muscle and knotted veins. Neither of them has a neck. Either one of them could crush me with his thumb. But getting past them is the most important thing in the world. Luckily, I have a secret weapon.

I raise my hand and squeeze the back of my ring.

Red shoots through the air, flying straight at the face of the security guard standing in front of the first door.

I get ready for the collision of marble and skull.

But the guard suddenly lifts his big meaty paw and . . . *catches Red in midair!*

I am stunned. No one has ever done that before.

The guard sees that I am stunned and smiles. To cause me further distress, he holds up a closed fist and starts to squeeze.

"Don't hurt him," I beg.

"Don't hurt him," echoes the second guard. Both of the giant slabs of meat start laughing at me.

They keep laughing until the guard with Red in his left hand suddenly swings his fist into his partner's face.

They both look shocked.

"You hit me!" gasps the recipient of the punch, rubbing his jaw.

"I didn't mean to," says the shocked guard. He tries to open his fist, but somehow it won't do what he wants. He tries to open the fingers of his left hand.

"It's stuck," he complains to his colleague. The other guard tries to help him pry open his closed fist.

I have a feeling I know what's about to happen.

The guard with the closed fist punches his friend in the face again.

"Stop hitting me!" yells the guard with the throbbing face.

"I'm not doing it," the guy with the closed fist shouts back.

His closed fist flies at his partner's face again, but this time, the wounded guard punches back.

And, just like that, the two guards are rolling on the ground, throwing punches at each other and ignoring both the doors they are supposed to be protecting and me.

I rush toward them and jump over their warring bodies. As I jump, Red flies back into my ring. I greet him warmly. "You, my friend, never fail to surprise me."

And I'm through the doors.

My senses are overwhelmed. The music hits me like a wave. The sight of the five boys who have taken up residence inside my thoughts and dreams singing on a stage five hundred yards away from me scrambles my mind.

The fact that they're singing in an intimate little venue capable of holding an audience of maybe one hundred people is unreal. Even more unreal, the hall is entirely empty except for me, L4E, and Jamie Brennan, who is standing in front of the stage, jumping up and down, screaming her little head off.

I let out a gasp of relief.

My spy senses were accurate. Jamie is here in Morgan Font's headquarters. I don't know how she got here, or what L4E are doing here, but these are questions for later. Right now, I need to get Jamie back to the White House, get Vanessa *out* of the White House, and remove my parents from the Trezekhastan Embassy.

I run across the floor of the small club. "Jamie!" I yell. She doesn't hear me over her screams and the blast of the music. I feel a burst of joy. My new friend. My favorite band. And we have them all to ourselves.

"Jamie," I bawl. She still can't hear me.

I'm close enough to reach out and tap her on the shoulder. I reach out. My hand is almost touching her . . .

I feel a sharp pain on the back of my head. My heels scrape against the ground. I'm being dragged out of the hall by my hair. It *hurts*. (Why did I let my hair grow long enough for someone to grab a handful? Probably because Mom kept telling me it was time to get it cut. But now is not the time to think about Mom.)

I try to twist around, try to aim Red at my assailant, but the pain is making my eyes water, and I'm fighting to keep my balance.

"Jamie!" I keep shouting. But she's screaming so loud she still can't hear me.

CHAPTER THIRTY-THREE

Brute Force

"Get off me," I bawl at the invisible assailant who dragged me out of the concert hall. I'm whirled around and thrown through a door into a room filled with Ping-Pong tables!

As I go staggering backward, I reach out and grab the edge of the nearest table to steady myself. I'm breathing hard and trying to blink away the tears of pain, anger, and embarrassment I feel welling up. I rub my eyes, and when the blurring fades, I see Starey Hayley wiping stray hairs from her palms.

I've wiped the floor with adversaries twice—*thrice*—

my age, and some demented *volunteer* just got the best of me by pulling my hair. Maybe that's my Achilles' heel. My Achilles' hair.

I burn with the fury of a thousand suns. Or, at least, I do inside, because the Ping-Pong room is filled with Font Force volunteers. At least twenty of them. Some big strapping high schoolers, others younger than me, all wearing the black T-shirt, all looking at their phones. And now, all looking up and staring at me with the exact same unblinking intensity as Hayley. My finger grazes the back of my ring as I mentally calculate how many of the volunteers Red can take down. The odds are not in our favor.

Hayley takes a step toward me.

"Liar," she spits.

"Good judge of character," I reply.

"You don't care about the future," she says.

"I care about *my* future," I tell her.

Hayley bares her teeth at me. "You're a spy," she states flatly.

I give her my game face. No reaction. No emotion. But, on the inside, I stop burning with the fury of a thousand suns and start getting nervous. How does a hair-pulling volunteer who hands out flyers and stickers know who I am? Oh my God, I *am* public enemy number one. The whole world knows I work for the CIA.

"For the Brennan campaign," Hayley goes on.

My anxiety immediately vanishes. Hayley knows *nothing*.

"You want to steal our speeches and leak information about what we're going to be talking about at the debates."

I laugh in her face.

"You bug-eyed hypocrite," I reply. Her shocked expression is highly enjoyable. I pluck a Ping-Pong ball from the table and toss it from hand to hand. "You throw false accusations at me when you're the one who kidnapped the president's daughter."

"Liar!" she shouts.

"Not this time," I shoot back. "I saw Jamie Brennan in the concert hall with L4E. You're in a huge amount of trouble. You should probably burn that T-shirt."

Hayley ignores me and addresses the volunteers. "This is classic Brennan. Deny, fabricate, avoid responsibility, blame others."

The Font Force radiates dislike in my direction.

"You're the one denying, fabricating, and . . ." I can't remember her whole list of false accusations. "All that other stuff. Whatever I've done, you've done a million times worse. You kidnapped . . ."

"I don't know what you're talking about," Hayley yells in my face. "I caught you trying to transfer files onto a flash drive. Stop talking about the president's daughter."

"I may be a liar," I bark back. "But I'm a good one. *That?* That was pathetic. I was in the concert hall . . ."

"What concert hall?" Hayley demands.

"There is no concert hall here," pipes up one of the younger Font Force volunteers.

"You're a spy," shouts another volunteer.

Something is not right. I don't just mean the lies. I look from Starey Hayley to the assembled Font Force, and they *all* have the same intense, wide-eyed expressions on their face. L4E are live and in the flesh *inches* away from where they are, and these kids are acting like nothing's happening. I can hear the boys singing their incredible catalog of hits, and again, there is no sign of excitement from these people. Are they even human?

The Ping-Pong room begins to boil over with tension. The Font Force are not content merely to stare anymore. They're starting to make their way toward me.

"Get the flash drive!" Hayley commands them.

"There is no flash drive!" I start to say, but it's like trying to reason with the undead.

I jump onto the Ping-Pong table. It immediately collapses. I flail around on the floor like spilled soup noodles, and curse the shoddy equipment in Morgan Font's multi-million-dollar headquarters. Font Force hands reach out to grab my wrists and my ankles. I try to squeeze my ring, but I'm being lifted into the air and I don't have a good aim. I unleash Red, and he smacks into the ear of the square-headed boy whose hands are locked around my ankle. He yells in pain and grabs his sore ear, but the other hand tightens around me.

"Get off!" I find myself yelling once more, as the Font Force swarms around me. Someone pulls a T-shirt over my head, ensuring I see only shadows through the black cotton.

"Take her up to see the campaign committee," I hear Hayley order her minions. She makes the words *campaign committee* sound deeply sinister. The hands of these zombie kids lift me into the air. I struggle and kick, but they hold me fast. I'm in uncharted territory here. Are they going to eat my brains? Are they going to make me like them?

CHAPTER THIRTY-FOUR

Lethal Weapon

Is this the end of Bridget Wilder's brief spy career? Is this how I go out, hoisted aloft by a mob of weird kids and carried off to an uncertain fate while my favorite band is performing in front of my friend a few feet away?

Then I hear . . . is that a whip cracking?

The next sound is a bloodcurdling scream of pain. It's not my scream or my pain, so that's a plus, but I can't see what's happening. Another whip crack, another scream, this one right in my ear. I'm dropped on the floor. *Ouch.*

"Stop!" I hear Hayley plead. "We're your friends."

The screams mount in volume and terror as I scramble across the floor on my hands and knees. My shoulder bangs into the leg of the Ping-Pong table that's still standing. I shuffle to my side, crawl backward a few paces, and then pull the black T-shirt off my head. From my safe little shelter under the Ping-Pong table, I see some Font Force volunteers throwing their hands over their eyes. I see others lying facedown on the floor. And I see Adam Pacific whirling a wet towel over his head like a lariat. He lashes out behind him and hits a volunteer in the face. The volunteer howls in pain.

"Get help!" Hayley yells at a pimply volunteer. The pimply kid starts to run from the room. Pacific lashes out with a second wet towel. It curls around the pimply kid's ankle. Pacific gives the towel a sharp tug.

"Waaah!" screams the pimply kid as his leg gives way and he tumbles to the ground.

Pacific crosses his arms. The wet towels make a *swish* sound as they fly over his shoulders. He surveys the damage he's done. I follow his gaze. The floor of the Ping-Pong room is littered with broken glasses. A couple of short-sighted volunteers crawl blindly across the ground. A girl rocks back and forward, her hand over her mouth. "My retainer," I hear her weep.

I see a huge, hulking high schooler with red marks

on his face looking stunned and shaken, and I see Hayley trying to text on her phone. Pacific whips a wet towel over his shoulder and then jerks it back in a sudden movement. Hayley looks down in amazement at her empty palm. She looks up in even more amazement to see her phone fly into Pacific's open hand. I'm not going to lie, it's pretty impressive. He takes a step toward her, spinning the towel as he walks. Hayley stares at it, hypnotized.

"Don't hurt me," she pleads.

"Don't give me a reason," Pacific replies.

He suddenly snaps his fingers at me. "Shirt," he says.

I throw him the T-shirt. He gives it to Hayley. "Put it over your head and then go stand in the corner."

"But . . . ," she begins.

Pacific gives the wet towel a practice midair crack. Hayley squawks in fear. She pulls the Font Force shirt over her head and stumbles blindly into the nearest wall.

He gives me a smirk. "You can come out now."

I crawl out from under the Ping-Pong table.

"Looks like I saved your butt again," he says.

Ignoring him, I say, "I take it that was one of the martial arts disciplines you created?"

"Towel-fu." He nods, looking pleased with himself. He gestures at the weeping, twitching human wreckage littering the Ping-Pong room floor, and says, "I took it easy on them. When I give it a hundred percent, you're looking at a bloodbath."

"You might have to give it a hundred and twelve percent," I tell him. "Something deeply sinister is going on here. These volunteers were going to tear me limb from limb like rabid dogs."

"Why do they have to be rabid dogs?" says Pacific. "Couldn't they just be dogs that don't like you? Which would make them ordinary dogs."

I ignore him. "We've got to get Jamie Brennan out of this building."

I pick my way through the moaning volunteers and walk back up the corridor toward the metal doors. The music that rumbled through the floor and walls is no more. I fear for Cadzo and the boys. Pacific follows as I walk over the fallen bodies of the two security guards.

"What happened to this pair?" he says.

"I have a martial art of my own," I reply. "Bri-jit su."

"Mine's better," he mumbles. *This guy!*

We walk into the concert hall. Five microphone stands are the only the evidence that L4E were once in this small room, a few yards away from me, close enough to touch. I think I might tear up again. Luckily, Pacific distracts me by running across the floor and jumping on stage.

He grabs a stand, throws his arm wide, and yells. "Howyeeez doin', America!" Looking over at me, he says, "They say that at the start of every show. They never know what city they're in."

As Pacific cavorts around the stage like a clown, my phone rings. Ryan.

"Tell me your mission's accomplished and you're on your way back to the embassy to get me out of this." He sounds scared.

"Ryan," I say. "Calm down."

"We didn't think this all the way through," he says, clearly making an effort to keep his voice down. "I'm a seasoned pranker, but even I can't keep up this pretense much longer. Mom and Dad are going to *disown* me if I keep acting like I'm trying to take over the embassy."

Oh God.

"I'm *so* sorry. I'm coming. We'll figure this whole thing out." What a bunch of meaningless drivel. But what am I supposed to say? Oh, wait, I know. "Ryan, listen, I've got an amnesia . . ." I can't think of the word for the thing-that-sprays-the-perfume-that-makes-you-forget. ". . . thing. I can wipe Mom and Dad's memories. It'll be like none of this ever happened."

"Seriously?" Ryan suddenly sounds *a lot* less frazzled. "I can do *anything*, and you can make them forget about it?"

Uh-oh.

"But I'm sure it won't come to that," I say. "I'll be back at the embassy soon. Just hang in there. You're doing amazing, and I super-owe you."

"You super-do," agrees Ryan. "And another thing . . ."

Beep. Someone else on the line.

"Ryan, I've got to take this." I accept the new call.

"Just checking in, peanut," says Vanessa. I hear the mumble of party guests and the clink of glasses behind her. "POTUS, FLOTUS, and I will be making our way to Georgetown University for the debates at five o'clock, FYI."

I check my watch. Three thirty.

Gulp.

"Not that I don't have every confidence in you," Vanessa continues. "But if you fail, if you're captured or killed, and you need me to start shooting people . . ."

"No!" I yelp. "Don't shoot, stab, or strangle anybody. I'll bring Jamie back in time for the debates, and then you can disappear."

I wait for her to reply. Instead I hear Vanessa call out, "Hey, everybody, who thinks we should make Family Day a national holiday? Let me hear a yee-haw, like we do it back home in Texas!"

I hear a loud *Yee-haw!*

"Vote for my daddy, and he'll make it happen."

I hear the first lady croon, "Jamie, that was *perfect*. I mean, it'll probably never happen, but I love your enthusiasm. You've really stepped up today."

"Thanks, y'all," Vanessa drawls. The call cuts out.

A clock starts ticking in my head. Suddenly, everything's urgent. Where would Jamie be? Where would *I* be if I were her—and I *have* been her.

"Pacific," I yell at the stage. "Find the band's dressing room. Now."

I follow him as he heads backstage. We charge down some rickety wooden steps, through a darkened corridor to a half-open white door and the familiar, wafting odor of deep-fried chocolate.

"I love that smell," mutters Pacific.

I push open the door.

A pudgy guy with a shaved head surrounded by video monitors, all of which show footage of Jamie, taps furiously on a computer keyboard. As he does, the images of Jamie move in reverse, and then they freeze, and then they fast-forward a few frames.

My stomach rumbles *loudly*. (It's been *hours* since I've eaten, and that deep-fried chocolate smell is getting to me.)

"Nice manners," mutters Pacific.

The pudgy guy stops tapping at his keyboard and revolves in his seat.

"How did you get in here?" he starts to say.

Whap!

A towel shoots out and hits him on the chin. His head rolls back, and he slumps in his chair.

I turn to Pacific as he jerks back a towel that has a knot the size of a fist.

"Fast knotting," I say.

"Probably seems that way to you," he mutters.

I make a mental vow to never again utter a compliment to Pacific.

With an effort, I roll the unconscious pudgy guy away from his video screens so I can get a clear view of Jamie. She is sitting in front of what looks like a large sheet of paper featuring a graphic of a white fist gripping a black lightning bolt.

I press the *play* button on the keyboard.

"If my captors' demands are not met within twenty-four hours, you will never see me again," says Jamie in a trembling voice, her terrified eyes staring straight into the camera. "*Please*, Dad," she implores. "I want to come home."

Pacific stands next to me, arms folded. Both of us stare at the multiple images of Jamie.

The scared expression leaves Jamie's face, and she suddenly bursts out laughing.

"Was that okay?" She giggles. "That '*pleasssee,* Dad' was kind of cheesy."

"It was great," offscreen voices assure her.

"Thanks, you guys." She smiles, and then the screens go black.

Pacific and I look at each other.

"What?" he says.

"Double what?" I add.

The pudgy guy's phone starts playing the *Star Wars* theme. Pacific and I both jump in fright.

"I wasn't scared," he says quickly. "I was doing an impression of you."

There is no start to this kid's charm.

The ringtone wakes the pudgy guy. Pacific goes for his knotted towel.

"Let me," I say. I aim Red at him. The pudgy guy sees the marble headed straight for him. He struggles to get out of his seat. Too late. Red pops him in the forehead, sending him back to sleep again.

I fish the phone out of the slumbering pudgy guy's shirt pocket. As I do, a text appears on the screen.

> Footage needs to be finished now. Font finishing up in hospitality then heading to Georgetown U.

I search Pudgy's phone. Not only do I find a floor-plan of the Font Foundation showing the hospitality suite on the fourth floor, but my unconscious pudgy friend has also made a note of the passcode that unlocks the suite.

"We struck gold!" I tell Pacific, only to catch him in the act of eating a deep-fried chocolate bar that I am certain he picked up *from the floor*.

"What?" he grunts, his mouth filled with mutated chocolate. "I'm hungry."

"Save your appetite," I instruct him. "We're going up to hospitality."

CHAPTER THIRTY-FIVE

Best Foot Forward

"There's a certain procedure spies follow when they're venturing into unknown territory, like we are now. You probably don't know what I'm talking about because you think you can rely on luck to get you through any given situation, but that's not going to cut it in this . . ."

Pacific drones on and on as we make our way up the stairs of the third floor of the Font Foundation, but I tune him out and concentrate on the thoughts crashing around inside my confused mind. One minute, I see Jamie screaming her head off at her own private L4E show just like in her fantasy. The next, she's a scared, trembling wreck begging the president to rescue her—*and then laughing about it.* Like it's a joke. Or not a joke. A game.

"She's playing a game," I say out loud.

"Are you even listening to the important spy advice I'm giving you?" says Pacific.

"Of course not," I reply. "This is all a game. Jamie vanishes. She pretends she's been kidnapped and held for ransom. But she isn't. She's having the best day of her life with her favorite band in the headquarters of her father's biggest rival."

"So what?" says Pacific, like a fool.

"So think, Spy," I shoot back. "Jamie hates life in the White House. She'd do anything rather than face another four years. So this is what she's doing. She's going to let Morgan Font go on live TV and tell the watching millions he saved the president's daughter from her captors. And the president's going to stand there with his mouth hanging open going, 'Um, um, um,' 'cause he didn't even know she was missing in the first place."

"You're completely wrong," says Pacific.

"Actually, she's pretty much correct in every detail," remarks a voice from behind us.

We both turn to see Morgan Font, live and in the

raven-like flesh, smiling up at us from a few steps below. "I'm impressed, Bridget," he says.

"I'd already figured it all out," breaks in Pacific. "She was just repeating what I told her."

"You might be the worst person who ever lived," I tell Pacific.

"If you could have kept your mouth shut, this guy wouldn't have been able to sneak up on us," moans Pacific. "You gave him the element of surprise."

"Put them in a quiet place, and we'll deal with them later," says Font.

Pacific and I both whirl around. Bearing down on us is a colossal beast of a man with tree-trunk arms. His big meaty paws grab both me and Pacific by our shoulders and lift us right off the ground.

Pacific lets out a high-pitched *waaah* that drowns out my own scream of fear and pain.

As I dangle, kick, and scream, I somehow have enough presence of mind to pull out my amnesia spray. The beast dangling me above the stairs smiles at the plastic tube in my hand. He keeps smiling when I squirt him. Then he falls forward and tumbles downstairs.

I jump from his grasp. Pacific, who is still going *waaah*, scrambles out of the big man's grasp.

I hear a crash and a muffled scream behind me. I look

around. The beast has fallen on top of his boss. Morgan Font lies trapped and struggling under the considerable weight of the giant man he sent to get rid of me. Ha!

I walk downstairs.

"Wilder, what are you doing?" I hear Pacific bleat.

I ignore him and look down on Font's thrashing legs.

"I wouldn't want to leave the Font Foundation without a souvenir of my visit," I tell him.

"Too heavy," wheezes Morgan Font. "Can't breathe."

"Maybe this'll help," I say. And then I pull off one of his shoes.

I head back upstairs, Font's strangled cries for help receding into the distance.

"A shoe?" says Pacific. "Have you gone mental?"

I walk past him and head toward the top of the fourth floor. I can already hear the music, the laughter, and the loud voices coming from inside the hospitality suite.

"Wilder," I hear Pacific attempt to whisper and shout as he hurries to keep up with me. "Procedure. Strategy. You can't just . . ."

I walk up to the locked doors and key in the passcode I retrieved from the pudgy guy's phone. The doors open.

No one in the spacious, luxurious hospitality suite sees me come in. They're all too busy enjoying one another's company. Beano and Lim from L4E are stuffing their faces with shrimp from the huge metal serving bowls that line the sitting room. Cadzo, Beano, and Kecks are talking, laughing, and filming Jamie doing the dance that *I* made famous when I was pretending to be her. They don't notice me make my way across the room toward them. Jamie doesn't see me because she's basking in the attention of her favorite boy band. She's so immersed in this dream scenario where she's the star and L4E are *her* adoring audience that she doesn't see me walk right up to her and throw Morgan Font's shoe right in her face.

CHAPTER THIRTY-SIX

True Colors

"Owwwaaa!" screams Jamie, more in shock than pain, because she was fast enough to block the shoe just before it made contact.

"B-Bridget?" she gasps, eyes wide. "But I thought you . . . How did you . . . ?"

Her face reddens. I watch guilt and embarrassment shut her down. She looks at the ground while her hands open and close. I really liked Jamie. I *still* really like her, but I want her to know exactly what she's done.

"You set me up, Jamie," I say, no emotion in my voice. "You made it seem like I had something to do with you disappearing . . ."

"But Morgan said . . ." Jamie's voice is far more fearful than it was when she was pretending to have been abducted. "He said it would be okay because he'd get elected and make everything right with the CIA. It had to look convincing . . ." Her voice trails off. Even she doesn't believe what she's saying.

"You wanted out of the White House, and you didn't care what you had to do or who you had to do it to," I say crisply. "You involved me, and my family, and my other family. So I'm taking you back before you can put your plan into action."

Jamie's face changes. She's clearly making calculations. "Let me fix this," she says, moving closer to me, dropping her voice. "Let me clear your name, and your family, and your other family. I'll say it was nothing to do with you. I'll pull a name from the FBI Most Wanted list and put the blame on him."

I shake my head. "I don't trust you, Jamie."

She gives me a sorrowful blink and touches a hand to her heart. "But we're *friends*."

"We're not friends. We like the same band, that's it."

And right then, I become aware that L4E are surrounding us, engrossed in our conversation, and filming every second of it. Now it's my turn to redden and stammer.

"Come on, Bridget," Jamie says, her voice turning harsh. "What do you care who's president? Does it matter if it's Chester Brennan or Morgan Font? Will it make that much difference to your life? The answer is, it won't. But it'll make a huge difference to mine—and you've been me, so you know what I mean. I can't face another four years. So I found a way out. Why can't you just be happy for me? Why don't you help me instead of trying to make me feel bad? I can't believe how selfish you are."

That last statement literally takes my breath away. I find some breath and say, "You know what, Jamie? I would like to take off my own shoe and throw it at you, but I like it too much to waste on your lying, selfish face. But just know this: *my shoe hates you.* You don't care how bad you're going to make your father look, you don't care what you're going to do to the country, you only care about the luxury you're going to be forced to live in, the private jet you'll fly in, the limousines you'll ride in, and all the places you get to visit. It might seem like torture to you, but so what—*shut up and suck it up.*"

Okay. I was not intending to be quite so forceful. Jamie looks like she's on the verge of tears. I grab her wrist and start to pull her away from the hospitality suite.

"No," she says, and digs her heels in.

A hand pulls us apart. Cadzo's hand. *Cadzo touched me! Oh my God!*

"Hey, hen, don't come in here starting a rammy," he says. "The wee lassie disnae wannae go wi' ye. End of."

"Honestly, I'm not trying to cause trouble," I manage to tell Cadzo. "I realize the young lady doesn't want to leave with me, but it's super important she gets back to the White House. I know you understand, because you've got such a huge heart and I love you so much."

Ah. That went a bit further than it should have.

Cadzo takes my hand in his. His deep-blue eyes stare into mine. I can die right now.

"I love ye, too, so I dae," he says. "See, if I wiznae geein' it laldy on stage every night, you're the kind of lassie I could imagine . . ."

His hand on mine. His eyes looking into mine.

"Yes?" I hear myself say from what seems like a hundred million miles away.

"Covering in shrimp." He grins.

"What?" I say.

And then shrimp rain down on me. Hundreds of wet, slimy shrimp. In my hair. In my eyes and my mouth. A metal serving bowl drops over my head, covering my eyes.

I hear loud shrieks of laughter. Someone bangs

serving tongs off the top of the bowl, causing my head to ring. I don't know what just happened. Or rather, I *do* know what just happened, but I can't bring myself to acknowledge it because my heart would break a hundred times over. I will myself to turn to stone. To feel nothing, to be nothing, to summon up the strength to get through this.

"Classic!" I hear Cadzo exclaim. "Signature shrimp gag!"

And then I hear a whip crack, and the laughter turns to screaming.

I push the metal bowl off my head and shake off the shrimp that continue to cling to my hair and my clothes.

Adam Pacific, who I left behind when I came storming into the hospitality suite, is wielding his wet towels like whirling helicopter blades. Beano is doubled up on the ground. Lim stumbles in circles, groping blindly. "Ma contacts," he moans. Kecks clutches his head, crying. Benj hides under a table, pretending to be dead. And Cadzo . . .

Cadzo keeps trying to get up and fight Pacific, but every time he almost gets to his feet, Pacific whips his towels around Cadzo's ankles and he falls back to the floor.

"Aah, ya tube!" moans Cadzo. "Git aff us!"

"*That's* for the Dumpster," growls Pacific, lashing Cadzo's ankles with the towels.

Cadzo tumbles to the ground.

"I'm gonnae batter ye!" wails Cadzo.

"*That's* for stealing my passport."

Whip!

Down goes the most beautiful boy in the world.

"I'm gonnae . . . I'm gonnae . . ." Cadzo's voice is choked with sobs.

Pacific draws back his towels.

"*That's* . . . ," he begins.

"You've done enough, Pacific," I say. "Time to throw in the towel."

With an effort, Pacific restrains his whipping arm. He inhales deeply and calms down.

"Thanks," I say.

"Are you okay?" he asks, looking concerned. "These guys think they can get away with anything, but when they did that to you, something in me just snapped . . ." Pacific stops abruptly. His expression changes. "I wasn't helping you. I was paying them back."

"I'm aware," I assure him. Pacific's jerkitude is nothing next to the horrifying shrimpy trauma I just endured. I'm definitely getting that haircut now.

"So," I say briskly. "Let's get what we came for and get out of this place."

At the same time, Pacific and I become aware that what we came for—i.e., Jamie—is no longer in the vicinity of the hospitality suite. In the distance, we hear shoes running downstairs and a piteous voice screaming "Help! Help!"

"Jamie!" I yell. I just found that treacherous little brat. She does not get to slip through my fingers again.

I start running after her.

Behind me, I hear the sounds of the hospitality suite doors being locked and heavy objects being shoved up against it.

Pacific runs down the stairwell alongside me. "Wilder," he growls. "This is all your fault."

CHAPTER THIRTY-SEVEN

The Getaway

The man-beast who collapsed on top of Font when I squirted him with my amnesia spray device is now conscious and trying to pull his dazed boss to his feet. Jamie stands on the third floor of the stairwell staring at both of them, her hands flapping in the air. "What happened to him? What did you do?"

"I don't know," moans the man-beast.

"I'll be fine," Font says through coughs. "I just need a minute."

Jamie suddenly lets out a piercing scream and points a finger at the stairs.

She's right to scream because Pacific and I are running down the stairs toward her.

"She's going to take me back to the White House," Jamie whines. "Stop her."

I shoot Red at Morgan Font's shoeless foot. Direct hit. He howls in pain and hops on his other foot. Pacific spins a towel over his head a couple of times and then lets it fly. The towel wraps around the man-beast's eyes like a blindfold. The big man roars in shock and frustration. I jump down the last few steps, grab Jamie by the wrist, and pull her after me. Once again, she tries to resist. I turn to face her.

"Don't put up a fight, Jamie," I say, through gritted teeth. "Look what I did to L4E, and I love them."

Technically, I didn't do anything to them, but my tough tone works on her. She lets out a scared little gasp, and her wrist goes limp in mine.

Pacific brings up the rear as we race downstairs.

"You're down a towel," I shout to him.

"One's all I need," he grunts.

"Are you a spy, too?" asks Jamie, turning around to look at Pacific.

"*Too*," he echoes. "I'm the only real spy here."

"So insecure," I say in a singsong voice that I hope gets under his skin. "So desperate and needy."

"Three times, Wilder," he retorts. "Three times now I saved you."

"Three times you were useful," I fire back. "As opposed to all the other times."

"Are you two, like, broken-up exes forced to work together?" asks Jamie. "'Cause I'm getting that vibe . . ."

"*No!*" I yelp.

"What, me and *that*?" shouts Pacific. "Never in a quadrillion years."

"Never in a *decillion*," I shout back. "That's a lot more."

"Never in a . . ." I await Pacific's brilliant comeback. I turn around to see him frantically searching the Font phone he confiscated from Starey Hayley.

"Looking for higher numbers?" I say. "How about duodecillion? Or quindecillion? Or how about octodecillion?"

"Shut up, Wilder," he mumbles.

I give Jamie a *can you believe what I have to put up with?* roll of the eyes.

"Total vibe," she says.

"Wilder, stop," Pacific says.

He's still looking at the Font phone. "Where are we going?"

Good question. Finding Jamie has been my priority,

but I should be thinking about the bigger picture. A whole battalion of Font Force volunteers might be lying in wait for us.

"There's a garbage chute on the first floor that lets us out behind the building," he says, holding up a map on the screen.

"I'm not sliding around in garbage," protests Jamie. "It's all right for you, you're already covered in shrimp."

"Lead the way," I command Pacific. I don't want to go down a garbage chute any more than Jamie does, but it's now just after four o'clock. I have less than an hour to get Jamie back to the White House before the first family departs for the debate.

Pacific takes a right turn and pushes open a door leading us down a corridor festooned with Font paraphernalia.

"Yes, it does matter to me," I say.

"What?" Jamie replies.

"It does matter to me who's president. It does make a difference to my life. It didn't forty minutes ago, but that's before I found out Morgan Font thinks faking an abduction is an awesome way to win an election."

Jamie gives me a condescending smile. "That's just politics."

"Is it?" I retort. "He flew L4E . . ." The words *taste*

funny in my mouth now. Like bile rising in my throat. I attempt to regain my composure. "He flew them here to give you your fantasy so you'd be even more inclined to do whatever he wanted. What if your own private show hadn't been your fantasy? What if having them turned into wax figures and mounted in a secret museum had been your wish?"

"Oh my God, that's an *astonishing* idea!" Jamie exclaims.

"Okay, it kind of is," I concede. "But that's not my point. Forty minutes in Morgan Font's headquarters has told me all I need to know about the world he wants me to live in. I don't like it."

"He's nice to me," she mumbles. "He listens to me."

"*Really?*" I laugh incredulously. "I wonder why. Don't act like you were so obsessed with being close to Cadzo . . ." *Ugh.* Just saying that name was like walking into an oncoming express train. *Focus, Bridget.* ". . . you didn't notice how weird and sheeplike the Font Force volunteers are, how they've all got those mad eyes."

"But that doesn't mean . . ." Jamie trails off. "Are you saying this stuff because you want to get me back to the White House and clear your name, or do you actually, deeply, and sincerely believe Morgan Font's a bad guy?"

"Both," I reply. "I want the Wilders and the

Wilder-adjacents as far away from DC as possible, and I want the same for Morgan Font."

Jamie says nothing for a few seconds. "They do all have those staring eyes," she agrees. "Like, they never blink."

I feel a great weight lifting from my shoulders. Jamie gets it. Maybe it's safe for me to like her again.

"In here," Pacific says. He's standing by the door at the end of the first-floor corridor, with a key in his hand that seems to be changing shape in front of my eyes.

"Nano*key*?" I squeal. "Why don't I have one of those?"

"They only give them to spies," he scowls, then points to his watch.

"All right." I nod. "Let's do this."

"Oh no," moans Jamie. "Garbage."

"Wilder'll go first," says Pacific. "It's her natural habitat."

"Didn't I find you tied up in a Dumpster like an abandoned puppy someone threw away the day after Christmas?" I remind him.

"*Total* vibe," I tell Jamie, and we both laugh.

Pacific holds the door open, and I venture inside.

I'm in a dimly lit room, medium-size, completely empty.

"Where's . . . ?" I start to say.

I feel something coil around my ankle. I look down and see a white towel. I try to kick it loose, but the towel is yanked away so quickly, it sends me stumbling forward. As I fall to the ground, a clear wall of plastic slides down from the ceiling to the floor. Behind me, the same thing happens. To my left, and then my right, more walls of plastic slide noiselessly to the ground.

On the other side of the plastic, Jamie stands staring at me with her mouth hanging open. Pacific is also staring at me, but his expression is different. There is no shock, no fear, in his eyes. Just an intense, wide-eyed stare.

"No!" I shout. "Pacific, no. You're not one of them."

"Morgan Font is the future," he says. "No one fights the future."

"Bridget!" Jamie yells. She rushes to the plastic wall separating us and throws punches at it. Her fists make no impression. Pacific's hand comes down on her shoulder. He starts to pull her away.

"No," she cries. "I don't want to. I made a mistake."

"We have to go," says Pacific.

As he drags Jamie out of the room, she reaches out a desperate arm to me. All I can do is push my pinkie up against the plastic wall.

"I'll find you," I promise her. "I'll come for you, and I'll save you. Pinkie swear."

The door of the room slams shut, and I am left alone, encased in a plastic cube.

Pacific. A double agent. A Font plant. I should have suspected. But double agents go out of their way to get you to like them. Pacific went out of his way to do the opposite. He antagonized me at every opportunity. *Maybe he is a better spy than me.*

How far back does this go? Did Font cut a deal with him to get his dad out of North Korea? Is . . . what's his name . . . Charlie Pacific in on it? He did try to kill Strike three times. Maybe we're all pawns in his game. Maybe Charlie Pacific *is* Morgan Font in a nanomask. How would I even know? My mind is all over the place, thoughts popping like popcorn.

Focus, Bridget.

"Here's where they want you to fall apart," I tell myself. "But you thrive in impossible situations, and besides, Pacific was so determined to get Jamie away from me, he didn't disarm me. I still have Red."

I aim Red at the plastic wall in front of me. He bounces straight off and rebounds into the back wall. I watch him pinball back and forward until I accept there is no further progress to be made with this approach. I hold up my ring, and he returns home.

"Nice try, buddy," I tell Red.

I pull out my phone. No service.

It's starting to look like Pacific knew exactly what he was doing when he neglected to disarm me.

Maybe if I walk in a circle, I'll spot a flaw in my plastic prison, something I can use to help me escape. Maybe if I tap or rub or pound my fists against the walls, it'll trigger some kind of secret combination that will . . .

I don't know how I'm going to get out of here.

I run at the wall facing me, and kick out hard. The impact of my shoe hitting the plastic doesn't even leave a mark. I bang my fists and yell, "Let me out."

Here's where you fall apart, the voice in my head tells me.

I crumple to the ground, exhausted and out of ideas.

That's when the lights go on in the room surrounding the cube. And Morgan Font walks in.

CHAPTER THIRTY-EIGHT

Hail to the Thief

"How's the foot?" are my first cool and defiant words to Font.

"How's the cube?" are his first smug and triumphant words to me.

"No Wi-Fi," I point out.

"I'll put my best people on it."

"Like Adam Pacific?" I say. "How long's he been working for you?"

Font checks his watch. "I'm going to say five minutes?"

I look at him in his dark-blue suit with his Stars and

Stripes lapel pin, and I curl my lip in disdain. Then I uncurl it. Five minutes ago? Five minutes ago, Pacific was looking at his Font phone, trying to find a higher number than decillion, and suddenly he turned into a decisive man of action, leading Jamie and me toward the garbage chute. And then I think back to the Ping-Pong room filled with Font Force volunteers staring at their phones and then attacking me like savage beasts. What do the two events have in common?

"It's the phones," I groan, feeling dumb and smart at the same time. "You turned Pacific into a mindless follower through the Font phone, the same way you turned all your volunteers into starey weirdos who don't see what's really happening. And that's why they gave me a form for my parents to fill in. You send phones to voters so you can control their minds."

Font touches his fingers together in light applause. "You're good." He smiles.

"You're not!" I respond.

He looks hurt, or pretends to.

"How did you do it?" I ask.

"I don't honestly know. I mean, I came up with the idea of sending out subliminal instructions via phone, and I let the tech guys hammer out the details. It's a mixture of a super-high-pitched frequency and a pattern of vibrations. The results are pretty impressive, though."

"Not really," I say. "It didn't work on me."

"You stole a tech guy's phone," he points out. "They put in a code to protect themselves against the subliminal signals. But don't worry, when I want to put my fingerprints over your squishy little brain, I'll do it."

I feel a shudder pass over me. "What about Jamie?"

"She reached out to me," Font says. "She came to me of her own free will."

"But you're too much of a coward to let the rest of the country do that," I shout at him.

He pushes his hands deep into his pockets and gives me an amused frown. "Don't get all judgey, Spy Girl. You're no different from me."

I gesture around my luxurious plastic prison.

"Our current circumstances may differ," he agrees. "But morally? You're not entitled to think you're any more of a saint than I am."

"Oh, I'm *so* much more of a saint," I snarl. "I'm Saint Bridget."

"My apologies," says Font. "You've never lied, cheated, stolen, and manipulated people to get the result you want? Because, being a spy, I assumed that's *all* you did."

"That's different," I shoot back.

"How?"

"I'm the good guy," I tell him. "I'm the one who saves the day and makes things right."

"So am I." He smiles. "This will be a much better, much more profitable, and much more peaceful country when I'm running it."

"That's what my dad said you'd say!" I exclaim.

Font leans an elbow against the plastic wall. "Does your father know you're a spy?" he asks. "Does he know where you are right now? Does he believe things about you that are only in his head because you put them there?"

"To keep him safe!" I shout.

"Just like me!" he shouts back.

"It's different!" I wail.

"It's exactly the same," he says in a calmer tone of voice. "I believe voting is too important to be left in the hands of voters. You believe being your parent is too important to be left in the hands of your parents. We both saw problems, and we both addressed them in the same manner."

"Yeah, but . . ."

I'm floundering here. How is it that I, the victim in the plastic cube, am on the losing end of this argument?

"You're such a politician," I mutter.

"I know you didn't mean that as a compliment, but

I'm going to take it as such," Font says.

He moves away from the cube and smooths out the arms of his jacket.

"I've enjoyed our little talk," he tells me. "The first of many to come."

That shudder goes through me again.

"There's going to be a big role for a smart girl like you once I'm president," says Font. "And you know who's going to be pleased about that? Your father."

He checks his watch. "Got to run. I have to pick up your friend Jamie, whose mind I am forced to control now that you've seen fit to fill it with doubt. And then I've got a debate to win, and another fake president's daughter to unmask. Big day for me, and America! See you soon, Bridget."

Font strolls away, whistling "Hail to the Chief."

I bang my fists on the plastic wall, knowing it won't have any effect, but my rage has to be directed somewhere.

I can only bang so long before my arms grow tired. I slump down on the ground and gather my knees up to my chest, thinking of the bad guys who were so sure they were smarter than me. Brian Spool from Section 23. Edward Dominion from the Forties. The non-redeemed version of Vanessa. That corrupt Little Chef,

Nelson Geiger. Dr. Klee, the insect-loving dentist and mind-controlling freak. Okay, the last two aren't exactly world-class villains, but they still make the list of bad guys brought to justice by Bridget Wilder.

Morgan Font isn't any different from my other enemies. He's got decillions of dollars at his disposal, and he's capable of washing the brains of an entire nation, but he's still a delusional bad guy with a massive ego and a weak spot I can exploit. If I ever get out of here.

Think positive, Bridget. That's what Natalie would tell me.

You're positively stuck inside that cube. That's what Ryan would tell me.

I wish I hadn't thought about Natalie and Ryan, because now I feel guilty and scared. *Even without his mind-controlling phone, Morgan Font is in my head.* I shouldn't have dumped my family at the embassy. They shouldn't have been in Washington. I shouldn't have taken on the fake Jamie job. But I did it because lying, cheating, stealing, and manipulating are what I do.

And then I think of something my father said to make me feel better about being sent to fake FBI camp. Dad hugged me. *This is nothing,* he said. *This is a bump in your road, and your road is going to take you to awesome places.*

My dad was smart enough to see through Morgan

Font. If he believes in me, it's time I believed in myself.

There *is* a way out of this cube. There *is* a way to stop Font from taking Jamie to the debate and using her to destroy the president.

I just need to think of it.

I just need to think.

Think, Bridget.

I hear a grinding noise.

The plastic wall in front of me is rising back into the ceiling.

So are the other three walls.

Oh my God, I'm telepathic!

The walls stop rising. They start to slide back down to the ground.

I'm not telepathic. Font, or one of his tech minions, most likely the pudgy guy whose phone I stole, is toying with me, trying to raise and then dash my hopes.

I'm not playing his game.

The walls start to rise again. This time there's enough room for me to slide my foot under, and if I can get my foot under, maybe I can squeeze the rest of me under.

The walls freeze, midrise. The grinding sounds get louder.

My non-stolen phone rings!

It's Dale Tookey.

"Dale," I gasp into the phone. "There is no one in the world I am happier to hear from at this minute. You won't believe . . . ."

"I can't believe you didn't tell me about the whole president's daughter thing," says a familiar voice. A voice I was *not* expecting to hear. "Aren't we supposed to be the spy twins?"

"Joanna?" I gasp. "But it said Dale Tookey. What are you, how are you . . . ?" Words fail me.

"So you know how people don't like you?" asks Joanna.

"Is that the only reason you're calling me?"

"This Ur5ula doesn't dig the idea of you and Dale T. still being kind of a thing . . . ."

"But we're not even a fragment of a thing," I protest. "He just gave me some intel that I really needed . . . ."

"Because he keeps tabs on you," says Joanna. "His head should be full of codes and hacks, but instead it's filled with Bridget Wilder."

"Really?"

"I know, hard to believe. But he's scared to make Ur5ula mad because she's a genius-level hacker. Get on her bad side, she could make your life miserable in a million ways. So he has to help you in secret. That's where I come in."

Dale still likes me. He's scared of Ur5ula. Can I gloat about these two interesting facts for a second?

"I hear you gloating." Joanna laughs. "Okay, here's the deal: Dale was hacking your phone, and then when he lost contact, he initiated a program that would override the building's power supply and get you out, but the building has its own program that overrides any attempt to override . . ." I hear Joanna exhale. "God, this is exhausting," she goes on. "I don't really understand what's happening. He's trying to get you out, is all you need to know. So is it working? Are you out of the cubicle yet?"

The walls come down.

"No," I tell Joanna. "And it's not a cubicle, it's a cube."

"Did you tell Jamie Brennan about me?" she asks.

I think back to the time I told Jamie how tough it was being friends with Joanna. Now I realize being friends with Jamie was *a lot* tougher.

"It didn't come up," I tell her.

The plastic walls start to rise a few inches off the ground.

"It's working!" I whisper into the phone. "But I need more space."

"Dale's trying to get you the time and space to escape, but you only have a really short window," Joanna tells me.

"The second you think you can get out of there without hurting yourself, take it."

The walls to the left and right of me rise slowly. The back wall remains frozen. The wall facing me descends to the ground.

"Aargh!" I groan. "Tell Dale to keep overriding the override. . . ."

The wall in front of me rises higher than before. It smashes straight back down like a jaw snapping shut.

"Is there a toilet in the cubicle?" I hear Joanna ask. "What happens if you're in there all night and you need to go . . . ?"

The walls surrounding me follow the same pattern. Up, up, and then crashing down.

My timing has to be right, or I'll end up trapped underneath a plastic wall that could slice me in two.

I time the rise and fall of the front wall. It rises up for one, two, three, four seconds, and then comes crashing down. Can I make it under the wall in four seconds? What if it falls faster next time?

Joanna's voice breaks my concentration. "Bridget, I need to say something. If anything happens, if you don't make it out of there, I want you to know I consider you one of my best friends."

One of? *One of?*

"Me too," I tell her. "Definitely in my top ten."

I start to breathe hard. I feel my heart punching its way out of my chest. This is not the state of mind I need to be in. I need to be ice and steel.

I hear Joanna say, "If you had to lose a limb, would you rather . . . ?" I hang up on her and concentrate on my escape.

I lie down on my side by the wall, ready to roll under and out.

It doesn't rise. I count one, two, three, four. Nothing.

Come on, Dale.

The back wall starts to rise. I roll over as fast as I can, and . . . it comes crashing down.

The front wall rises. I roll away. It smashes back down before I make it out.

As fast as Dale can take control of the building, the building regains control. All I can do is try to make my escape in the seconds between the continual shift in power.

The left-hand wall rises; I crawl over to it.

It falls to the ground before I'm able to slide under.

The front wall rises. I crawl on my hands and knees to the center of the cube. I aim Red at the front wall. As it descends, Red fills the one-inch gap and prevents the wall from reaching the ground. The grinding sound gets louder as the plastic wall keeps pressing down on Red.

Fear suddenly grips me. I drop down on my knees and, to my horror, see cracks start to appear in the little marble who has stayed by my side and seen me through so much.

"Red, *no!*" I cry.

I did this to him. I put him in this position.

"Stop!" I bang my palms on the front wall. "Let him go. I'll stay here. I won't try to escape."

I feel plastic move under my palms. The front wall is rising. It keeps rising.

There's enough space for me to duck under. I swing down low and move out from under the gap. As I leave the cube, I grab the broken remains of Red. Two jagged pieces of glass and a few fragments.

"I'm sorry," I whisper.

I try to attach the remains to the front of my ring. Some of them stick, others drop to the ground.

I choke back a sob.

The door of the room bursts open, and a group of Font Force volunteers come running in. Right at the front, with eyes unblinking, is Adam Pacific.

CHAPTER THIRTY-NINE

Boys Don't Cry

"It's your phone!" I yell at Pacific as he comes thundering toward me, spinning a towel over his head. "That's how Font controls you. Get rid of it!"

Starey Hayley runs into the room just behind Pacific. "Get rid of her!" she commands him.

I pull out my amnesia squirter—I remembered the word!—and aim it at Pacific. The towel wraps around my hand, whipping the weapon away.

No squirter. No Red. I'm defenseless.

I raise both fists and one knee. I can at least get in a couple of decent kicks and punches before I'm overpowered.

Pacific suddenly slumps to the ground and lies there, motionless. Starey Hayley, who hasn't removed her mad, vengeful eyes from me since she came stomping into the room, trips over Pacific's body. The rest of the volunteers are suddenly a little less bloodthirsty, and a lot more scared. Two Font Force members lie on the ground, but I'm still standing. Plus, I see what they don't. I see that the amnesia squirter went off before it was towel-fu'd from my hand.

I swoop down to the ground and grab the atomizer. *Atomizer!* I remembered the word!

"She killed them," a Font Force member whimpers.

"No, I . . ." I start to deny the accusation, then I decide this is a time for drama rather than honesty.

"You want me, Font Force?" I cry out, waving the amnesia atomizer around. "Come and get me, but there's going to be a lot less of you standing by the time you reach me. Because you'll be lying on the ground." I gesture with the atomizer at Pacific and Starey Hayley. "Like these two."

The Font Force members stop in their tracks.

"She didn't squirt me," Starey Hayley points out. "I tripped."

"Let me rectify that right now," I say. I aim the atomizer at her. The rest of the Font Force volunteers scamper for the door.

"Call the FBI and the CIA!" I hear them scream. "Call the police, the fire department, and the sanitation people!"

Hayley looks down at the still-motionless Pacific, then back up at me and my amnesia-squirting weapon.

"Any last words?" I ask. "Any favorite quotes or lines of poetry?"

Hayley's face twitches. She starts to blink and then rubs at her eyes.

"I didn't want any of this," she says. "I just wanted the city to keep the dog park open. I emailed Font, and I ended up here."

Huh? I look at Hayley's miserable, confused face and I realize: extreme terror just overcame mind control. That's useful, but I don't have time to roam the nation, waving my atomizer in people's faces to scare them into waking up.

I motion to the open door. "Get out of here," I command Hayley. "Run and don't look back."

"What about the dog park?" she asks.

"I'll handle the dog park," I lie.

Hayley scampers out the door.

Which leaves me alone in the room with the limp body of Adam Pacific. What do I do here? Should I just leave him? Do I try to revive him? I kneel down and reach out my index finger till it hovers a half-inch from his nose. I feel weird about touching him.

"Dad?" he says, sitting up suddenly.

I lose my balance and tumble backward, flailing on the floor before I pull it together and scramble to my feet.

Pacific gazes around the room and then up at me. He looks lost.

"The Font phones," I tell him. "They control your mind. Not just you. Everyone. Well, except me."

Pacific looks at me like he has no idea what I'm talking about.

"You were one of the Font Force," I explain. "But I shot you with my amnesia atomizer." I hold up the tube as proof. "You don't remember the last half hour, but you towel-fu'd the Font Force, L4E, and some guy the size of a monster truck." I get up and gesture to the open door. "Let's go get Jamie. Font's got a head start, but if we hurry . . ."

Pacific remains on the ground.

"My dad was going to show me a technique that makes it impossible to be mind-controlled," he says quietly. "I remember him saying he had faith in me, that this was the thing I was going to excel at." Pacific doesn't look at me, but I can see his eyes start to mist over. "'Cause I wasn't ever going to be great at any of the other skills he tried to teach me. No good at languages. Never learned to swim. Can't shoot a gun. Scared of being locked in tight spaces."

The arrogant, obnoxious facade Adam Pacific shows the world has vanished. In its place is the sensitive, vulnerable guy beneath. But it's totally the wrong time for that guy to make his appearance. Right now, I need the jerk.

I squat down beside Pacific. "You're being too hard on yourself," I tell him. "What you did with those wet towels . . ."

"That's all I have," he retorts. "I'm a one-towel pony. I got tossed in a Dumpster by a boy band."

"I got covered in shrimp by the same boy band," I remind him (and oh, how the memory stings!). "And you stuck up for me. You won't admit it, but you did. You saved me from the worst moment of my entire life. You've saved me a lot."

He turns his head away from me.

"But I couldn't save my dad," says Pacific. "I couldn't do what you did. You saved Strike. You figured out where he was, and you found him. I don't know how to do that. I don't know if he's alive or dead."

He wipes his eyes. I don't know where to look or what to say. I feel horrible for him, and I understand his pain. But the time is now four forty-five, so the sharing will have to wait for another day.

"Listen, Adam," I say, touching his arm. "I don't know you very well, and what I do know I don't really like. But I'd be in trouble without you, which tells me we're a good team. So why don't you bottle up your emotions, put your game face on, and help me put together a plan to stop Font from using Jamie to end the president's career?"

"Right," sniffs Pacific. He gets up off the floor, rubs the back of his hand across his eyes and nose, and picks up his towel. He gives me a nod, and we head out the door.

"Sorry about your dad," I say as we go.

"Sorry about your face," he retorts.

There's my guy!

We make it two, maybe three, steps into the first floor corridor when a deep growling voice says, "FBI. Keep your hands where I can see them."

CHAPTER FORTY

Mind Games

An actual-to-goodness, square-jawed, broad-shouldered, tough-as-a-tank FBI agent is waiting for Pacific and me midway down the corridor. She points her gun at us.

"You've got a lot of people looking for you, Bridget Wilder," she barks. Wow. I can hear that voice of hers in the soles of my feet. It's probably the wrong time to ask her to record my voice mail message. "You and your friend are coming with me."

"I wouldn't call us friends exactly," I correct her. "We're like reluctant partners who have to work together to bring down the bad guy. Wilder and Pacific."

"Pacific and Wilder," says Pacific. He shoves his hands in his pockets and affects a cool-guy posture.

"You see why we don't get along?" I ask the FBI agent.

"This is what's going to happen," she says. "You're going to very slowly take all your weapons and your communication devices out of your pockets, and you're going to kick them to me."

"You heard that part about us working together to bring down the bad guy?" I ask the FBI agent. "Indicating that we're not the bad guy?"

Ms. FBI is unmoved. "Kick them to me," she repeats.

Pacific kicks his towel toward the FBI agent. I slide my atomizer. Pacific shoves the phone he took from Starey Hayley to the agent. I go to slide her my phone, but not before I touch the screen and activate Pacific's Font phone. The FBI agent kicks Pacific's towel aside. She grabs my atomizer and phone, and finally, Pacific's phone.

"Hands in the air," the agent instructs us. "Walk toward me and . . ."

She stops talking. Her eyes go wide. An intense look falls over her face. She drops my gun and phone.

I nudge Pacific. "Do what I do," I whisper. I widen my eyes and adopt as intense an expression as I can manage. Pacific does the same.

"Morgan Font is the future," I intone.

"Font is the future," echoes the FBI agent, whose mind fell into Morgan Font's trap the second she picked up Pacific's phone—which I, of course, activated.

Pacific and I continue to act like mind-controlled volunteers.

"Font's enemies are everywhere," I tell the brainwashed agent. "You need to help us get out of here."

"I will help you," says the agent robotically.

She gestures for us to follow her. As we go, I pick up my stuff and text Joanna.

Get Dale to find Font's current location. Also, I got out alive.

The FBI agent leads us to a flight of stairs at the end of the corridor. Oh look, there's a man in a suit pointing a gun at us.

"Secret Service," shouts the guy. "Stand down."

The brainwashed FBI lady faces off against the Secret Service agent. "Morgan Font is the future," says the FBI agent. "Are you an enemy of the future?"

"What's wrong with you?" demands the man.

"It's her phone," I call out to the Secret Service agent. "It's controlling her mind."

"Get it away from her!" yells Pacific. "Grab it now!"

The Secret Service man registers the intense, unblinking stare of the FBI agent. He moves like lightning, kicking the phone out of the FBI agent's hand, snatching her gun away, and catching the phone, all in one smooth motion. But I'm faster. I activate Hayley's Font phone. The Secret Service guy's face goes blank. These phones are the work of the devil, and they need to be destroyed, but, I have to admit, they're fun toys to have. With a mere touch of a screen, I have transformed the Secret Service man and the FBI agent into obedient zombies. And I immediately realize that's way too much power for me to have.

I get a text from Joanna.

Font's on the E Street Expressway. Congrats on not being dead.

I feel Pacific's hand grip my shoulder. "Wake up, slacker," he grunts. "I've got a plan."

"You?" I say.

"FBI. Secret Service. Get us down to the garage. Disable anyone who gets in our way."

The two agents lead us down to the bottom of the first-floor steps.

"Your plan is we steal a car?" I ask Pacific.

"You're not thinking big enough," he says.

"An elephant?"

He spreads his arms. "Bigger."

The brainwashed agents push open a blue door, and

we follow them down more steps that take us to the Font Foundation parking garage.

What's bigger than an elephant? I wonder, as I glance around at the vehicles in the dark garage.

And then I see five faces that used to make my heart race but now make my stomach churn, larger-than-life, plastered across the side of a huge bus with a Stars and Stripes background. The neon words *All Over America* are printed under the familiar faces.

"Is that L4E's tour bus?" I ask.

"Not anymore," smirks Pacific, as he heads toward the massive vehicle. "Now it's ours, and we're going to drive it to the White House."

CHAPTER FORTY-ONE

Get on the Bus

There are other, smaller, vehicles in the garage that would have been easier to navigate through traffic. But I understand why Pacific headed straight for the L4E bus.

"That band stole something from us," I tell Pacific. "In my case, my heart, in yours, your dignity. Relieving them of this big, lumbering beast of a bus is the least we can do."

As the brainwashed FBI agent drives the L4E *All Over America* machine out of the garage and toward the E Street Expressway, Pacific guides me through the interior of the vehicle. The front of the coach has a seventy-inch TV screen and leather couches customized in Scottish tartan. The next section of the bus is occupied by the band's sleeping quarters.

In the far-off days of an hour ago, being near such hallowed ground would have made me stammer and tremble. Now, it means nothing to me (though I do reach out and touch what I imagine to be Cadzo's pillow as I leave the sleeping section).

Pacific walks me through a space with a full-size pool table and into the kitchen. Well, I say kitchen. The space is filled with a huge stainless steel fridge with two sliding glass doors that provide an unspoiled view of the mountains of frozen burgers, frozen pizzas, ice cream containers, sodas, meaty nuggets, and Scottish Mars Bars inside. Next to the mega-fridge is a rectangular chunk of metal.

"It's a deep-fat fryer," Pacific informs me.

"So they can fry their chocolate bars?"

"So they can fry *everything*."

Pacific leads me to the last section of the bus. It's a recording studio big enough for an actual grand piano.

"In case they ever got inspired," says Pacific. "But I never saw any of them come in here."

"You can't fry a piano," I point out.

Pacific laughs. Not at me, but at something I said, which is a first.

"Waste of an instrument," he says.

Pacific sits down at the piano stool and starts to play scales. His hands move up and down the keyboards, and then he begins to play a melody that's sort of sad and wistful. After a few bars, he picks up the tempo, and the tune he's playing becomes more rhythmic and hard-hitting.

If only I'd practiced on my flute, I could have been this good, I think.

Pacific changes to L4E's latest hit, "No One Is More Perfect Than You (Girl)," but slows it way down and makes it seem a lot cooler. I can feel the bus judder and screech and I can hear the horn honk as the FBI guy at the wheel drives us to the White House, but right now I'm more interested in listening to Adam Pacific.

"You're not a one-towel pony," I say. "You can do *that.*"

Pacific stops playing. He gives me a surprised look, as if he'd forgotten I was there. I see his face revert to that half-sneer I've grown to know and dislike.

"It's nothing," he mutters, getting up from the piano.

I'm going to need the jerk side of Pacific in a few minutes, but I don't need him right now.

"It's *not* nothing," I say. "Play something else."

He starts to walk out of the studio. I don't know why I want this moment to last a little longer, but I do, so I start singing the first song that comes into my head.

"Here come the spy twins on an another adventure, here come the spy twins coming to your town . . ."

Pacific looks at me like I just lost my mind. Which I very well might have. Here's a guy who does nothing but put me down, and I'm making myself into a target for him. But nevertheless, Joanna's song is nothing if not appropriate to where I am right now, so I sing it again.

"Here come the spy twins on another adventure . . ."

Pacific goes back to the piano. He instantly finds the right chords to go with my reedy warble. And he harmonizes with me. "Here come the spy twins coming to your town, here come the spy twins on another adventure, nothing's going to stop us now." He added that last bit!

"We're already better than L4E." Pacific laughs. He starts improvising a new verse.

My phone vibrates. A text from Joanna. I feel myself go red. Why?

R U watching TV? If not, watch NOW.

I grab a remote and turn on the giant TV hanging down from the studio ceiling. I glance around and see a remote control on the mixing desk. Pacific stops playing.

"What?" he says.

I press *power,* and there it is. Shaky phone footage of L4E being whipped by towels. Also, of me with a shrimp bucket over my head. The footage freezes on Pacific mid towel-fu. I flip to more channels. This is everywhere.

"Breaking news," says the anchor onscreen. "The teenager accused of assaulting pop group Live 4 Eva has hijacked their tour bus . . ."

The footage changes, and I see the L4E tour bus driving on the Whitehurst Freeway.

Police sirens start to shriek behind us.

On the TV screen, we see six police cars and two motorcycles chasing the bus.

I turn to Pacific. He's frozen to the spot, eyes fixed on the screen, a stricken look on his face.

"If my dad sees this," I hear him whisper.

Oh no.

I grab his arm. "He'll think he's got an awesome son," I tell him as earnestly as I can manage. "And he'd be right." *Wait, do I think he's awesome? Just because he played the piano? A cat can play piano.*

"What's happening here?" bawls the Secret Service agent as he runs into the studio. "How did I get here? What are you two doing on this bus?"

I check out his face. No intense stare.

I check his hands. No Font phone.

Mind control clearly works better and longer on impressionable young volunteers than hardened Secret Service agents. I whip out my amnesia atomizer and squirt him in the face. The agent slumps to the floor.

"Better shoot the FBI chick, too," says Pacific.

"Then who's going to drive the bus?" I ask.

Pacific squirms and shifts from foot to foot. "Remember when I said the band turned on me when . . ."

"You pretended to be Beano's brother to get free stuff," I finish his sad sentence.

"That's not the only thing I did," he says.

I'm about to ask what else he could possibly have done, when I realize.

"This isn't the first time you stole the bus!"

CHAPTER FORTY-TWO

Cut to the Chase

D o I have misgivings about Pacific driving the L4E tour bus? My misgivings have misgivings.

"You drive like a maniac," I tell him.

"I haven't killed anyone yet." He laughs. "That deer was just stunned."

He honks the horn to punctuate his horrible joke.

"Slow down!" I yell at him. "You're driving way too fast!"

His reply is to yank the bus without warning across all three lanes of the Whitehurst Freeway.

"It would be good if we could get there in one piece," I shout at him.

He honks the horn again.

"Stop honking the horn!" I demand.

This is a terrible mistake, but it was either let Pacific drive or let the cops catch us. The Secret Service agent is amnesia-snoozing in the recording studio where I tied him up with guitar leads. The FBI agent is sleeping off her amnesia in the bathroom. I left them nice little handwritten notes for when they wake up and wonder where they are.

Right now, the police cars are surrounding us in a kind of U-shape, but Pacific's erratic driving is preventing them from getting ahead of us and blocking our path.

"I wish they would try to stop us," whoops a way-too-excited Pacific. "I wish they'd put a wall of police cars in front of me." He punches the dashboard and shouts, "BAM! I'll knock that wall down."

"Keep your hands on the wheel," I beg him.

"Bam!" he repeats happily.

The giant TV screen at the front of the bus shows the president's motorcade heading into Georgetown University. The streets are lined with patriotic Americans, some cheering, others booing. The passenger window of the president's limousine opens. Jamie—which is to say, Vanessa in her nanomask—leans out to wave at the people on the sidewalk and film them on their phone. This earns her loud shrieks of approval. I still don't entirely trust her, but there's no denying that she's committed one hundred percent to the role.

The news report shows film of Morgan Font's limo driving up Canal Street, only a matter of minutes behind the president. The tinted windows don't open. No one knows what's in that car. No one knows Font has a ticking time bomb in the shape of the real Jamie Brennan waiting to blow up her father's career. The time on the TV screen is five twenty. Georgetown U is less than ten minutes away, but the traffic is going to become increasingly dense the closer we get to the location of the debate. The police are going to be all over us, too. I can't do anything about the traffic to come, but maybe I can do something about the cops.

I hurry down the bus.

"Where are you going?" Pacific calls after me.

"Kitchen," I respond.

"Grab me something tasty," he shouts.

I rush into the mini-kitchen area of the coach, and switch on the big steel fryer. Hanging on a hook at the side of the fridge is an apron with a pair of rubber gloves shoved into the pocket. I put on the apron.

The kitchen starts to heat up as the oil inside the fryer starts to hiss and spit. I pull on the rubber gloves and slide open the fridge door. I open a box of Scottish Mars

Bars, throw them into the fryer, and retreat a few paces as the chocolate hits the hot oil. Welcome to *Cooking with Bridget*!

The stench makes me cover my face with the bottom of the apron.

"You read my mind!" yells Pacific. "A deep-fried Mars Bar is *exactly* what I need right now."

I don't plan on there being any left over.

I tiptoe toward the fryer and peek down into the boiling furnace. I pick up a steel ladle from the side of the fryer and plunge it into the fiery depths. I carefully transport my ladleful of deep-fried chocolate out of the kitchen and into the main body of the coach. I slide open the window and hurl the contents of the ladle at the nearest cop car. Direct hit! The brown bubbling mess splatters across the windshield of the cop car to the right-hand side of the bus. The car swerves crazily across lanes.

I charge back into the kitchen, fill my ladle of doom, and repeat the process, engulfing the cop car on the other side of us with fried chocolate goo. The driver slams on his brakes. The police car behind rams straight into him.

"Ha!" I hear Pacific yelp with laughter from the front of the bus. "Wilder, did you see what happened? I guess the cop cars got splashed with mud or something . . ."

I walk back through the bus, carrying my chocolate-dripping ladle, until I'm certain he can see me in the rearview mirror.

"Guess again," I say. I don't have a huge need for validation, but I want Pacific to be aware that I'm as deadly with a ladle as he is with a towel.

A familiar face appears on the TV screen. Secret Service Director Adina Roots. She's being interviewed outside Healy Hall, the building on the Georgetown campus where the debate is due to take place. The interviewer gets up in Roots's face about the Secret Service repeatedly dropping the ball in terms of providing A-plus security for the first family. Roots flares her nostrils at the reporter and assures him the Secret Service will be all over the campus. No one's getting anywhere close to this debate unless they have a good reason for being there.

My first impulse is to ditch this big bus. My second impulse is to use this big bus to cause a distraction and get the Secret Service to drop the ball again.

I go up to the driver's seat and stand next to Pacific.

"Back when you pretended to be Beano's brother to get free stuff . . ."

He sighs. "That again?"

"No judgment," I assure him. "Did you do the accent?"

"Wha' ye blethering aboot, hen?" he says in full-on Glaswegian. "I gied them the patter, so I did."

"What are you talking about, girl?" I translate. "You gave them your best lines." I smile at him. "And you said you weren't good at languages. Okay, I want you to be Beano again. Fire up the bus PA and start broadcasting to DC. Tell them there's a free L4E show at Healy Hall in Georgetown U, happening right now!"

Pacific looks confused. "But that'll cause chaos. The streets will be filled with . . ." His confusion fades. ". . . screaming, demented kids, which is exactly what we need."

He holds up a hand to be high-fived. Our hands make contact with a loud smack. Just for the slightest second, our fingers intertwine, and then he puts both hands back on the wheel. Did I feel a little shiver there? If I did, it was probably just professional respect between two spies on a dangerous mission. I hurry back down to the sleeping section of the bus to put the next part of my plan in motion.

In my long-dead days of being an L4E devotee, my life was spent waiting by my phone for the boys to grace me with little snippets from their exciting lives. Now that the veil of fandom has slipped from my worshiping eyes, I know L4E for what they are: a bunch of mean, sloppy, overindulged teenage boys. Which means they probably left their laptops lying around and, if that is indeed the case, I can send out invitations to the spontaneous Georgetown U show from their official accounts.

"Hey, youse, it's yer man Beano frae the L4E. Wur oan wur way tae play a free show at Healy Hall in Georgetown University," bawls Pacific into the bus PA. "Aye, ye heard us right. Free! So whit are youse waiting for? Git doon there noo!"

I stifle a laugh. He sounds just like the real thing. I wonder if he'd record my voice message in that accent. Wait . . . why do I care? I shake it off and go back to the mission at hand, which is searching the sleeping quarters of the band I now despise to find their laptops.

I search two beds and find nothing except a mess of boxer shorts, old socks, chip bags, gum wrapper, and filthy T-shirts. Cadzo's bed is next. My heart has hardened to him, but still I find I need to take a couple of seconds to steady my nerves before plunging my hand beneath his sheets. Nothing incriminating lurks down there, or under his pillows, or shoved down the side of . . . wait a minute . . .

With trembling hands, I retrieve Cadzo's laptop. Do

I know him well enough to guess his password? I know that he's the member most likely to quit the band and go solo. I try *SoloCadzo*. Nope. *Solocareer*. Wrong. *Myownvoice*. No.

Think like the obsessive fan you once were. I type *Nothingwithoutme*. Bingo.

I'm about to start spreading the word about the fictitious free show when I see file marked *We Love Our Fans*.

Aww, I think. *That's sweet*. I can't stop myself clicking on the file. I see a bunch of video clips. Once again, I can't stop myself. I see Lim hugging a fan. As he hugs her, he sticks a sign that reads I FARTED on her back. The rest of the band crack up. The image changes to a clip of Beano pushing a fan into a fountain. Each clip gets worse. My shrimp trauma was simply the latest in a pattern of outrages against fans that started a long time ago. The last clip is of the band sitting on the bus surrounded by screaming fans banging on the windows, begging for attention. The boys ignore them. A chant of "we love you" begins.

"Aye," say the members of the band in unison. "And we cannae stand youse."

I think I have a lump in my throat.

I try to push the horrific image out of my mind and

execute my mission. I begin filling L4E's social media accounts with details of the Georgetown U show. And then I hear the sound.

My first thought: *The cops are back with reinforcements.* But it's not police sirens I'm hearing. It's the sound of screaming. Loud, sustained, high-pitched screaming.

"Wilder!" shouts Pacific. "Look out the windows."

We're on Canal Street. But we might as well have been transported to a parallel universe, one populated exclusively by screaming girls. They're jumping up and down on the sidewalks. They're on the road, running out into traffic. They're swarming out of office buildings and stores. I see schoolgirls. I see school*teachers*. And then I feel the thump.

Hands and fists are thumping the bus. I feel it on both sides. I feel it from above.

"Wilder, someone's on the roof!" yells Pacific.

"Great!" I call back. "Our plan is a huge success."

I see an entire basketball team. I see women abandon their cars in the middle of the street to join the pursuit of the L4E bus that's headed to Georgetown University for a free show that doesn't actually exist. There's no way this clever plan can go horribly wrong, is there? I've taken on terrifying bad guys in the past and come out on top. But Morgan Font is a different breed of enemy, and the stakes are way higher than I've ever faced before. This time, the stakes are the whole country. Am I really a good enough spy to stop America falling into Font's hands?

Pacific honks the horn and lets out a whoop of excitement.

At least one of us thinks we're good enough . . .

CHAPTER FORTY-THREE

Simmer Down, Furious Moppets

As Adam slowly maneuvers the bus down the street, I hear a bunch of thumps, and a smash. Did that smash come from inside the bus? I hear screaming, louder this time, and the sound of feet hitting the ground. Those sounds definitely came from inside the bus.

"Cadzoooo!"

Someone's on the bus?

"Wilder, what's going on back there?" yells Pacific.

"I got it," I shout back.

Of course, now that I've said I got it, I actually have to go and get it. I hurry through the bus, and there in the kitchen is our uninvited guest. She doesn't look any older than eleven, the same age as my sister, Natalie. But unlike the always-composed Natalie, this little creature wearing a school uniform that's a size too big for her is a red-faced, sweaty, gasping bundle of anxiety who is crazed enough to smash her way inside a slowly moving bus.

"Where are they? Where's Cadzo? Who are you? Is Lim here? I love Lim. *Lim!*"

"You'll see them all at the show," I lie. "But I have to ask you to leave the bus now. This is private property."

"Shut *up!*" she screams. "Shut your fat ugly face. *Liiim!*"

"Wilder!" Pacific shouts. "What's going on back there?"

"I got it!" I reply.

The little girl runs at me with palms outstretched, ready to shove me out of the way. I grab my ladle and thrust it at her like a sword. Angry tears squirt from her eyes.

"I love Lim, and you won't let me see him, and it's not fair. I hate you. I HAAATTTEEE YOUUU!"

"Simmer down, furious moppet," I say. "L4E may seem like the most important thing in the world right now, but . . ."

My wise lecture dies in my mouth as another red-faced girl squeezes through the broken window and into the kitchen.

"I can smell them" are her first words. She sniffs the air and then looks at me. I see her clench her little fists.

"*She's* trying to keep us from seeing the band," whines the first intruder.

A third L4E fanatic hauls herself through the window. This is getting out of hand. All three of them eye me with blistering hatred.

"Get out of my way or I'm going to rip every hair out of your head and shove them all down your throat," threatens the latest member of the group.

"That's not going to happen," I tell her. (But imagine if it did? Yuck!)

All three girls transform into hissing, spitting, feral cats. They fly at me. One of them grabs my ladle.

First Red, now my ladle!

"Wilder!" yells Pacific.

"I got it!"

I do not "got it." I turn and run from these banshees. As I flee toward the front of the bus, I hear more feet landing in the kitchen, followed by more screaming voices. It's like an infestation of ants.

As I charge toward the tartan couches, the bathroom

door opens. The FBI agent I shot with my amnesia atomizer staggers out. I jump past her and dive onto a couch.

"Hey," she starts to say. "How did I get here?"

She doesn't manage another word. The rampaging L4E fans are on her, shoving, kicking, biting, and scratching.

"Watch out for the one with the ladle," I advise her.

Pacific cranes around in his seat, looking horrified. "The bus is filled with crazy fans."

"So the plan half-worked," I say.

The gates of Georgetown University's main campus are in sight. A swarm of university cops, local police, and gray-suited guys whose dark glasses and earpieces identify them as Secret Service agents attempt to hold back the crush of shrieking girls trying to clamber over the locked gates.

I grab the bus's public address microphone. "Officer down, repeat, officer down," I intone, my voice electric with urgency. "Request backup now."

I see the local cops pointing at the bus.

"Pull over," I tell Pacific.

He brakes outside the main gates. We open the bus door and gesture frantically to the cops, who stop trying to hold back the kids and hurry toward us. They eye me and Pacific with suspicion, but the sight of a full-grown woman trying to calm a baying mob of shrieking teens, one of whom is pounding her on the knees with a ladle, is their priority.

As the cops board the bus and go to the FBI agent's aid, we make our escape, hurrying off the bus and making our way toward the mob of girls.

"It's four fifty," I say to Pacific. "We've got ten minutes. Let's split up, melt into the crowd, and try to get into Healy Hall unnoticed. Then find Jamie and get her away from Font before our time runs out."

"That's a lot," he says.

"Yeah, but there's two of us," I remind him. "Wilder and Pacific."

"Pacific and Wilder," he replies, and holds out a fist to be bumped. I bump it. There's that little shiver again. Professional respect. And then Pacific eases himself into the swelling crowd of weeping kids.

I take a few steps back and watch the mob shaking the gates. I wonder if I'm agile enough to pull off a Cheerminators routine here. What if I jumped on the shoulders of a hysterical L4E fan and then tried to somersault over the gates and into the campus?

"Don't even think about it," breathes a man's voice. I feel a hand come down on my shoulder. I immediately stamp hard on his foot and shove my elbow into his belly.

"Ow," he yelps. "Take it easy with that elbow."

I whirl around to see a campus cop clutching his stomach. The guy's face may be hidden behind dark glasses and a police cap, but I know that belly.

Strike.

CHAPTER FORTY-FOUR

School Visit

"an't this thing go any faster?" I say to Strike, as he drives his official campus police department golf cart toward the looming gothic spires of Healy Hall at a mind-bending twenty miles per hour.

"If we went any faster, someone might notice us," he replies. "But right now, we're just a campus cop and a random girl riding on a slow-moving golf cart. Why single us out for attention when there's so much more going on?"

Strike is correct. The cluster of emotional L4E fans are still gathered outside the front gates. Countless TV reporters on the lawn are talking to their camera crews about this evening's debate, which is only minutes away. Secret Service agents, White House staffers, and Morgan Font campaign team members all mill about, chattering urgently into their headsets. Font Force volunteers hand out phones to debate attendees making their way to the venue. No one gives us a first, let alone a second, look.

I go to glance at my watch.

"We'll make it in time," Strike assures me. "Do you know how often I've saved the world with seconds to spare?"

"A lot, I hope."

"So relax," he says.

I relax for 0.00000002 of a second. "I heard the CIA put you and Irina in a box," I pipe up. "Obviously, you made it out."

"Note to self: probably not a good idea to get back in business with an agency that doesn't trust you." He gives me a rueful smile.

"So, the Forties?" I ask.

"Under new management." He shrugs.

"And you and Irina?"

"We might need to go off the grid for a while."

"Does that mean I'm not going to see you?"

"It might be better," he says. "For you and your

family. Once the trust is gone, it's hard to get back."

"We're doing important stuff here," I tell him. "We're saving the country from a madman who wants to be president."

"We're never going to be short of madmen who want to be president," Strike replies. "People who are always there for you and put their needs before their own? Not so many of those. Don't lose them."

"Are you firing me from being a spy?" I shout.

Strike opens his mouth, but before words emerge, he is dragged from the golf cart and thrown onto a motorcycle driven by Adina Roots.

"Strike!" I wail.

He tosses me his police cap.

"Bridget!" he shouts back at me. "Save the world! Press the green button on the wheel."

What green button? What wheel?

"Bridget," shouts Roots. "Don't press the green button. Get off the cart and turn yourself in."

I look around at Roots as she snaps handcuffs around Strike's wrist. "Thanks for believing in me," I tell her. "Thanks for thinking I might have been set up. I'm being sarcastic. And now I'm pressing the green button."

I jam the police hat down over my face and toss her a non-respectful salute.

"Get her!" Roots commands. I hear the sounds of motorcycles roaring toward me.

I press the dime-size button in the center of the golf cart steering wheel.

Things That I Would Really Like to Happen Right Now:
1. The golf cart sprouts giant monster-truck wheels and I get to crush all the vehicles in my way.
2. The golf cart goes into suction-wheel mode and allows me to ride straight up the walls of Healy Hall without falling off.

Things That I Would Really *Not* Like to Happen Right Now:
1. The golf cart explodes.

The golf cart does not explode, but it jolts and shakes, and then it sinks into the ground. That's because the wheels are gone. That is correct: I am being pursued by Secret Service agents on motorcycles, and I am sitting in a golf cart whose wheels disappeared because I pressed the green button without first thinking to ask, "What happens when I press the green button?"

The cart stops sinking into the ground. I feel another

jolt and then the cart rockets into the air.

I let out a scream of terror and grip on to the sides of my hard plastic seat. I feel my phone vibrate. Hello, Joanna, perfect time to call.

"Hi," I say. "And that's both a greeting and a description of my current location."

"You're in a drone cart," Joanna replies. I can hear the relish in her voice as she gets to explain something about the spy world to me. "It's a prototype Strike stole from the Forties on his way out. Dale forwarded the instructions to me because I'm now known in the world of international espionage as Bridget Wilder's handler. Should I have a special handler name? Or maybe it should be a letter. J's probably too obvious. Maybe a number? Seven?"

"Okay, fine," I yell. "How do I drive this thing, Seven?"

"It has a switch on the dash with four settings," says my new handler. "Memorize this: F for Forward . . ."

"R for Reverse, U for Up, and D for Down. Got it," I say.

"You have to steer it like a car, or it'll keep going up and finally it will fall from the sky and you will be squashed like a bug. Splat!"

"That puts my mind at ease," I tell her. "Where am I going?"

"Head to the fourth floor. That's the location of Gaston Hall, the auditorium where the debate's taking place."

I click F and the drone cart lurches to a halt, and then shoots straight at a concrete spire. I yelp with fright and click R. The cart drops like a stone. I feel the contents of my stomach splashing their way up into my throat. The prototype drone cart doesn't work. Like everything else that ever came out of the Forties, it's defective.

I look at the dashboard. Oops. I clicked D when I meant R!

"I hope the next spy I handle is more competent than you," I hear Joanna grumble.

I switch to U, and the cart ceases its rapid descent and floats upward again. A plan takes shape in my head. I will pilot my strange little vehicle up to the fourth floor, where I will hover outside the window of Gaston Hall. The moment Font shocks the president by bringing out mind-controlled Jamie Brennan, I will fire my amnesia atomizer, and Jamie will forget all the lies she's been programmed to tell. Victory will be mine.

"I need full concentration," I tell Joanna. "But thanks, Seven." I click the phone off.

My cart drifts skyward, and two floors below my final destination I pass a window where I think I catch a glimpse of Morgan Font and Jamie sitting in front of mirrors having their makeup done. Victory is prematurely mine. I switch to D so I hover level with the window. I keep one hand on the switch and slide the other hand into my pocket for the squirter. The cart suddenly lurches forward. Did I touch F by mistake?

The drone cart smashes through the window. I throw my hands over my face to protect myself from the shards of glass spraying all around me. When I take my hands away, I'm in a long dark room filled with old and expensive-looking paintings. The corner of the room nearest to me is illuminated by makeup mirrors ringed with searingly bright bulbs. I look down on Font, who does not seem at all surprised to see me, and Jamie, who has a vacant, faraway look in her eyes. The makeup people, who continue applying powder to Font's and Jamie's faces, have the same vacant look.

I aim my atomizer at Jamie and gaze down at her kidnapper. "Three words, Font," I tell him. "Nick. Of. Time."

Font remains unruffled. "Three more words, Bridget," he replies. "Meet the Wilders."

He gestures to a shadowy corner of the art room. My mother, my father, Ryan, and Natalie are pushed out of the darkness by three large men carrying large guns and wearing extra-large Font Force T-shirts. My family look terrified but they do not seem like they've been brain-washed. Morgan Font wants them to experience every minute of this.

"Oh my God," I moan.

"Oh my God!" shrieks my mother.

My father just stares at me in the hovering drone cart.

Natalie dissolves into tears of confusion.

Ryan puts an arm around her shoulder and gives me a helpless shrug.

Font gestures to me to land the cart. I touch the D switch and hit the ground with a thump.

"I don't have to give you the big 'hurt me and I'll hurt them' speech, do I?" he asks me. "We're on the same page with what's happening here, right?"

I feel my family's wide, disbelieving eyes on me as I clamber out of the cart.

"You were supposed to stay in the embassy," I tell them.

"Who *are* you?" breathes Natalie.

Font laughs. "I tried to tell them, but they wouldn't believe me. 'Your daughter's a superspy,' I told them. 'Who, Bridget?' they said. '*Our* Bridget? Nah.' Being underestimated is a very effective cover, Ms. Wilder."

I feel my mother's eyes on me. I don't want to look at her. This is the time I need to be strong and smart. If I look at my mom, I won't be either of those things. But I know how confused she must be, and how hurt.

Font puts on a serious face, and turns to me. "Foreign governments can't gain access to the Trezekhastan Embassy, but my money opens every door. The ambassador was happy to hand your family over."

He waves the makeup girl away. "Enough," he says. Font gets up from his seat and examines his reflection. He tries a few expressions—proud, offended, passionate, sincere.

"You probably want to spend some time with your daughter," he says as he guides Jamie from the room. "Assuming she really is your daughter. Because it doesn't seem like you know her very well."

I want to go after them. I want to stop Font and save Jamie. I can't. I can't do anything. Not when the people I love most in the world are trapped in this room. Not when there's a chance they could come to harm if I attack their captors.

My family are trapped in a room with three men who have guns trained on them. I can't help but notice that, except for Ryan, they all look a lot more scared of me.

CHAPTER FORTY-FIVE

Of All the Times the Stupid Chickens Had to Pick to Come Home to Roost, Why Now?

I am a liar. We know this about me. I lie a lot, and I'm good at it. But of all the individuals I've hoodwinked, the most consistently gullible has to be Bridget Wilder. Right from the start, I told myself that this would never happen. That my two worlds would never collide. That I could take part in spy missions without my family ever knowing or ever being involved.

Sure, there were unexpected detours along the way. First Joanna and her cousin in Brooklyn, and then Ryan. But there was something cool about having a small intimate circle who knew my secret: it bonded us, and, if

I'm *really* honest, I liked picturing them thinking about me and imagining the action-packed adventures I was having. I liked the new way they looked at me, like I was someone *special*. It was the exact opposite of the way my mother, my father, and my sister are looking at me now. They stand in a tight huddle, their eyes gazing in my direction as if I were an animal that snuck into their house and they're calculating how to expel it before it attacks them. I can see Ryan wants to come to my defense, but he's not sure what to say without implicating himself as another liar lurking under the Wilder roof.

"What's that thing?" my mom suddenly says.

Is she talking about me? Is that what I've become to her: a *thing*? Then I see she's looking at the vehicle in which I made my dramatic entrance.

"It's a prototype drone cart," I tell her. "Maybe in a few years your courier company will be using them instead of vans."

"What does it run on?" asks my dad.

"Who cares what it runs on!" yells Natalie. "She flew through the window in it. She pointed a gun at a presidential candidate . . ."

"Who kidnapped you," I remind her. "And it's not a gun, it's a . . ." I've forgotten the word again. "Squirter."

"How does a presidential candidate even know you?

Where do you get a flying car . . ."

"Prototype drone cart," I mutter.

"All those things Font was saying about you," Dad says. "They're true?"

"Yeah, but, Dad, all these things you told me about him, about how we'll all be in trouble if he gets into power, *they're* all true, too. But it's much, much worse. He's planning on brainwashing people into voting for him. I've got to stop him."

"You?" Natalie laughs harshly. "How are you going to stop anybody? Who made you a spy?"

"Does Irina have something to do with all of this?" my mother asks.

"No!" I respond too fast. "Well . . . yes, but . . ."

She throws her hands in the air. "I knew it. I knew there was something I didn't like about her."

"How long have you been doing . . . whatever you're doing?" asks Dad.

"Were you a spy when they adopted you?" chimes in Natalie. "How far back does this go?"

My mother looks shocked at the suggestion. I see her mind working, doing the calculations. I am even more shocked.

"Mom, *no!*" I shout. "How can you think that way even for a minute?"

"How do I know what to think?" she says, near tears. "All those times you lied to me. Right to my face."

"Leave her alone," Ryan interrupts. "She hasn't been a spy for very long, less than a year. If she lies to you, it's because she wants to protect you. She protected me."

I have mixed feelings about what my brother just said. I am filled with gratitude, but I am also primed for an explosion of parental outrage.

"You *knew*?" shouts Mom.

"Are you a spy, too?" asks Dad.

"I've played my part in spy action." He smiles. "That whole invading-the-embassy thing? That was me buying time for Bridget to save the president's daughter."

Which I'm not doing a great job of right at this emotion-packed moment.

"See, I would believe Ryan as a spy," says Natalie. "That makes sense. But *Bridget . . .*"

I glare at her. "You're not the only one things happen to," I say.

"And I would never want to be," she fires back. "I always tell people, you'd like Bridget if you got to know her, but then you do insane things like soak the first lady with a fire extinguisher . . ."

"That was to save her from being stung by a fly with a lethal mutant stinger attached."

Natalie gives me a sad look. "Do you know how hard it is to be your sister?"

My mouth falls open. "Do you know that the Secret Service thanked me for doing that and recruited me to stand in for Jamie Brennan? Do you know that it was *me* who called you to choreograph Jamie's big viral hit dance number? It was *me* who got you the private jet. It was *me* who danced with you at the hotel. It was *me* you hugged when everybody was cheering, and . . ." I look at Mom. "It was *me* you talked to on the phone when you said Bridget didn't really have a thing . . ."

I see Mom replaying the conversation in her head. She looks shaken.

"Take that back," blurts out Natalie, her face reddening. "The first lady called me personally. It was all her idea."

I walk up to her. My face inches from hers. "It was all my idea."

Natalie tries to push me away. I stand my ground, which infuriates her even more.

"Are you so jealous of me you'd try to ruin my most cherished memory?" she yells.

"This isn't about you," I shout back. "This one time something isn't about you."

One of Font's men lumbers forward. "I think we're

going to need to separate you."

"I thought my family was bad, but these guys never shut up," one of his colleagues says, nodding.

The first Font guy gestures with his gun for Mom and Natalie to follow him, but Dad puts himself in front of them.

"Very noble," smirks the guy.

I put myself in front of Dad and point my squirter in the guy's face.

"I'm guessing you're not a standoff veteran," the guy says calmly. "Here's what generally happens. The first person to shoot usually dies, and the people she's trying to protect usually die, too. Your move."

"Bridget, please," Dad says. "Put the squirter down."

"I'd take your father's advice." The guy grins. "He seems like a smart guy. In fact, why don't I take that little piece of plastic out of your—*aaah!*"

The Font guy never reaches the end of his sentence. The end of a long white towel flies into his open mouth. His gun is whipped from his hand by a second towel. It flies in the direction of the broken window. Adam Pacific catches the gun as he jumps through the window. He points it at the other two Font men and lands on his feet beside me. I fight a smile. Now both of us are guarding my family, and we're both pointing weapons at the Font guys.

"I guess I'm gaining standoff experience," I tell the Font guy who is staggering in a circle, trying to pull the towel out of his mouth.

"Saved you again, Wilder," says Pacific.

"One-towel pony," I reply.

"Better a one-towel pony than a no-towel corpse," he retorts.

"Excuse me," Mom breaks in. "Who *is* this?"

"Adam Pacific, the Wilder family of Reindeer Crescent, Sacramento," I mumble. "Wilder family, blah-blah-blah."

"Dude, much respect re: the towel thing," says Ryan. "You need to *sensei* me on that."

"Are you a spy, too?" asks Natalie.

I wince. This is the perfect cue for Pacific to say something mean.

"I'm no Bridget Wilder," he says. "But I do what I can."

"Did you just say something nice?" I ask, amazed. "How did that feel? Was it weird?"

"Like eating smoked eel," he replies. "Tastes weird. You can't chew it or swallow it. Leaves a nasty taste in your mouth."

"Oh my God." Natalie giggles. "You two are totally into each other."

"We are not!" Pacific and I reply in unison.

"Um, standoff," Dad reminds us.

"Right," I say.

Pacific and I point our weapons at the two Font men. They point their weapons at us. This is not an ideal situation. My little squirter has almost no bullets, and Pacific, as he admitted in a moment of weakness, has never fired a gun. If my family weren't standing behind me, I'd hurl caution to the wind and take out both of these Font lackeys, but my family *is* standing behind me—literally, if not figuratively—and I can't take the chance.

"Shoot them!" coughs the Font guy who has finally removed the towel from his mouth.

"We're professionals," the guy wheezes at his partners. "We have kills to our name. They're two little kids. What've they got?"

Above their heads, a ceiling panel opens. Vanessa drops down and lands on the shoulders of one of the gunmen.

"They've got me," she says.

She reaches down, grabs the bottom of his Font Force T-shirt, and yanks it over his head. As he reaches up to pull himself free, Vanessa jumps off his shoulders, snatches the gun from his hand, and joins Pacific and me. The guy with the T-shirt over his head stumbles around making muffled sounds of anger. The last armed

Font man now looks a lot less confident.

"Hey, V," says Pacific.

"Hello, Adam," Vanessa says. She gives me a curt nod. "Peanut."

"You're supposed to be at the debate," I say.

"I had an inkling you could probably use a hand," Vanessa says. "So I took a pee break, ditched the nano-mask, gave my handlers the slip, *et voilà*."

She glances around at my stunned family.

"Hello, Mr. and Mrs. Wilder, how very nice to meet you again, even though the circumstances are somewhat trying."

"You." Ryan gulps. He looks horrified at the sight of his fake ex-girlfriend.

"Don't be scared, Ryan," Vanessa says sweetly. "I'm nice now."

Ryan looks to me for confirmation.

"Everyone else seems to think so." I shrug.

Dad suddenly strides out in front of the last armed Font guy.

"Hey, bozo," he barks. "You're working for the losing side. My daughter and her gang of underage spies just ate your lunch without firing a shot. Save yourself further embarrassment and limp out of here."

The Font guy looks taken aback at Dad's tough-guy

approach. He turns to his coughing partner, and the one with the T-shirt still stuck over his head, and mutters, "I hate politics."

The coughing guy stamps his foot in frustration, and they both run out of the room.

Pacific pokes me in the ribs. "Wilder, I don't trust those guys. They might be recruiting backup goons. I'll keep eyes on them." He grabs his towels and hurries after the men.

"Guys?" says the remaining Font man, from beneath his T-shirt. "You still here?"

He follows blindly in their wake, walking into a makeup mirror as he goes.

I give my father an admiring smile. Ryan and Natalie look equally surprised and impressed. Mom does not. She's caught in a place between anger and fear, and she seems unable to access any other emotions.

"Tick-tock, peanut," mutters Vanessa. She points up at the ceiling panel from which she emerged so spectacularly. "There's a passage that will take you right up to the backstage area."

"And this'll get you there faster," says a familiar voice.

Irina strides across the room. She elbows the remaining Font in the head as she passes, knocking him to the ground.

"Great," moans Mom.

"Mrs. Wilder," sniffs Irina. "Always a pleasure." She does not say this like she means it.

Irina hands me her arrow-shooting gun device.

"Go save the day," she tells me. "I'll stand guard here."

"Don't you think you've done enough?" Mom says.

"You never gave me a chance," snaps Irina. "From the moment I met you, I knew you didn't like me."

"Hey," I shout. "We're an extended family. Extend each other some understanding."

With that I fire the arrow into the ceiling. The steel wire hurtles upward. As it embeds in its target, I feel a pressure shoot up my arm. I am pulled into the air and through the ceiling.

"Oh my God, Bridget!" I hear various family members beneath me scream. I squeeze both my hands together and cling on for dear life as the wire rockets me up the passage, which curves left and then right. I don't know where I'm going, but it smells bad, and it's so narrow I have to press my arms to my sides. As I continue to rise, I hear a muffled, echoey voice. The voice becomes clearer. It's the president. The debate has begun.

Bright light comes streaming down the passage. Up above me, the arrow is embedded in a loose floorboard. I dig my feet in at the side of the passage and work my way up the last few feet until I'm able to push the floorboard aside.

All around me are the legs of important people watching the debate on a large TV monitor Nobody sees my head peering out of a hole in the floor. Nobody sees me take off my dust-covered glasses and wipe them on the nearest pant leg.

"Thank you, Mr. President," says a female voice from the monitor. "Mr. Font, same question. Gas prices."

"I'll address that important issue in a second, if I may," I hear Font reply. "But first, I'd like to ask the president a question. Sir, do you know where your daughter is right now?"

I hear a chorus of gasps and *Whaaats* above me.

I pull myself out of the hole, scramble to my feet, and try to get a look at what's going on in the monitor. No one notices me. I'm shorter than everyone else in the room, and I'm nowhere near important enough to grab anyone's attention. All the campaign staffers and reporters crammed into this backstage space are furiously texting and whispering on their phones.

I get as close to the monitor as I can, and I see the look of confusion on the president's face.

"I'm not sure I understand why that's in any way relevant," he replies.

"It's extremely relevant to our national security, and the safety of our loved ones," says Font.

As President Brennan stands behind his podium, looking out at the packed auditorium, Font steps out from behind his and approaches the president.

"I know Jamie's safety and security are as precious to you as every American daughter's safety is precious to every father. That's why you had a CIA operative wear a mask and pretend to be her during public events."

The gasping and *whaaat*-ing increase.

The cameras zoom straight in on Jocelyn Brennan, who sits stone-faced in the audience, next to an empty seat where the Vanessa version of Jamie should have been. The cameras cut back to the president's baffled face.

"This is . . . can we move on to something more appropriate?" the president splutters.

"Mr. President, I can't think of anything more appropriate. I'm here today to tell you the CIA operative who passed as your daughter was a double agent working for enemies of our great nation. Enemies who abducted your daughter and were prepared to make you pay a ransom for her safe return."

The audience is gasping louder than the freaked-out staffers and reporters backstage.

President Brennan is unable to form any words other than "I . . . I . . . I . . ."

"But Morgan Font does not stand by while enemies of freedom prey on America's children. Morgan Font rescued your daughter, Mr. President."

Font turns to the side of the stage. "Jamie, come and hug your father."

Every head in the backstage area turns. Two of Font's men lead a trembling, terrified Jamie toward the stage.

This is my chance to stealthily save the day and vanish into the shadows like the super-professional spy I am.

Font holds out his hand, ready to walk Jamie to her baffled father.

Every eye in the backstage area is fixed on Jamie and Font. No one sees me squeeze my way past. No one sees me pull out my squirter, and take aim at Jamie . . .

Someone screams "Gun!"

And then a bus lands on me. Or at least that's what it feels like.

I'm thrown face-first onto the ground. The squirter flies out of my hand, and a huge weight presses down on me.

I feel hot breath in my ear. "I told you the first person to shoot dies."

CHAPTER FORTY-SIX

The Fall

A super-professional spy would not have let a hired killer walk away because he got towel-fu'd and then shouted at by her dad. A super-professional spy would have taken the hired killers prisoner, so there was no chance one of them could slam her to the ground just as she was about to thwart his employer's evil scheme.

But, as it turns out, I'm no super-professional spy. I'm a barely breathing, barely conscious gimmick whose run of good luck just ended. The big brute who tackled me has pretty much crushed the life out of me. I have no plan to escape from this. I have no backup, no Red, no squirter, no way to save the day.

The Font guy's massive weight lifts off me. I see a blurry circle of faces staring down. I recognize White House Chief of Staff Hayes Oberman. He shakes his head in disbelief.

"Take her away," he says. Two Secret Service agents pick me up as if I were a stray leaf blown backstage by an errant gust of wind. I don't struggle or try to plead my case. There is not an ounce of fight left in me.

And then I hear the entire auditorium gasp in shock.

"Oh God," groans Oberman. "She's fallen over again."

The Secret Service guys stop moving but keep their hands on my arms. Their eyes go to the stage, where Jamie is lying flat on her face, motionless.

I twist around to get a look at the TV monitor. I see a slow-motion replay of Jamie being led by Font toward the president. He opens his arms to his daughter. She takes a step toward him and then falls down.

Mrs. Brennan cries out in horror and jumps out of her seat. She runs to the stage and crouches over the fallen Jamie.

Even the hardest-hearted White House staffers and journalists look moved to tears by the mother-daughter scene playing out in front of them.

I'm not moved to tears, though. I laugh out loud.

"What's wrong with you?" snarls Oberman.

"Why am I laughing?" I grin at him. "Because I know something you don't."

I gesture at the Font man who brought me down. "When that goon tackled me, my amnesia squirter went off and hit Jamie in the back. That's why she fell over. When she wakes up, she won't remember the last hour. But she *will* remember all the bad stuff she knows about Morgan Font."

Oberman stares at me, not sure what to believe. I've got a little wiggle room here, so I start wiggling.

"So you can have your men drag me off and throw me in a cell. Or you can wait till she wakes up, and realize that I just saved Jamie Brennan *and* your job. Either way, today's going to end with you apologizing to me. The question is, when do you want to do it? Now or later. 'Cause later's *really* going to ruin your day."

Oberman flinches. That confidence and swagger? I got it from my dad. Thanks, Jeff Wilder.

He gestures to the Secret Service agents to unhand me.

On the stage, the president and the first lady are both crouching over Jamie, rubbing her back and stroking her hair.

Font stands alone and awkward on the stage. The

audience he had in the palm of his hand a matter of seconds ago doesn't even see him anymore.

He walks to the edge of the stage. "Ladies and gentlemen, I have footage that will be shocking to some of you, but I think we have to see it to understand the threat this country faces, that our children face."

He gestures to a huge video screen at the back of the stage. "*This* is what I saved Jamie Brennan from." The screen fills with static, and then the audience sees . . . Lim from L4E sticking an I FARTED sign on a fan's back.

"What is he doing?" Overman says.

"He's showing the clip of L4E being mean to their fans that I had Dale Tookey upload in place of the clip he thought he was going to show."

Oberman just says, "Oh." (Don't make your fans mad, boy bands. They'll get their revenge in the end. They'll either grow out of you, or, if they're like me, they'll do something a little more malicious.)

On the stage, Font is shouting "No, no, no, no!" at the screen.

"We cannae stand youse," chorus L4E in front of their biggest-ever global TV audience.

"That's not the right clip," shouts Font. "Someone's getting fired over this." He makes an appealing gesture to the audience. "The same people who abducted Jamie did this. The enemy is everywhere. President Brennan can't stop them. But I can. I got Jamie back."

"No, you didn't," says Jamie.

The whole auditorium inhales in surprise as Jamie slowly, shakily, gets to her feet.

The president and the first lady hold on to her hands.

Font contorts his features into a grotesque smile. "Thank God!" he exclaims. "You're safe and well, and back with your family. That's all I ever wanted."

"That's almost true," Jamie says. "Except you left out the part about the deal we made."

"Jamie, you've been under a lot of pressure," Font says. He looks at the president and the first lady. "She needs rest. Maybe we should start this over another time."

Jamie shakes loose of her parents' hands. She walks toward Font, her posture more aggressive and defiant with every step she takes.

"I wanted out of the White House and you wanted in, so we came up with a plan. I'd pretend to be kidnapped. You'd pretend to rescue me. We'd both get what we wanted."

The audience gasps in unison.

"Oh God," I hear Oberman groan.

"Ready with that apology?" I ask him.

Onstage, Font's makeup is starting to run under the heat of the TV lights, and the burning realization that his dirty secrets are about to be revealed to a worldwide audience.

"The poor child . . . how much she must have suffered . . . seeing what they've done to her . . . I will not rest until the subhuman creatures responsible are hunted down and made to pay . . ."

"I was stupid," shouts Jamie. "I made a mistake. I trusted the wrong guy."

She turns to her parents. "You don't know who he is, who he *really* is . . ."

"Don't listen to her," Font implores the audience.

"He's right." Jamie nods. "Don't listen to me. Listen to someone else who knows what Morgan Font is all about." She walks off the stage.

"Bridget?" she calls. "Are you back there?"

I feel my face burn. I can't blow my cover. If I go out there everyone in the world will know I'm a spy.

Jamie hurries to the backstage area and grabs me by the arm.

"Jamie, I can't," I whisper. "You're doing great. You don't need me."

"I won't say anything about you being a spy," she promises.

I have to trust Jamie. She believed me. She turned

against Font and put the fate of the nation above another term of being miserable in the White House. Now it's my turn.

Jamie leads me on to the stage. Hundreds of eyes are suddenly on me. I feel horribly self-conscious. The nice green dress I've been wearing since the White House is crumpled, torn, and stained. It doesn't make me feel much better seeing audience members holding up phones to film me. I notice that, in the first few rows, people are brandishing Font phones.

The president and first lady stare blankly in my direction. My appearance on the stage is just one more of the evening's unexpected surprises. Jamie walks me toward her parents. We stand by their side.

Font's reaction is louder and more aggressive. "Her?" he bawls. "You're bringing a known liar to back up your baseless accusations?"

He approaches the audience. The people in the front row rear back in fright, and I don't blame them. Font is a seething mess of sweat and melting makeup. He clenches and unclenches his fists. The smile he attempts to keep on his face makes him look like a psychotic clown.

"She's going to tell you fairy tales about me brainwashing voters with my phones," he laughs. "Stories about me controlling the minds of my young volunteers. The Font Force is the heart of my campaign. The accusation that I would . . ." He throws up his hands in disbelief.

"But let me tell you a true story," he says, leaning forward, as if to bring the entire auditorium into his confidence. "About a girl who had her childhood ripped away from her. A girl to whom lying, cheating, and manipulation come as easily as breathing does to the rest of us. A girl who shows one face to her family and a whole other face to those she's ordered to take down."

I see Font growing in confidence. He thinks he can turn my presence on his stage to his advantage. Font points at me. I feel my face redden.

"President Brennan allowed his covert intelligence agencies to turn this girl into the monster you see before you. Think what he'll allow if you give him a second term."

I hear sporadic boos from the crowd.

That was pretty good. That was the work of a man who thinks on his feet. Font made the audience take a good look at me. I'm not a pretty little package. If anything, I'm a suspicious package, and he just succeeded in making me seem more suspicious. I could use the I'm-just-a-scared-little-girl approach and *maybe* win the audience back to my side. But why should I? Morgan Font never treated me like a scared little girl before. He paid me the respect of treating me like an equal. He deserves the same treatment from me.

I squeeze Jamie's hand and then I walk across the stage until I face Chester Brennan, who towers over me. I glance back at Chester Brennan.

"Hey, Mr. President," I call out. "You ever used a Font phone? You should. Fifty gigabytes of free storage, rollover data, unlimited international texting."

I pull Starey Hayley's Font phone from my pocket and toss it to the president. He barely knows where he is by this point, but high school sports hero muscle memory kicks in and he catches the phone.

"Hey, Jamie," I say. "Call your dad."

Jamie takes out her phone.

"NO!" Font suddenly screeches. He sprints across the stage and snatches the Font phone from the president's hand.

President Brennan does not give it up. The two candidates start shoving each other. I scoot to the front of the stage and address the audience.

"Mr. Font called me a liar," I tell them in a loud, clear voice. "I would never say that about him. I think every word he told me is true. He told me his phones emit a high-pitched frequency and a series of vibrations that make people act the way he wants them to act because, and I think these are the words he used, 'I wouldn't want to lie to you.' I think he said, 'Voting is way too important to be left in the hands of the voters.' Or something like that."

The booing starts with one or two people. Then it spreads across the entire auditorium.

A Font phone lands on stage and shatters on impact. A second phone is hurled from the audience. It hits the ground near Font's feet.

Font stops trying to pull the phone from the president's hand. He turns his full attention to the auditorium, where a hail of Font phones are crashing onto the stage. The audience are on their feet, throwing phones at him.

"Stop!" he screeches. "It's not true. None of what she said is true."

A phone hits him in the face.

"Why are you listening to her?" Font yells, batting away the phones that fly onto the stage. "She's just a kid."

"Here are a few more kids," shouts a voice from the back of the auditorium. "Listen to them."

Font, the president, the first lady, Jamie, the audience, and I all follow the sound of the voice.

It's Strike.

He's marching down the steps in the center of the auditorium, a handcuff still dangling from his wrist, leading a procession of young Font Force volunteers. Starey

Hayley stomps down the steps with a look of blazing fury in her intense eyes. She wears her Font Force T-shirt, but it's been altered with a few words in Magic Marker. The shirts worn by the former volunteers now read *Font Forced Me to Do His Dirty Work.*

I take off my police cap and toss it to Strike, who catches it and puts it on his head.

The former volunteers take up position at the foot of the stage, their accusatory T-shirts staring Font in the face. Font takes a few steps forward. He has to kick broken Font phones out of his way. I can see him sizing up the situation, working through all the angles, searching for a way to emerge on top. He stops walking. His shoulders slump. He experiences an unfamiliar sensation: defeat.

And just in case there was the slightest chance of him not grasping who is responsible for ending his presidential hopes, I lean in close to him and say, "I'm the good guy. I'm the one who makes things right and saves the day."

Font looks angry for a second, and then he gives me a condescending smile. "This doesn't change anything, little girl. I've still got more money than anyone else. I can still remake the world the way I want it. You'll still end up working for me, and you won't even know it."

He holds his head high and starts to saunter offstage.

I stick my foot out and trip him up.

Yes, that's correct. Bridget Wilder, the famous spy, just tripped up the bad guy on stage, in front of a live audience. I couldn't help it.

Font goes flying. He tries to clutch at air, but he lands face-first. The auditorium *erupts*.

The ex-volunteers are howling, even Starey Hayley, who I don't believe I've ever seen smile before. The Brennans are cracking up. Strike is cackling. Up at the top of the auditorium, I see Ryan, Vanessa, Pacific, and Irina. They're laughing, too.

"Shut up," snarls Font. He clambers to his feet, slips on a broken phone, and falls face-first again.

"I told you phones were bad for you!" the first lady calls out to the audience. They give her a standing ovation.

My work here is done. I step around Font, give Jamie a high five, and walk off the stage.

I head into the backstage area, where the first person I encounter is Hayes Oberman. He hands me my squirter.

"Great job, fake Jamie."

CHAPTER FORTY-SEVEN

Aftermath

"Never come back to Washington," First Lady Brennan tells me as we leave the Oval Office. Her smile lets me know that she's joking. The steel in her eyes lets me know that she's really not joking. Immediately after the debate sputtered to a close, there was an emergency meeting in the White House where everybody blamed everybody else for what had happened. But despite all the finger-pointing and accusations, one fact remained true: since Font went down in flames, the president's second term is all but guaranteed.

"Four more years," Jamie sighs.

"Four more years," repeats Vanessa enviously.

"Say good-bye to your friends, Jamie," instructs the first lady.

Jamie turns to Vanessa. "I didn't really get to know you."

"You'd have liked me." Vanessa smiles. "Everybody does."

Jamie takes my hand. "I'll call you."

"She won't," says the first lady. "Give my best to your family, Bridget."

"Can we have a minute, Mom?" Jamie gestures to the first lady to back up and give us some space.

She keeps holding my hand. "You were right about everything. You were right about Font. You were right that I was selfish."

"I was wrong about Cadzo," I say sadly. "But you came through when it counted. You could have done what Font wanted. Instead, you did the right thing."

Jamie smiles. "I didn't want to make Bridget Wilder mad at me. Last time I got a shoe in the face."

"This time, you get a friend," I tell her.

Jocelyn Brennan pulls Jamie's hand from mine. "Minute's up," she snaps. "We have an election to win. We're building a dynasty, Jamie. It won't be long before you're the one we'll be campaigning for."

And with that, FLB hauls her daughter off into the heart of the White House. Jamie looks back at me with anguish on her face.

"Awww," mocks the snooty blonde standing next to me.

"What are you going to do now?" I ask Vanessa.

"Well, since your name and face are trending worldwide, there's a gap in the market for a young lady spy. I'm already entertaining offers." She gives me a quick air-kiss on both cheeks. "See, peanut, we're always looking out for each other."

I watch her walk away as if she's on the red carpet. "I don't trust her," Irina says. "But there's something about her I like."

Strike exits the Oval Office and joins us. "The shocking news is the CIA wants us back. The even more shocking news is that we've finally learned from our mistakes and we're not going back."

"You're out of the spy game?" I ask.

"No one's ever really out," says Irina. "But it's time for me to stop paying lip service to the idea that I can do something else, and actually see if there's anything I can do. Your mother said she'd help me look for career options."

She notes my expression of extreme surprise. "You

bond quickly when you're waiting for your daughter save the country," she tells me. "We tried hating each other. Now we're trying the other thing." Irina touches my cheek. "I'll be around."

Strike and I watch her go.

"What about you?' I ask. "What's the plan?"

At that moment, Pacific comes out of the Oval Office.

"I'll let him tell you," says Strike.

Pacific smiles when he sees me. He immediately catches himself, and reverts to his above-it-all smirk, and then he wipes the smirk away and goes back to the original smile. Which I like.

"Not bad, Wilder," he says. "You destroyed Font and L4E, and ensured the president a second term. All in under two hours."

"We did that," I remind him. "We are a hot team. Pacific and Wilder."

"Wilder and Pacific," he corrects me.

I get a little flush when he says that. The little flush makes me say something I didn't know I was going to say.

"I know my name and face are out there," I tell him. "But people just think I'm this crazy random chick; they don't connect me to spy action. Once the hubbub dies down, maybe we can connect on another mission. We make a good team."

"Agree." He nods. "But right now, I want to do what you did. I want to find my dad. Strike's going to help me."

Oh. His dad. Charlie Pacific, who may be dead, or may be in North Korea. Which means this may be the last time I ever see Adam Pacific.

"But I'll be back," he tells me, and holds out a fist to be bumped.

I pull him close to me and hug him tight.

"Stay in touch, Adam," I whisper. "Be safe, and if you need me for anything. *Anything . . .*"

I let the sentence trail off. We hold each other for another moment, and then Pacific pulls away. He rubs at his eyes, and then touches a fist to his heart and holds the fist back out to me. This time, I bump it.

Pacific leaves. Strike returns.

"I'll watch his back," he assures me.

"Who's going to watch mine?" I ask him. "You're going off the grid. Irina claims she's pursuing new career opportunities. I don't even know if I'm going to see you again."

"You can't get rid of us that easily," says Strike. "But right now, you've got to concentrate on protecting your family. They know about you. That makes them vulnerable. It makes them targets."

"I'll fix it," I tell him.

He pulls me in a for a quick hug, and then I watch him hurry after Pacific.

A lot of emotional good-byes there, but I'd gladly endure a hundred more if it meant putting off the next item in my to-do list.

"Tick-tock, peanut," I say under my breath, and then I hurry away from the Oval Office and go in search of my family.

I find them outside the East Wing waiting to board the stretch limousine provided by the first lady to ensure the Wilder family make their flight to Sacramento.

Dad and Ryan look pleased to see me. Mom and Natalie less so.

"Your secret spy meeting over?" says Mom. "Can we go now?"

"So I heard you and Irina talked?" I say, trying to make cheery conversation.

"You could learn a lot from her," Mom replies. "She knows there's no future in the spy business."

"You're trending worldwide, Bridget," Natalie tells me, holding up her phone. "They're calling you *#weirdphonegirl*. So embarrassing."

What a proud and supportive family.

She goes back to thumbing through the texts on her

screen. Without looking back up, Natalie says, "Thanks. For giving me the chance to teach Jamie Brennan how to dance. She was kind of stiff and uncoordinated at first, but she surprised me. There's a lot more to her than I thought. I . . . think maybe I admire her."

I blink in surprise. The limousine driver opens the passenger door. Natalie hurries in, then Dad, then Mom.

"Hang back for a minute," I tell Ryan.

He gives me a worried look. "Trust me," I tell him. Then I climb into the back of the limo.

Dad is busy opening a bag of white-cheese popcorn from the free food tray when I shoot him with my amnesia squirter.

Natalie sees Dad slump down onto the long, black leather couch. She gasps once, and then I squirt her, and she loses consciousness.

Mom whirls around to see me with my squirter pointed straight at her.

"Bridget," she gasps.

"Mom, this is my thing," I say. And then I shoot her. Nothing happens. I squirt again. Nothing.

The atomizer is empty.

CHAPTER FORTY-EIGHT

Mommy and Me

This is awkward. The journey from the White House to Dulles Airport is about half an hour. We're maybe five minutes in. Ryan sits up front with the driver. I sit in the back with my comatose father and sister. Mom is fully conscious, but even though I've explained about the amnesia gun—thanks, by the way, Vanessa Dominion, for dumping your cheap, shoddy, malfuntioning spy gadget on me: I was supposed to get ten squirts and it expired on seven!—and how Dad and Natalie will wake up feeling fine, with only the previous hour wiped from their minds, she still looks like she's in a state of shock.

I want to call Strike, or Irina, or Vanessa, or one of the weirdos from the Forties' Research and Development department. *Anyone* who can airlift me more amnesia spray, because *this* is an intolerable situation.

I like Ryan knowing my secret. Dad may not have fully understood what was going on, but he was on my side. Natalie needs to remain the star of the family because that takes the spotlight off me, and I've found I work better in the shadows. But Mom. Mom is the *last* person I wanted to ever find out about my secret life. Not only did she find out, but she discovered in the worst possible way. Do not point a weapon, even an empty amnesia squirter, at your mother, unless you want the image of her horrified face tattooed on your mind for the rest of your life.

Dad and Natalie are going to wake up in a few minutes. They're going to wonder how they went from being in the Trezekhastan Embassy to the back of a limo. I'm going to try to convince them that the banquet laid on by the embassy staff was so excessive that they fell asleep. But before they wake up and I send some more lies into the atmosphere, I have to talk to my mother.

"Mom?" I say.

Nothing. Not a word.

Fine. I'll do the talking. "This was too big. Me in the

White House, pretending to be the president's daughter. I know that now. I shouldn't have taken it on. It's not what I normally do, and the minute I found out you were caught up in it, I should have walked away. But I became friends with Jamie, and then I found out who Morgan Font *really* is and that the whole country was in danger, just like Dad said! I had to finish the mission, Mom. But I'll never say yes to something on that scale again. Not that anyone's going to ask me. You should have seen the first lady's face when she said good-bye—"

"I remember when we first brought you home," Mom suddenly says. "I was worried you wouldn't be able to sleep, that you'd have nightmares from being in unfamiliar surroundings. I remember worrying that you wouldn't be able to eat anything I made for you. I remember worrying you'd be scared of Ryan. I worried you'd trip over your shoes and crack your head open. I worried you'd catch cold. I was going to get a kitten for you, but I worried it would suffocate you in your sleep. I worried you would be scared of the dark. That you'd choke on a button. There were a hundred more things. And that was the first day we brought you home."

"Mom." I don't know what else to say. There is no persuasive argument, no winning her over.

"I can't, Bridget. Knowing this about you paralyzes me."

"That's why I lied all those times!" I blurt out.

Mom's eyes and mouth grow wide in shock and anger.

I try a desperate save. "But, Mom, one day I'll take driving lessons, and then I'll go to college, and then get my own place, maybe start my own family. These are all huge, traumatic things for you, but you're not going to stop me from doing any of them."

She gives me an exasperated look. *"Really?* Those are your examples? Yes, I will continue to worry through every stage of your life, but I get to share those worries with your father, and every other parent I know. Who do I talk to about this other thing?"

I point to the front of the limo. "Ryan?" I suggest.

Mom makes a snorting noise.

"Irina? You're sort of friends now."

She ignores this suggestion and glares at me. "Who do I go to when you're . . ." Mom claws the air, frustrated at being lost for words.

"Climbing the rope ladder of a helicopter as the assassin I'm chasing tries to cut me loose?"

"Thanks." Mom scowls at me. "Thanks for putting that picture in my head."

Dad starts to stir. Natalie yawns.

Mom leans in close to me and grabs my hand. "No more, Bridget," she says. "Promise me."

CHAPTER FORTY-NINE

The Final Chapter

I returned to Reindeer Crescent a massive celebrity. And then, four days later, Cadzo dropped his debut solo song, "How Many Ways Can I Say I'm Sorry? (I'm Really Sorry)," and the world moved on.

And now, two weeks removed from my time in Washington, it feels like none of it ever happened. I'm back to being an adequate student, an unexceptional daughter, and a not-bad friend. The secret I share with my mother has created an uncomfortable tension between us. Her eyes glimmer with suspicion every time I leave a room. But it's also weirdly made us closer.

"What's the intel on that?" she's taken to asking me every time there's a political scandal on the news.

This morning I wake up to find I have a new Instagram follower. Ruth Etting is her name. I click on the screen and discover that Miss Ruth Etting is an English exchange student, staying in Westlake, Texas, with Molly Costigan-Cohen and her family. The pictures of Ruth make her look like a brunette Vanessa Dominion, but far less smug, far more approachable. Her favorite quote is "Shut up and suck it up."

Hmm.

"So, if Jamie's in Texas wearing a nanomask, who's in the White House?" asks Joanna as we walk to school.

I think back to the offer Jamie made me: "Do you have a backup mask? We could swap. You could stay on as me. I could go back to your life and pretend to be you." I couldn't say yes. Apparently Vanessa couldn't say no.

"Take a guess, peanut," I drawl in an accurate approximation of Vanessa's voice.

"Everyone gets what they want," marvels Joanna. "Except you."

I have no reply to that.

"And another guy dumped you and left," she points out.

"There was no dumping," I inform her. "It wasn't like that."

"But you wanted it to be," Joanna prods.

"We might have caught each other's cold a little bit" is as far as I will go.

"Are you done as a spy?" she asks. "Like *done*, done?"

"I promised my mom," I reply. "Sort of." (I didn't *exactly* promise. I said the word "okay." Which could be interpreted in a variety of ways.)

"You know that sounds lame, right?" Joanna says, poking me in the arm to make her point. "What if the pilgrim fathers had said, 'I promised my mom'? Would America even exist? Would any of us even be here?"

"What do you actually do in school?" I ask.

"I hope the next spy Seven handles doesn't have a mom," she grumbles.

"Where did Seven come from?" I ask. "Is it your shoe size?"

Joanna ignores my question and screeches, "What is *that* about?"

I follow her pointed finger.

A block ahead, I see a man and a boy wheeling a large metal trolley filled with tall, white wedding cakes up a driveway. The door of the house opens, and a group of women hurry out to help drag the trolley into the house.

I notice that the man has a bushy beard and the boy has an egg-shaped head. A white van passes us. The words *Tastes Like Cakes* are emblazoned on the side. I do not get a look at the driver, but I have good idea what's going on.

"Martin Geiger!" I say out loud.

"Food-based bad guy," I remind myself. "Poisoning the competition in the fast-food market didn't work out for him, so now he's moving into wedding cakes."

"Call the cops?" suggests Joanna, holding up her phone.

We could. We absolutely could. But we're so close. And I've got history with the Geigers. This is me being a concerned citizen taking a stand against local crime rather than . . . that other thing I don't do anymore.

I start to run in the direction of the house.

Joanna runs after me. "Spy action, right?"

"Not if we don't call it that," I say.

"What do we call it?" she asks.

"Being the good guys, making things right, and saving the day."

Joanna grins. "I know a song that's perfect for such an occasion."

I know it, too.

"Here come the spy twins on another adventure," belts out Joanna. I'd tell her to lower the volume, but the guys we're pursuing are hard of hearing.

"Here come the spy twins coming to your town," I join in, and I'm singing it for Adam Pacific, Dale Tookey, Vanessa Dominion, my long-lost friend Red, and even Ur5ula. All of us with our secrets, our gadgets, our double lives, and our mountains of lies.

"Here come the spy twins on another adventure, nothing's going to stop us now."

Acknowledgments

Thanks to Tina Wexler, Maria Barbo, Lori Majewski, James Greer, Lola G., Clare English, Kitty Page, Rebecca Schwarz, and everyone at Katherine Tegen Books.

Read them all!

She's no ordinary spy.
She's Wilder. Bridget Wilder.

 KATHERINE TEGEN BOOKS
An Imprint of HarperCollins Publishers

www.harpercollinschildrens.com